HAPPY DAYS AHEAD IN THE CORNISH VILLAGE

SARAH HOPE

Boldw**oo**d

First published in Great Britain in 2024 by Boldwood Books Ltd.

Cover Design by Head Design Ltd

Cover Illustration: Shutterstock

A CIP catalogue record for this book is available from the British Library.

Paperback ISBN 978-1-80549-080-7

Large Print ISBN 978-1-80549-081-4

Hardback ISBN 978-1-80549-079-1

Ebook ISBN 978-1-80549-083-8

Kindle ISBN 978-1-80549-082-1

Audio CD ISBN 978-1-80549-074-6

MP3 CD ISBN 978-1-80549-075-3

Digital audio download ISBN 978-1-80549-077-7

Boldwood Books Ltd
23 Bowerdean Street
London SW6 3TN
www.boldwoodbooks.com

For my children,
Let's change our stars
xXx

1

Picking up her watch from the bedside table, Megan checked the time before turning back to the mirror and dabbing another layer of concealer under her eyes. She had forty minutes to get to Wagging Tails Dogs' Home if she was going to arrive on time. Forty minutes to finish her make-up, brush her hair and get the bus to West Par before running up the road to where the dogs' home was located.

And at this rate, she would be running. Literally. She'd missed the bus she'd planned to take thanks to the battery on her mobile dying because the charger Lyle had let her take was the dodgy one from the kitchen drawer. She wriggled the cable in the charging port and sighed. Nope, it still wasn't working, and she didn't have time to go and buy a charger now. She'd just have to hope she didn't miss the call she was expecting from her solicitor.

Still, she'd get her car back from the garage tomorrow. It was just bad timing that she'd booked the MOT for the same day as the volunteer induction morning.

Turning back to the mirror, she pulled the hairbrush through her hair, tugging at the knots. What had happened to her? A couple of months ago, she'd never have had knots, she'd never be trying and failing to cover the bags under her eyes. Her hair would have been trimmed and styled, her eye bags covered with the tiniest dab of expensive concealer.

Megan looked beyond the reflection of the poorly hidden tell-tale signs of tiredness towards the room behind her, staring back at her from the mirror; the double bed, two bedside tables holding two identical lamps and nothing else. How had she got here? From living in a large detached five-bedroomed house to this? Living out of a bed and breakfast in Trestow, Cornwall?

Squeezing her eyes tight, she pushed all thoughts of her old life out of her mind. When she opened them again, she plastered a fake smile on her face. She could do this. She could. She had to. She had to make amends. However small and insignificant they might be, she had to try.

With the smile still in place, she grabbed her handbag and room key before heading out, letting the heavy fire door click shut behind her.

* * *

Megan took a step forward before pausing again. Of all the ideas she'd had, this was the worst. What had she been thinking? That she, Megan Trussel, could try to make up for all the upset and upheaval her ex, Lyle, had put the staff, volunteers and dogs at Wagging Tails through? What could she do apart from muck out a few kennels or walk a dog or two?

Plus, she was completely inexperienced. She didn't own a dog. She never had. The only time she'd really had anything to do with one was when their neighbour had asked her to pop in and let their dog out after being called to a family emergency. After that, they'd asked her to walk the soppy spaniel a handful of times when they'd been out all day but that was it, she hadn't even had one as a child. What use would she be? What if the dogs picked up on her inexperience? Or what if she just wasn't a dog person?

She kicked at a stone on the floor, watching it skid across the lane towards the hedgerow on the other side. They probably wouldn't trust her to walk any dogs, anyway. And she wouldn't blame them. She wouldn't trust someone whose spouse had attempted to force them out and bulldoze down the dogs' home.

'Megan?' a voice called from behind her.

Turning, Megan smiled as Sally, the dog trainer and girlfriend of Lyle's ex-business partner, walked towards her, a small Jack Russel at her feet.

'Hi.'

'It is you!' Sally told the dog to sit and grinned at Megan. 'What are you doing here? I thought you were living up north still?'

'No, me and Lyle split a few months ago. Just after all this business, actually.' Megan waved her hand, indicating the dogs' home at the end of the lane.

'Ah, yes, Andy mentioned that. What are you doing down here, though? It's a long way from your home.'

Megan nodded. Home. Now that was a word she hadn't used for a while. And what did 'home' even mean? She'd certainly never felt very much at home in the big, bland house she'd shared with Lyle. In fact, she hadn't felt particularly at home with him for a few years now, full stop.

She shrugged. 'I don't really know, to be honest. I stupidly thought I might volunteer here for a while. Try to make up for everything.'

'Oh.' Sally looked at her, the surprise in her eyes unmistakable.

'You don't think it's a good idea, do you?' Megan looked down at the small Jack Russell sitting by Sally's feet.

'No, I didn't mean it's not a good idea. I'm just surprised, that's all. You don't have to make up for Lyle's actions.'

'I know.' Megan nodded. And she did know. As soon as she and Sally's partner, Andy, had discovered Lyle's intention for the dogs' home, they'd worked together to expose him and bring a halt to his plans. But still, she should have realised what he'd been up to before. If she had, she could have saved a lot of stress and heartache. She did need to make up for that, for her own naivety.

Sally looked from Megan towards the gate leading into Wagging Tails and back again. 'Come on, you'd better get in before Flora starts giving her talk. And I need to get this little one up to the top paddock to help practise some socialising with Susan and one of the other pups we have.'

Should she go through with this? She'd come this far. She'd been staying in the bed and breakfast in Trestow for five weeks now, waiting for the perfect opportunity to show herself at Wagging Tails, waiting to gain enough confidence to return to the place that had cost her her relationship.

No, that wasn't true. Her marriage had been over way before then. She and Lyle had been living separate lives for the past few years. What he'd done, or attempted to do, to Wagging Tails had merely been the last straw, had been the catalyst for her to act, to no longer make excuses for him, to no longer imagine a time when things would be better between them.

Yes, discovering what he'd had planned for Wagging Tails had given her the kick to walk away, but it certainly hadn't been the reason she and Lyle were over. No, that was down to him.

'Ready?' Sally held out her arm, ready to link arms.

Megan nodded. 'As ready as I'll ever be.'

'Great.' Sally glanced down at the dog by her heels. 'Come on, Rex, let's go and meet the new volunteers.'

'Do you think there'll be a lot of people?'

Megan looked down at the sign hanging on the gate as they walked through. The words 'New Volunteers Welcome Day!' were emblazoned in bright yellow on a background of green.

'I'm not sure. I think Flora said she was expecting about ten, but if they all show up...' Sally shrugged.

'That's a good number, then.' Megan paused as Sally closed the gate behind them.

'Yes, it is. Of course, not everyone will become regular volunteers. Last time Flora put on a volunteer day, we had maybe fifteen people turn up, but only six are still volunteering on a regular basis.'

'Really? How come?'

'People always have good intentions, but I guess life just gets in the way sometimes.' Sally glanced across at Megan. 'Six is still a lot of volunteers to gain from one of these drives, though, which is why Flora asked Darryl to advertise it in the *Trestow Telegraph* again.'

As they crossed the courtyard, Megan could see a cluster of people making their way from the small car park towards the door into the reception area. Good, at least she hadn't missed the beginning of the induction through her dithering.

'Go on, you'll be fine.' Sally touched Megan's forearm and nodded towards the door.

'Thanks.'

Letting a flicker of a smile catch the corners of her lips, Megan began to walk towards the door, pausing to watch Sally head towards the paddocks. She was here now, she might as well go in. Reaching the door, Megan slipped in behind someone else, muttering her thanks and quietly closing the door behind her.

She looked around. The small reception area was crammed full of people, presumably all prospective volunteers like herself.

'Again, for those just arriving, thank you all so much for coming.' Megan recognised Flora's voice. 'It's so lovely to see so many of you wanting to give up time from your busy lives to come and help us out. We're currently at full capacity and so all the help we can get will be very much appreciated.'

Megan pulled her mobile from her back pocket ready to switch it to silent only to see the blank screen and remember the battery had run out.

'Do you want to come in front of me so you can see better?' The man in front of her turned around and stepped slightly to the side, indicating the small space in front of him.

Automatically shaking her head, Megan smiled. 'No thanks.' The last thing she wanted was to draw attention to herself. Even though Sally had said she thought this was a good idea, she still didn't know how Flora would react, whether she'd be happy to see her or whether she'd ask her to leave. No, she was more than comfortable standing at the back behind the other volunteers. The last thing she wanted was to be called out in front of a group of strangers.

The man nodded and turned back around, concentrating on Flora's talk.

'...and so, without any further ado, I'll give you a tour of Wagging Tails before we come back inside to discuss the boring bits. We'll start outside and then you can have a chance to meet the dogs inside after our tour.'

Megan followed the group outside, stepping into the summer sun. As the reception area emptied, Megan positioned herself behind a couple standing nearby.

'That's it. This way. We'll begin at the paddocks where you can all meet our lovely trainer, Sally, and our longest standing volunteer, Susan.'

The couple in front of Megan moved forward, leaving Megan standing there at the very moment Flora walked past. Megan swallowed as Flora paused in front of her, her words caught in her mouth for a second before she nodded slowly and made her way towards the front of the crowd.

What had that meant? Should she just go now? Save herself the embarrassment? No, she was here for a reason. The very reason she was staying in Trestow. If she didn't at least stay until the end of the induction and see what Flora had to say, then it would all be for nothing. She'd have travelled all this way for no reason.

As the other volunteers surged forward, following Flora as she led them towards the bottom paddock, Megan followed at a short distance. It wasn't as though she had anywhere else to go. She no longer had anywhere to call home and the friends she'd thought she'd be able to rely on for support she hadn't heard from. Lyle had probably made up some story or other to explain why she'd left him. That was the thing with Lyle, however bad his situation, however much he was in the wrong, he was quick to spin it so he always came out on top, so he was the one in the right.

'That's it, come on through. This is our bottom paddock, a safe space for the dogs to exercise off lead. It's all enclosed and secure so they can let off some steam. When we have a new arrival, we assess them and those who are friendly with other dogs will have the opportunity to socialise.'

'Can all the dogs you have be exercised together?' A woman towards the front of the group shot her hand up.

'No, but don't worry, when you arrive for your volunteering session, there'll always be one of us around who will tell you who can and can't be exercised together. Plus, when we look round the kennels, you'll see each kennel has a clipboard, information such as that will always be written on there, too.' Flora shut the gate behind them all.

'Will we be able to choose who we walk?' the woman called out again.

The man walking next to Megan turned to her and shook his head, his dark hair bouncing. 'Let me guess, she only wants to walk the cute ones.'

Megan grimaced. It sure sounded like it.

'Up to a point. All of our dogs need to be exercised each day, and that needs to be done fairly. All the dogs in our care deserve our attention and love. As a volunteer, some of the dogs will be off limits, such as our resident dog, Ralph, who must be walked by someone he is familiar with at the quietest times of the day.' Flora led the group across the paddock. 'We have a list we tick after each walk so we know who has had their walk and who hasn't.'

'What if we can't commit to a certain time each week?' A man towards the front of the group spoke up. 'Can we just turn up?'

Flora paused. 'We prefer people to commit to a regular time. Just so we can make sure we have an even spread of volunteers. With only the two paddocks, there's a limit to how many dogs we can walk at once so we wouldn't want people to just turn up or they might find it's a waste of their time. Of course, if you can't commit to a regular time slot, we can try to work around you and come up with a solution. We just ask to be kept in the loop, so to speak.'

'Of course, thanks.' The man nodded, seemingly happy with Flora's answer.

Flora steered them towards the gate to the top paddock and waved towards Sally and Susan, who made their way towards them.

'This is Susan and Sally.' Flora introduced them.

'Hi, everyone. Lovely to meet you all.' Susan waved as the small Jack Russell Megan had seen Sally walking earlier bounded up to the gate.

Turning back to the group, Flora raised her voice again. 'We won't go into the top paddock as Susan and Sally are socialising two of our newest arrivals, but as you can see it's much the same as the bottom paddock. Now, if we head back to the reception area and the kennels, we'll grab a cuppa, and I can answer any other questions you may have.'

Turning, Megan followed the group back through the bottom paddock.

'Megan, isn't it?'

Jerking her head up, she caught her breath. It was Flora.

'Yes. I'm sorry, I can go. I just...' She shoved her hands in her pockets.

'You'd like to volunteer here?' Flora began to walk beside her, matching her pace.

Megan nodded.

'Good to have you here, then.' Flora indicated the people ahead of them. 'I'd better get to the front. Shall we have a quick chat after the induction? If you have time, of course?'

'Okay.'

'Great.' Flora smiled before quickening her pace and weaving her way towards the front of the group.

Megan could feel the tension melting from the knots in her shoulders. Flora hadn't asked her to leave. That was a start.

2

'Here you go.' Flora placed a fresh mug of coffee in front of Megan and slipped into the chair next to her. The kitchen was now empty, the last of the volunteers having signed up for their first volunteering shifts and left. 'Thank you for staying behind. I think it's best we have a chat before you begin volunteering, don't you?'

'Thank you.' Megan took the mug and wrapped her hands around it, the heat from the ceramic warming her skin. 'Honestly, I don't have to volunteer here if you'd rather I didn't. I half expected you to tell me to leave when you first spotted me. And I understand. I really do.'

'I'm not going to ask you to leave. I'm just curious. Why do you want to help out here?'

Glancing down into her coffee, Megan swallowed. There were so many reasons, many of which she didn't fully understand herself. How could she explain something that she didn't understand?

'It feels like the right thing to do,' she said tentatively. 'After everything that happened... the way Lyle tried to force you to sell, what happened to Sally and her dog...'

'You feel responsible?'

'No, yes. Yes, I do. I should have realised what was happening. I should have guessed what he was doing. I was living with him.' She laughed, a short hollow sound escaping her lips. 'I was married to him. I should have known.'

'I think he was just a rather good showman. He had Andy fooled too.'

Megan nodded, automatically touching her ring finger, still uncomfortable with the sheer absence of the wedding ring which she'd been wearing for the past fourteen years. 'That's right.'

'It must have all been such a shock to you.' Flora smiled sadly.

'It was. But it shouldn't have been. I don't know how I didn't see what he was like earlier. How could he have kept such a secret from me? How didn't I realise what sort of person he really was?'

'Love does that to people. Love covers up the most damaging secrets.'

'I suppose so.' Megan took a sip of her drink, the sharp taste of black coffee welcome. Flora was right, she knew she was.

'I don't want you volunteering because you feel you have something to make up to us. Because from where I'm sitting, you don't. You've been as much fooled by that man as we have. And lost a lot more because of him, too.'

Megan took another sip of her drink. 'I do feel as though I have something to put right. Even though I wasn't aware of what he was doing and his underhand tactics, I was still part of the problem. I was still supporting him.'

Flora sighed. 'I don't think that's true. As soon as you discovered what he was up to, you and Andy worked so hard to bring his plans to a stop. And you succeeded. If it wasn't for you, Wagging

Tails would likely still be trying to put up a fight against him. Or worse.'

'Still, I'd like to volunteer. Please?'

'I'm not going to stop you from volunteering, but I'd like you to make that decision because you want to, not because you feel you have to.'

'I do. I do want to.' Megan looked out of the window. The sun was shining, and she could just about make out a couple of figures and dogs in the top paddock. Sally and Susan must still be up there. She laid her hands, palms down, on the table in front of her and looked down at them. 'I feel as though I don't have any control over my life any more. Everything I thought was real wasn't, and everything I thought I wanted in life, I realise I don't. This is the one thing I can do to try to feel better about myself. I would like to volunteer here. I want to make a difference. Even if it's an insignificant one.'

Frowning, Flora nodded slowly and pulled the sign-up sheet towards them. 'Let's get you signed up, then.'

'Thank you. I appreciate it.' Megan smiled as relief flooded through her. It probably seemed disproportionate to Flora, but this, Wagging Tails and trying to make up for the part she may or may not have played in Lyle's attempt to destroy it, was all she had to cling on to at the moment, all she had to build her life around.

The kitchen door opened slightly, and Megan saw Ginny peering through. 'Sorry to interrupt, but can I just have a quick word please, Flora?'

'Of course, lovely. I think we're done here, anyway.' Flora turned back to Megan and patted her hand. 'You fill this out and finish your coffee and I'll go and help Ginny. Take your time.'

'Thanks.' Megan picked up the pen and looked down at the sheet. A list of names and available time slots stared back at her. Most people had indicated that they wanted to volunteer at the weekends and the majority had highlighted just one or two hours. What was she supposed to write? That she was available every day, all day?

She downed the rest of her coffee. She might as well be honest and write that she could volunteer whenever. There might be a time or a day that Flora and the team needed more help. And it wasn't as though she had anything else to do with her time. Apart from staring at the four walls of her room back at Honeysuckle Bed and Breakfast, that was.

After scribbling her name and contact number down, she paused and looked down at the list again. Huh, there was someone else with a lot of time on their hands too. Someone else who had signalled that they could be flexible with their volunteering time. Someone called Jay had indicated he was free most days. Every day apart from a Friday and Saturday. She wasn't the only one after all then. That was a relief.

There, done. Hopefully, they'd think she was just happy being flexible rather than literally not having anything else to do, but she'd be happy volunteering every day if they needed her.

Standing up, she placed her empty mug in the sink and made her way towards the door. She could hear Flora and Ginny's voices on the other side. They must still be discussing whatever Ginny had needed Flora for. She picked up the sign-up sheet. She'd hand it to them on her way past.

Pushing the door open, she found both Flora and Ginny standing behind the counter, Flora flicking through a notebook, her reading glasses perched at the end of her nose and her forehead creased.

Megan placed the sheet of paper on the edge of the counter. 'Here's the form.'

'Thanks, Megan. I'll let you know as soon as I've taken a look through and come up with a rota.'

'Great. Thank you.' Megan paused, unsure whether to dash away or say what she wanted to.

'Everything okay?'

'Yes, I just wanted to say thank you for not dismissing me.'

Flora smiled. 'Of course not, lovely. We're happy you want to help us, aren't we, Ginny?'

'Absolutely. We couldn't operate without our volunteers.'

Megan nodded and turned away.

'Megan, mind your lace. It's undone,' Flora called.

'Oh, thanks.' Bending down, Megan began to tie her lace.

'Ah, I just don't understand,' Flora said, her voice filled with exasperation. 'I'm sure it was this notebook I'd written it all in.'

'Let's try another one,' Ginny replied. 'Maybe you wrote it in the red one? I'm sure it was that red one which has been lying about for days.'

'Maybe. Yes, yes, let's take a look in there.'

Megan pulled the bow in her lace tighter. They'd obviously lost something.

'We do need to come up with a better system, though. We can't keep relying on notebooks to scribble our outgoings in. We have this problem every year when we sort out the finances. We need to have a better system.' Flora's voice was firm. Not with Ginny, but herself.

'You're right. We really should get one of those computer programs and just fill it in every time we spend something. It would make life so much easier. Or even an Excel spreadsheet.'

Megan tucked the end of her laces into the top of her trainer. Maybe there was a way she could help Flora, really help her, after all.

'Umm, I'd love to agree with you, Ginny, but I've no idea what an Excel spreadsheet is. It might as well be an alien spacecraft to me.' Flora chuckled.

Standing up, Megan turned back to the counter. 'I could help you with that if you like?' she said. 'I'm a trained accountant, and I'd be happy to get your finances in order. I could set up a system and explain it all to you.'

'Oh, are you?' Flora closed the notebook.

'Yes. And I wouldn't charge you. I'd do it all for free.' Megan looked from Flora to Ginny and back again. 'I haven't officially worked for over ten years, but I used to help Lyle out with his accounts.'

Flora nodded slowly.

Megan clasped her hands in front of her, the searing heat of self-consciousness flooding her face. Why had she said that? If it wasn't bad enough that she'd mentioned his name, to then say that she had done all his accounts would have made things worse.

'I mean, I kept the accounts that he told me about. I know now that he wasn't transparent about his finances, but I didn't know at the time.'

'Right.' Flora's eye twitched, her forehead creasing ever so slightly before she relaxed her expression again as Megan continued.

'But I am an accountant, and I can do this for you. I promise I wouldn't have offered if I didn't think I could. I know I can.' She shrugged. 'I'm good at what I do. I just need to be given all of the information and not be lied to. Not that for one minute I'm suggesting you will. I mean, Lyle. If he hadn't lied to me, I could have done my job properly...' She let her voice trail off and turned around. 'Sorry, I should go.'

'Wait.' Flora held up her hand. 'Are you sure you wouldn't mind? It'd save us a lot of headaches if you could sort the accounts for us, but I'm afraid I've never been the best at keeping on top of things. Not things like finances. As long as we have money in the bank to keep the dogs fed and the bills paid, then I don't tend to worry too much about documenting everything until we have to.'

Megan smiled. 'Yes, I'm sure. I'd be happy to help.'

'There are receipts everywhere. In the drawers, stuffed into notebooks, scribbled lists of expenses.' Flora held her arms open, indicating the countertop strewn with notebooks and papers.

'I can collate them all for you and enter them into a system. Once that's done, I can show you all how to use it, so it's not a huge job at the end of the financial year.' Megan stepped forward.

'You mean no more all-nighters trying to find evidence of all expenses?' Ginny raised her eyebrows. 'That sounds like bliss.'

'Ha ha, we're not that bad.' Flora shook her head.

'Umm, I beg to differ.' Ginny laughed. 'Honestly, what you're offering to do sounds fantastic, but Flora's not joking when she says all the information is spread around.'

'That's fine. In the past I've worked with people with really shocking ways of storing income and outgoings, so I'm sure I can cope. I'd love to help.'

'Great. Well, we accept, and quickly before you change your mind.' Flora smiled, the skin around her eyes creasing with kindness.

'When would you like me to start?'

'Whenever is convenient for you, lovely.'

'Okay, I'll come in and make a start tomorrow then, if that's okay?'

'Perfect.'

Nodding, Megan pulled the door open and stepped outside, the heat of the summer sun enveloping her. She grinned. She could actually help. She could actually make a difference. She was needed. For the first time in a very long time, she was needed.

3

Megan yawned as she pulled out another mound of paperwork from the bottom drawer beneath the counter. Yep, these were receipts too, although judging from the way some of them had begun to yellow and curl at the corners, they might well be from years ago.

The bell above the door tinkled, announcing someone's arrival. That would likely be Flora. She'd said she wouldn't be long and would come back to talk Megan through the charity's monthly spend. Reaching up, she placed the pile of receipts on the counter before watching them flutter down to the floor.

'I'll help you with those.'

Megan frowned. That wasn't Flora. That was a man's voice.

Looking up, she realised it was one of the others who had attended the volunteer induction morning. She shuffled along as he knelt down to help. 'Thank you.'

'I think we've got them all.' With a handful of receipts, the man straightened his back.

Megan stood up and let the receipts fall from her hands into a heap on the counter.

'Shall I?' The man nodded downwards.

'Oh, yes please, and thank you.' She held out her hands for the receipts.

'It's my first day here,' he said. 'By the looks of things you've been here a while? I'm sure I saw you at the volunteer induction morning?'

The man smiled, a slight dimple showing beneath his dark stubble.

She looked up from the mound of untidy paperwork. 'Yes, I was there, and this is my first morning of volunteering too.'

The man looked down at the receipts, open notebooks and scattered papers on the countertop as confusion swept across his features.

Megan smiled. 'I know it looks as though I've been here ages with all this lot, doesn't it? I've volunteered to get the books in order.'

'Ah, I see.' The man chuckled. 'Well, I definitely don't envy you.'

'Umm.' Megan tilted her head, focusing on the mess in front of her, and smiled. This was just what she needed. Something to keep her mind busy and to test her accountancy skills. She looked up at the man. 'If I'm honest – and I know this probably sounds terrible – but I'm actually looking forward to figuring it all out.'

'It doesn't sound terrible. Well, to me it does because anything complicated to do with numbers brings me out in a cold sweat, but everyone's different.' He held his hand out towards her. 'I'm Jay.'

Taking his hand, she replied, 'Megan.'

'Pleased to meet you, Megan.' Jay shook her hand, his grip firm and strong.

'And you.' She nodded before taking her hand back. 'What are you helping out with?'

'Oh, I'm guessing walking the dogs, but I'm not fussy. I can turn my hand to most things.' He looked down at the countertop and grimaced. 'Apart from accountancy, of course.'

Megan laughed. 'Don't worry, I won't force you to help me.'

'That's a relief!' Taking a slight step back, Jay glanced out towards the courtyard. 'I'm not really sure what I'm meant to do now. I know Flora told us all there'd be a checklist of dogs to walk, but do I just go and fetch one or should I go find her?'

'She popped out to pick up a dog, I think,' Megan said. 'Although she's been over an hour, so I'm sure she'll be back soon. You've just missed Ginny, she's taken one of the dogs out on a walk. Sally and Alex should be about, though. They'll likely be up in the paddocks.'

'Maybe I'll take a wander up there. I'd feel more comfortable checking with someone. Unless, of course, you know what I should do?'

'No, sorry. I've no idea.' She shrugged.

'Right, I'll do that then.' Jay walked towards the door before turning and holding his hand up. 'I'll likely see you in a few minutes.'

They both looked towards the window as a vehicle drove down the lane before turning into the courtyard.

'Hang on, that's Flora in the van, turning in now.' Megan indicated out into the courtyard as the Wagging Tails' van drove in, pulling up just outside the door.

'Ah, perfect timing.' Jay grinned before stepping outside.

Back to her task, Megan began sorting through the receipts, discarding any from previous years into a separate pile.

Yes, this was just what she needed. She knew Flora was embarrassed by the state of the home's finance records, but all Megan saw was something to focus on and the more complicated it was, the more likely it would keep her mind from straying to the conversation she'd had with the solicitor that morning.

The bell above the door tinkled as Flora and Jay rushed through, Jay holding the leads of two dogs whilst Flora carried a small pup, possibly a Bichon Frise although Megan couldn't be sure as the poor thing was covered in mud.

'That's it, Jay, if you could take those two through to the kennels, you'll see there's an empty one. The third one down I think it is. I'll take this little one straight through to get cleaned up. The sooner this is all off of her, the better she'll feel.' Flora nodded towards the door leading through to the kennels as she used her elbow to open the door to the washroom.

'Here, I'll get that for you.' Megan rushed to the door and swung it open for Flora.

'Thanks, lovely.'

'That's—'

The shrill sound of the landline phone filled the room and Megan rushed back to the counter to pick it up.

'Hello, Wagging Tails Dogs' Home, how can I help you?'

'Can I speak to the owner, please?' A husky voice filtered down the line.

Megan glanced towards the now-closed washroom door. 'I'm afraid she's a little busy right now. Can I take a message?'

'No, sorry, but I really need to speak to whoever is in charge. It's urgent. Is there any way you could get them to the phone?'

Megan frowned. The man at the end of the line sounded desperate. 'One moment and I'll go and see.'

'Thank you.'

After carefully laying the phone down on the countertop, Megan hurried towards the washroom door and pulled it slightly ajar. Flora was standing next to the deep tray of the dog shower, the Bichon Frise cowering as far back as possible.

'Sorry, Flora, there's someone on the phone and he says it's urgent.'

Flora looked over her shoulder at her. 'Could you take a message and tell them I'll ring them straight back, please?'

'I tried. He sounded desperate.'

'Right. Are you all right to carry on here then, please?' Flora nodded towards the dog.

'Yes, okay.' Megan frowned. She'd never even had a dog before, let alone showered one. She inched forward until she was standing next to Flora.

'Thanks. He's very nervous, but he's been very gentle. Just try to get as much mud and grime off as possible, would you? Make the little sweetheart a little more comfortable.'

'I'll do my best.'

As Flora stepped away, Megan took the showerhead and looked down at the small dog.

'Hey, little one. So, it's just you and me now, then.'

She held her hand under the water, checking the temperature, before moving the showerhead so the water dribbled onto the dog's coat. The bottom of the white porcelain shower tray instantly turned a murky brown as the water seeped through the dog's fur.

'That's it. We'll get you nice and clean, shall we?'

The dog looked up at her, his deep brown eyes penetrating hers as he slumped against the cold shower tray.

'Shall we use some shampoo?'

Holding the showerhead in one hand, she took a yellow bottle from the shelf and gently tipped it upside down, waiting as a few dollops of shampoo dropped to the dog's fur before replacing it. As she gently rubbed the shampoo in, her fingers caught in large matts.

'Oh, you're not just dirty, you're matted too.'

How could someone let a dog they're responsible for get into such a state? Owners were supposed to love and care for their pets, not neglect them. She gently rubbed the fur as more dirt was dislodged and the once brown fur began to take on a shade closer to the typical white of a Bichon Frise.

A short, quiet knock sounded on the door before it opened. Turning her head, Megan realised it was Jay.

'Flora sent me in here to see if you need any help?'

'I think we're about done now. I've washed him but look at how matted the fur is.' She turned the water off before indicating the matts.

'That looks painful. I wonder if he can even walk with that much matting around his legs. If he can, I imagine it would hurt.'

Jay picked up a towel from the shelf beside him.

'I wouldn't be surprised if he can't. How could anyone let him get into such a state?' she said, voicing her earlier thoughts.

She took the towel from him and began to gently rub the dog's face dry.

'I don't know. Someone who certainly doesn't deserve the love and loyalty of a dog, that's for sure.'

Megan nodded.

Wrapping the towel around the dog, she could feel the dog's bony body and realised that although he looked quite well fed, the bulk of his size was simply the matted fur.

'He's ever so skinny, too.'

Jay glanced down at the floor. 'Poor thing.'

'Can you grab the door for me, please?'

'Yes, of course.' Jay stepped forward and held the door open as Megan carried the dog through to the reception area. Flora was still on the phone, her voice full of concern.

'...of course. We can work with that.' Covering the mouthpiece, Flora whispered across to them. 'Take him through to the kitchen and dry him off there, would you, please?'

Nodding, Jay moved towards the kitchen door and opened it, letting Megan carry the dog through. Then he hurried in and pulled a chair out for her.

'Thanks.' Lowering herself, Megan drew the dog onto her lap, the towel still wrapped around him. She could feel him shaking beneath the thick fabric. 'Aw, he's shaking. Poor thing.'

'He probably doesn't know what to make of this place yet. If he's been mistreated, he might assume that's how everyone acts.' Jay flicked the kettle on and held up a mug. 'Do you fancy a cuppa? We might as well quench our thirsts while we wait in here.'

'A coffee would be great, please. I didn't actually manage to get one before I left this morning.'

'Really? I don't think I could function without my morning coffee fix.' Jay chuckled as he spooned coffee granules into the mugs.

Megan smiled as she rubbed the towel against the dog's body. She was normally the same. She could almost taste the coffee from the expensive machine Lyle had given her for Christmas a few years ago. A fresh coffee had been so engrained in her morning routine for so long and the tiny sachets of cheap instant the bed and breakfast offered just weren't the same. Mixed with a pot of long-life milk, it wasn't even worth calling it a coffee.

'I used to be the same,' she said.

'Ah, you're trying to cut the caffeine habit, are you? I hope I'm not sabotaging it by making you one.'

'Something like that, but no, you're not sabotaging anything. This is very much appreciated. Thank you.' Taking the mug, she took a sip, the bitter taste hitting the back of her throat. It still wasn't quite what she was used to, but it was nowhere near the mellow liquid from the bed and breakfast.

'It looks as though he's settling.' Jay nodded at the dog, who had now laid his head on Megan's jeans.

'Yes, he's not shaking as much now either.'

Looking down at him, she wondered what his story was, what circumstances Flora had rescued him from. Did he know he was safe now? Or had he settled simply because he was used to being scared? She sighed.

Jay frowned, deep lines appearing across his forehead. 'Are you okay?'

'I was just wondering if he knows he's safe now and understands he's been rescued.'

Megan stroked the dog between the eyes, possibly the only part of him not covered in knots and matts. His eyelids flickered open before slowly closing again.

The door opened and Flora hurried into the kitchen.

'Sorry about that, Megan.' Flora paused by her chair and looked down at the dog in her lap. 'One minute I'm asking you to help with the accounts, the next I'm asking you to shower a dog.'

Megan smiled. 'I don't mind. I've got most of the dirt off, but he's covered in knots.'

'I thought he was. Sweet little thing. The most nervous of the three of them.' She shook her head. 'I've got to rush off now. One of our recent adopters is having a few behavioural issues with their dog, so I promised I'd pop round as soon as I can.'

'Is there anything you'd like me to do whilst you're gone?' Jay placed his mug on the table.

'Could you make up a bed for this little one in here, please? I'd like to keep an eye on him before he goes into the kennels, and I need to see how he is with the other two he came in with. And then Sally should be popping back in when she's finished her training session, so you can ask her to show you the ropes. Is that all right?'

'Of course.'

'Thanks. Finish your coffee first, though.' Bending down, Flora fussed the small dog before straightening her back and heading towards the door. 'Oh, and maybe you could give this one a name?'

Megan nodded as the door clicked shut.

Looking down at the dog in her lap, she smiled.

'What do you think, then? What should we name him?'

'Umm...' Jay tapped his fingers against his chin. 'Something strong maybe? A name meaning strength?'

'I like that. Set him up positively for his new life.' She took another sip of her coffee.

'Not that I know any names which mean strength.' Jay smiled, the dimple reappearing in his cheek. 'Do you?'

'I'm not sure.' She closed her eyes for a moment. When she'd been thinking about having children, she'd always thought she'd find a name that meant something positive, something that could possibly help determine the child's future. Of course, Lyle had been adamant that children would ruin their relationship and come between them. The truth, though, was that him not even being willing to discuss the idea properly, or much else, to be truthful, had caused a rift between them, a rift that had only grown over the long silent years of their relationship. Since then, though, there was one name she'd held close to her heart. A name she'd always imagined they'd have called their son if they'd had one.

'How about Angus?'

'Perfect.' Jay leaned forward and gently fussed over the dog.

'That's decided then.' Megan looked down at the pup. 'Your new name is Angus. A new name and a new start in life.'

4

Megan stared at the screen of her mobile for the eighth time in the last ten minutes and sighed. She needed to ring her solicitor, she needed to find out how things were going.

She tapped the phone against the tabletop. She was relieved the divorce papers were being served today but she couldn't help feeling sick, worrying about Lyle's reaction. She didn't want a fight. She wanted peace. She wanted to wake up in the morning without all of this stress and worry hanging over her head. She wanted to wake up without the nagging feeling that Lyle was going to pull another stunt. She wanted to wake up in her own bed, in her own home. Wherever that might be and whatever that might look like.

Sighing, she turned her mobile over, screen down, and slid it across the table before turning to the ancient laptop she'd borrowed from Flora. The Excel spreadsheet flickered back at her. She needed to push Lyle out of her mind. And she needed to focus.

The creak of the kitchen door sounded, and she looked behind her. Jay was standing in the doorway.

'Morning.'

Megan smiled. She'd enjoyed spending some time with him yesterday.

'Morning. You're back volunteering again today, are you?'

'I am indeed. And you?' He nodded towards the laptop and the paperwork spread across the table.

She grinned. 'Yep.'

'Do you know how little Angus is doing this morning?'

'Flora took him to the groomers earlier, and he's like a different dog already! He seems a lot more confident and inquisitive about his new surroundings.'

'Oh, that's great news. I couldn't stop worrying about him last night.' Jay leaned his elbows on the chair opposite her.

She looked at him. She could believe that. She'd seen him out of the window walking the dogs yesterday and she'd noticed that every few steps, he'd pause and fuss them before continuing.

'I think there's a staff meeting in here now.'

'Oh really? I'd better get out of the way then.' Standing up, Megan closed the laptop and began tidying the paperwork.

'No, you should stay. Ginny told me to come in and join in, so I imagine it will be the same for you.'

'Oh, right.' She frowned. Would it?

She looked towards the door as it opened again. This time, Ginny and Flora walked inside. Megan piled the papers on top of the laptop and picked it up.

'You'll stay for the staff meeting, won't you, Megan?' Flora asked as she flicked the kettle on. 'It only seems right, being that you and Jay are both going to be spending a lot of time here. It would be good for all of us if you're in the loop, so to speak.'

'I can do.' As she lowered the laptop back down, Megan dithered. Should she sit down again? Were there enough chairs for everyone?

'Tea? Coffee?' Flora began taking mugs from the cupboard.

'Tea for me, please.' Jay pulled out a chair and sat down.

Following Jay's lead, Megan sat back down as Sally, Alex, Susan and Percy filed in.

'Coffee please.'

'Did you say you'd baked some of your flapjack, Susan?' Percy took a pile of plates from the cupboard and set them in the middle of the table.

'I certainly did.' Susan picked up a large Tupperware container from the back of the work surface and set it down next to the plates.

'Lovely.' Rubbing his hands together, Percy looked around the table. 'Flapjack, everyone?'

'Sounds perfect.' Jay grinned as he stood up and began handing the plates around.

Once the mugs and flapjack were distributed, Flora sat down at the head of the table.

'So, today I've asked Megan and Jay to join us. As you know, Megan is rescuing us from the paperwork nightmare of the accounts and Jay has volunteered to come and walk the dogs every day apart from Saturdays for the time being. Is that right, Jay?'

Jay nodded. 'Yes, just not a full day on Fridays.'

'Of course. That's right.' Flora smiled kindly.

Megan looked across at him. He was volunteering every day? He'd spent the entire day at Wagging Tails yesterday and left only shortly before she had. Was he going to be spending all day here each day? When she caught his eye she quickly looked down at the slice of flapjack on her plate, the tinge of self-consciousness sweeping across her face.

'As you know, we've got a busy few weeks ahead of us as we get the home ready for the extension and I'm excited to tell you we finally have the plans.' Flora pulled a sheet of paper from a cardboard folder in front of her.

'You're getting an extension? That's great news.' Jay rubbed his hands together.

'Yes. I had meant to mention it on the induction morning, but it completely slipped my mind.' Flora laughed as she tapped her forehead. 'Darryl has been doing a terrific job fundraising for us through the local paper.'

'That's really impressive.' Jay took a sip from his mug.

Flora nodded. 'It's more of an outbuilding than an extension.'

'A glorified shed. That's what I call it.' Percy shuffled in his chair and leaned forward. 'Not that that's a bad thing. No, it's good. It's a great way of getting another few kennels without the expense of a brick extension.'

Megan looked at Flora. 'How many extra kennels will there be?'

'Four!'

'I'm actually quite interested in how it'll be put together.' Leaning back in his chair again, Percy stroked his beard. 'I'm sure I read that it comes already constructed with the insulation and everything already in place and then the walls are slotted together.'

'It sure does,' Susan said, joining the conversation. 'Malcolm has a summer house in his back garden that is the same sort of thing, and it's super toasty, even in the winter.'

'He was telling me about that,' Ginny said. 'It sounded nice and the kennels we're getting are going to be a lifeline for so many dogs.'

'Exactly. And this is what's so great about having two more people on board on a regular basis.' Flora glanced at Megan and then Jay. 'At least for the moment, anyway. I know realistically we can't expect you both to volunteer here full time forever but, and I know I speak for everyone here, we're very grateful that you've decided to dedicate the free time you have now to Wagging Tails. Very grateful.'

'Here. Here.' Percy raised his mug as a stream of coffee sloshed down the side.

'Careful.' Standing up, Flora moved to tear a sheet of kitchen roll from the roll by the kettle, which she passed across to Percy.

'Thanks, love.' After mopping the puddle of coffee which had collected on the table, he wiped the side of his mug. 'It's true, though, what Flora's saying, we're grateful you're giving your time to help the dogs in our care.'

'You're very welcome.' Jay lowered his mug to the table. 'After I read the article in the paper about what you'd all gone through at the hands of that awful man, Luke – no, Lyle, was it? – I knew what I wanted to do with my time off.'

Lyle? A newspaper article? Megan's stomach dropped. His attempt at closing down Wagging Tails to make way for his housing development had been in the paper? As she kept her eyes fixed on her coffee mug, Megan could feel the fierce rush of heat flooding across her face. Jay didn't know who she was, did he?

She held her breath, waiting for someone to tell him, waiting for the disgusted look, the disapproving stare, as though she were guilty by default because she'd been with Lyle.

'Oh, that's all in the past now.' Flora's voice cut through the silence. 'Back to the list of tasks we need to do to get ready for the build.'

But Jay continued, not taking the hint. 'It must have been such a worrying time. How awful for a developer like that, someone who, I imagine, would have a lot of money anyway, to then use such underhand tactics to try to force a charity out of their home.'

Jay shook his head, the flush of anger coursing across his face.

Megan swallowed, a hard lump stuck in her throat. She knew it hadn't been her fault. She hadn't even known what Lyle had been up to until the last minute, and she definitely hadn't approved when she'd discovered what he'd been planning. She'd stopped him. Eventually. With the help of Andy.

She focused on a tiny coffee granule stuck to the rim of her mug. She'd helped. She'd done all she could.

'It's in the past, Jay.' Flora spoke, her voice quiet but firm as she pushed the sheet of paper into the middle of the table. 'And this is our future. Take a look, everyone. In two weeks we'll have enough space for four more pups.'

Susan shifted in her chair and peered at the plan. 'It does look amazing.'

With her hands now tightly clasped in her lap, Megan glanced across at Jay, averting her eyes almost as soon as she looked at him. He had pushed his chair back and was standing, leaning across the table to get a better look at the plan. What if he did know who she was? What if he'd brought Lyle's name up to see her reaction? To shame her even? But if that was the case, why hadn't he mentioned it earlier? He'd waited until everyone was here to express how he felt. What must he think of her?

'Take a look, Megan.' Susan patted her forearm and pointed towards the plan.

Closing her eyes for a moment, Megan tried to clear her mind, to push all thoughts of Lyle and what he had done away. Jay's comments may have made it clear how he felt towards her, or if he didn't know already, how he would feel when he found out, but everyone else had welcomed her with open arms. She needed to focus on that.

Opening her eyes again, she smiled at Susan and focused on the plan. 'Yes, it looks amazing.'

'I'm guessing we need to clear the area so the builders can lay the foundations?' Susan sat back in her chair.

'I'll be doing that.' Percy crossed his arms. 'Laying the foundations.'

'Yes, so the area needs to be cleared of grass and dug down a little too.'

Megan sat quietly as Flora explained the tasks that needed to be completed before the new kennels arrived. Every so often, she heard Jay speak, asking questions about this or that, his voice friendly. That's how he'd spoken to her yesterday and earlier this morning, so why had he talked so much about Lyle?

Surely, he'd have known how uncomfortable it would have made her feel, but then Megan had to stop her thoughts from spiralling. Shaking her head, she reminded herself that he might not have realised yet who she was.

5

'Megan?' Flora placed her hand on her shoulder. 'The meeting is over now.'

Megan blinked and looked around the kitchen as Susan, Jay and Ginny filed out of the door whilst Alex and Percy loaded the used mugs into the dishwasher. In front of her, Sally was opening a folder.

'Sorry, I was miles away.'

'I know you were, lovely.'

Pulling the chair out next to Megan, Flora sat down.

'I'll catch you later.' Alex closed the dishwasher door and left as Percy turned his attention to wiping flapjack crumbs from the kitchen counter.

'Jay didn't mean anything by what he said about Lyle.' Flora smiled kindly. 'He doesn't know you were his partner.'

'He doesn't?' Megan gripped her mug, the ceramic cold against her hands, the coffee having cooled a long time before.

'Well, not unless you told him yourself. None of us has mentioned anything to him. Or anyone else, for that matter.'

'You haven't?'

'Of course not. Your business is your business, not ours.' Sally paused, pen in hand.

Megan looked from Flora to Sally and back again. Why wouldn't they have said anything? She'd have deserved everyone knowing.

'Thank you.'

'No problem,' Sally said. 'We're really grateful to you for volunteering.'

'Especially for doing the books!' Flora chuckled. 'Seriously though, we are grateful. It must have taken a lot for you to have come back here, not knowing how we'd react.'

'I take my hat off to you, I do. You've got guts coming back after what Lyle did.' Percy sat back down at the table.

Megan nodded. 'I did worry you'd all turn me away.'

'Well, as long as you know that you're welcome here. We all know what you and Andy did to save Wagging Tails.' Flora patted her hand. 'And we're here for you. You must be going through a tough time after splitting up with him.'

'Yes.' Percy looked at her and frowned. 'He might have been an awful man and I for one think you're better off without him, but a relationship has still ended.'

'And we all know how tough that can be.' Sally looked across at her. 'So if you need to talk or vent, then we're all here for you.'

'Absolutely.' Flora laid the palms of her hands on the table and pushed herself to standing. 'But don't worry about what Jay said. He wasn't aiming it at you at all.'

'Okay. Thanks.' Megan breathed a sigh of relief.

The last couple of days here at Wagging Tails had been a breath of fresh air. Quite literally. She'd been so used to spending time on her own, whilst she'd been living with Lyle and since she'd moved out, that suddenly being surrounded by people was both strange and comforting at the same time. And Flora was right, everyone had made her feel welcome. Maybe she herself was the one who was struggling to forgive the fact she hadn't realised what Lyle had been up to earlier and how corrupt he was.

'Right, I'm off to take Angus to see Mack at the vet's and to hopefully be given a full bill of health.' Flora tucked her chair in.

'I'll go and make a start of clearing that patch for the kennels.' Percy followed Flora out.

'I don't suppose you fancy a walk down to the beach, do you?' Sally closed her folder. 'I need to take Ocean and Splash out to see how they are with other dogs when they're together.'

'Are they the two who came in with Angus?'

'That's right. They're super lovely and get on so well together.'

'I'd love to come then.' Megan pushed her cold coffee away and stood up. She hadn't actually been down to the beach yet even though she'd been staying in Trestow for the last few weeks.

Megan looked towards the sea as they walked down the cobbled lane leading to the cove. The sun was beaming down on the blue water, which reflected the sun's rays, as a handful of people walked along the water's edge.

'So far, so good.'

'They've been brilliant, haven't they? So calm even when we met that puppy being walked back there.' Sally stooped down to fuss Ocean.

'Do you think they'll be rehomed together?' Megan glanced down as Splash, a small Yorkshire terrier, paused as the cobbles gave way to the sand.

'Possibly not. It's so difficult to find people wanting to adopt a pair of dogs. Still, it's good to check to see how they walk together as it might come in handy to know if the potential adopters

already have a dog.' Sally looked down at Ocean, a West High-
land. 'You never know though, someone might come forward for
the both of them. It would be nice for them to stay together.'

Megan looked across at Sally. 'So what's the real reason you
asked me on the walk, then? You already know they get along
together because they share a kennel, and you could have walked
them both together yourself, anyway.'

'You got me.' Sally held her hands up, Ocean's lead tucked
around her wrist and between her fingers. 'I wanted to check in
on you, see how you're doing with everything.'

Maybe she should be annoyed, but it was nice of Sally to ask.
None of her so-called friends from home had even bothered to
get in touch with her. Not that she blamed them. When she'd
moved in with Lyle, she'd moved away from her family, her
friendship group, and although she'd been welcomed into his
social circle, she'd never quite felt comfortable with them and
maybe they hadn't quite been as accepting of her as she'd
believed. Besides, she hadn't been the one to tell them she and
Lyle had split up so she dreaded to think how he would have spun
the story.

Megan looked across at Sally. 'I'm okay.'

'Are you sure? You've had a lot of upheaval recently and, as
Percy said, none of us liked Lyle, but he was your husband.' She
paused as Ocean slowed down. 'You loved him and now...'

As they walked towards the sea, the sand became wet and
Megan could feel her trainers sink, the millions of tiny grains
moving beneath her.

'I did love him, yes. Once, a long time ago, but honestly?
Towards the end of the relationship, I knew he had changed, I
knew he was no longer the man I'd vowed to spend the rest of my
life with, I just didn't realise quite how much he had changed and
quite how much I'd end up hating him.'

Bending down, Sally coaxed Ocean to move along the beach, before looking back at Megan. 'Why didn't you leave him before then?'

Megan shrugged. There hadn't been one reason, there had been a million different ones.

She cleared her throat. 'He was my world. I'd been with him for fifteen years and spent pretty much my entire adult life with him. I'd have lost everything – our friends, our social circle, my home. Everything.'

'I understand.'

Megan laughed, her voice catching in her throat. 'As it turns out, I've lost everything, anyway. Maybe I should have found the courage to leave him years ago.'

'Do you wish you'd left him before?'

'Yes, and no. I don't know.' Megan looked down at Splash as she pulled at the lead, seemingly desperate to get to the water. 'Part of me does. Part of me feels as though I wasted all that time I stuck with him.'

'If you had, though, Wagging Tails would have likely been bulldozed by now.'

'That's what I keep telling myself.' Megan bent down and fussed Splash behind the ears. 'I think this little one wants to go for a paddle.'

Sally smiled. 'She seems to love the water. You should have seen her this morning when Alex was cleaning out their kennel. Neither of them seems to be house-trained yet, so he had the hose out and Splash was absolutely loving it! Jumping up to catch the water and everything.'

'Aw, she was given the perfect name then.'

'She was! She's come out of herself so much since they first arrived.' Sally began walking across the sand towards the water's edge. 'But back to you. How are you holding up now?'

Megan watched as Splash lunged forward again, diving straight into the water, the seawater quickly reaching her shoulders. 'I'm not sure. Lyle was away from home so much towards the end of our relationship that, quite honestly, I don't really miss him much, but I miss being with him. That doesn't make sense, does it?'

'Umm...' Sally shrugged.

'I mean, I miss knowing he's there for me, that it's not just me on my own against the world, that I have someone to fight my corner.' Megan walked along the wet sand, the water seeping in through the tops of her trainers. 'Not that he would have been there for me anyway, but it's more the thought of being completely alone that I struggle with sometimes.'

'I understand.'

'It's strange because on the one hand, I feel totally free, as though I can do anything I want and go anywhere I want without having to think of anyone else, but on the other hand, it's daunting. I've not been alone since I was at university and then I lived with housemates. I'm completely alone now.'

She swallowed. Now she'd said it, it somehow felt real all of a sudden. She *was* alone. Her parents had emigrated to Spain years ago, she had no siblings and her so-called friends had all dropped her, perhaps worried that the impending divorce was a contagious disease which could threaten to ruin their marriages too. That, or they had just sided with Lyle.

'You're not alone. You have us.' Sally reached out and gave her a quick hug around the shoulders.

'Thanks, but you know what I mean. I guess it's that my life has been well and truly turned upside down. I don't miss Lyle, not one bit, but I miss the safety net he provided. I miss the future I thought we'd have. And now I don't know what my future looks like from one minute to the next, let alone where I'll be in five years' time.'

'Have you thought about what you'd like to do? Long term?'

'No.'

That wasn't true. She had.

'Sorry, I have actually. I've thought about it since the moment I shut the door on my marital home, but I'm no clearer what I want to do. What I do know, though, is I want to find somewhere to settle. Somewhere to put proper roots down.'

'How about here?'

Megan scrunched up her nose. 'There's too many memories here.'

Sally nodded slowly. 'I guess so.'

'I want to have a completely fresh start. I wanted to come here and volunteer, find my bearings, so to speak, and it just felt like the right thing to do. I know I can't make up for the way Lyle treated you all, but I hope I can make a slight difference, however small.'

'You don't need to make up for anything. And I know Flora's spoken to you about that before. You really don't. If anything, we owe you. If it hadn't been for you revealing his plans, then the home would no longer be here. You don't owe us anything.'

'Still, it feels right.'

It did. When she'd left Lyle the first place she'd thought of running to had been West Par. Well, not quite the first. She'd initially spent a couple of months in her and Lyle's holiday home on the Norfolk coast, but somehow it hadn't felt right. When they'd been together, she'd spent a lot of time there on her own anyway and as hard as she'd tried she'd just not been able to relax, she'd always felt as though he might walk through the front door without a moment's notice. No, coming here she at least could tell herself she was beginning her new life away from him.

She didn't need to look over her shoulder, or worry that he'd walk through the door of the bed and breakfast at any given time. West Par would be the last place he'd think she was.

As they walked across the beach, Splash and Ocean's leads taut as they played in the sea, Sally linked her arm through Megan's and pulled her close. 'Well, I'm glad you came. And I know for one thing, Flora's relieved she doesn't have to try to sort the finances out!'

Megan laughed. 'Glad to be of assistance.'

6

Perching on the edge of the bed, Megan balanced her plate of scrambled eggs, toast and grilled tomatoes on her knee and pulled her phone from the pocket of her jeans. She shovelled a forkful of egg into her mouth before hitting the Call button to ring her solicitor.

As she listened to the rhythmic tone of the call waiting to be answered, she looked out of the window. It wasn't the prettiest view, and if she strained her eyes, she could see into the top floor of the bank opposite, the staff members sitting on uncomfortable-looking plastic chairs pretending to listen to whatever was being discussed in today's morning briefing, but it was fine. She didn't need ocean views or the sight of mountains or hills. This was just right. Besides, in some small way, being able to see other people going about their daily lives made hers feel a little less lonely.

'Morning, Perkin's Solicitors, Evan speaking. How may I help you today?' Evan's authoritative voice boomed down the line, a comforting mixture of confidence and friendliness.

'Hi, Evan, it's Megan. Megan Trussel. I'm ringing to see if there's been any movement on the divorce petition, please?'

'Megan! Hi. Yes, there certainly has! It's all written and being delivered today.'

Megan nodded. Lyle was going to find out she'd filed for divorce. Today. He'd find out today.

'Okay, thank you.'

'Can I help you with anything else?'

'No, no. I don't think so. I think that's it. Thank you.'

'No problem! Have a great day.'

Standing up, Megan placed her breakfast on the little desk below the television and stood at the window.

She looked down at the pedestrianised street below. Mums pushing buggies and dads carrying young children rushed down the street, checking their watches every so often, determined not to be late for the school drop-off. A man carrying a briefcase meandered slowly, stopping every so often and peering into shop windows. Had he left too early for work and was trying to kill time, or was he trying to savour the last few minutes of freedom before being shackled to a desk he'd rather not be sitting at?

Lyle was going to get the divorce papers today. He was going to know she wanted to divorce him. The final axe to their marriage served. She gripped hold of the windowsill. This is what she wanted. This is what she'd wanted for the last few years. To be free to start her life over. And yet, now it was happening, now she'd taken that step to end things formally, she couldn't help but feel a little pang of regret.

Stepping back, she lowered herself down onto the bed and sank into the plush duvet. This would be the first day of the rest of her life. Yes, that's how she needed to look at it. She should be excited. The world was her oyster.

She could feel a single tear sliding down the skin of her cheek and she reached up, using the back of her hand to rub it away. She wasn't going to cry. She'd done all the crying she needed to when she'd discovered what Lyle had been up to with Wagging Tails. She'd cried herself to sleep every night that week at the realisation that Lyle was never again going to be the man she'd married. Now was the time to celebrate.

She lowered her head to her hands and stared into the darkness of her cupped palms. It was time to celebrate; she knew that, but surely it was normal to spend time grieving for what could have been?

A sharp tapping on the door to her room broke the silence. Pulling it open, she smiled as the young girl who took care of all the housekeeping shuffled from foot to foot.

'Shall I come back later?' She indicated the bucket of cleaning products by her feet.

'No, it's okay, thanks, Lisa. I'd better get off, anyway.'

Lisa nodded as she picked up the bucket and walked into the room. 'It's another lovely day out there today. It's going to be a hot one, I reckon.'

'Is it?' Megan glanced back towards the window. Lisa was right, the sun was already high in the sky, having taken its place ages ago, probably. She hadn't noticed when she'd been looking earlier. Turning on the spot, she searched for her mobile. Where had she put it?

'Are you looking for something? I'm usually good at finding things. Found a diamond ring in the room next door yesterday. They were ever so grateful as they'd only got engaged last week. Gave me a fifty-pound tip for that. Can you imagine having a spare fifty-pound just to tip someone for doing their job?' Lisa placed the bucket on the desk.

Megan smiled sadly. Yes, she could imagine it. 'My phone. I can't remember where I put it.'

'Is it the one in your hand?' Lisa pointed to Megan.

Looking down, Megan shook her head. Yep, there it was. 'Ah, thanks. I don't even remember picking it up.'

'One of those days today, then?'

Megan sighed as she slid her mobile into her pocket and picked up her room key. 'Something like that. See you later.'

'Have a good day,' Lisa called over her shoulder as Megan headed to the door. 'It can only get better.'

Pausing outside the room, Megan turned and watched as Lisa began polishing the bedside table. Maybe she was right. Today could get better. Today and the rest of her life would be better now that she was officially divorcing her lying husband.

Megan hit the Enter key on Flora's laptop and watched as the cursor jumped to the next box in the spreadsheet and waited there, patiently flickering away as she searched the paperwork for the next number to input.

She leaned back in her chair and rolled her shoulders, trying to loosen the tension she told herself was due to spending the morning scrunched over the table rather than the phone call with Evan and the nagging apprehension as she imagined Lyle receiving the official-looking brown envelope and tearing it open to reveal the divorce papers.

The slight creak as the kitchen door opened brought her back to the present.

'I'm not going to disturb you too much if I come and sit in here for my lunch, am I?'

Looking up, she could see Jay frowning as he held his lunch box up.

'No, no, disturb away. Please.'

'Thank you. It's too warm for me to be sitting outside.' He smiled. 'I don't like the heat much.'

'Oh, I love the hot weather. Although the heat here isn't the same as abroad.'

'No, you're right. It's getting too humid here for it to be particularly pleasant.' Jay nodded towards the kettle. 'Cuppa?'

'Good idea.' Megan stood up. 'I'll get them, though. I need to stretch my legs and give my brain a break.'

'A difficult day with the numbers?' Jay raised his eyebrows at the laptop, and papers strewn across the table.

'Yes. It's my own fault. I just can't concentrate today.' She flicked the kettle on.

'Ah, one of those days then.'

Megan laughed. 'You're not the first person to say that to me this morning! But, yes, I'm definitely longing for this day to be over already.'

'Sorry to hear that. I hope it isn't anything that bad on your mind.'

'Mmm...'

Should she tell him? Wasn't the saying something along the lines of 'a problem shared, a problem halved'? Although it wasn't a problem – the divorce papers – it was a solution.

She spoke quietly as she watched the steam escape the spout of the kettle. 'My ex will be receiving my divorce papers today.'

Jay whistled under his breath. 'Are congratulations in order or commiserations?'

She poured the water into the mugs, the small mounds of coffee granules instantly dissolving in the heat of the water. 'Definitely, congratulations, which is why I don't know why I'm feeling so weird about it all.'

'Because it's the end of an era in your life. The end of something which was supposed to last forever. The loss of the future you thought you'd have.' Jay's voice was kind, his words a statement, not a question.

Sitting back down, Megan slid his mug across to him. 'Yes. You sound as though you know what you're talking about?'

'Thanks.' Jay took a sip of his coffee. 'It's been two years since I divorced my wife.'

'Oh, sorry to hear that.'

'Don't be. It was my decision. Albeit a decision I was forced into.' He lowered his mug onto the table and unwrapped his sandwich. 'She cheated on me. I only found out by accident, and I've got to admit it floored me for a few months. I didn't even let on that I knew what she was up to. I figured if I just carried on as normal, it might all go away, I might find out that she'd ended things with him, and we could get on with the rest of our lives.'

'It didn't? I mean, she didn't end things?'

'Nope.' Jay shook his head and laid his sandwich on the Tupperware box. 'Quite the opposite. My wife introduced him to our daughter, who was four at the time. She came home, super excited to tell me that Mummy had taken her to a theme park and then proceeded to tell me how much fun Mummy's friend Patrick had been and that he'd even bought her an ice cream.'

'Ouch. That's awful.'

'Yep.' Jay rubbed his hand over his face before shaking his head. 'And suddenly I knew that I couldn't carry on the charade of pretending we were a happy little family a moment longer. I found a solicitor the next day.'

'Sorry, that must have been really difficult. Especially with a young child involved.'

She looked at him. The usual glisten of happiness in his eyes had been replaced with a dullness instead.

'It was, but I know it was for the best. In the long term. I didn't want Mia to grow up thinking that was what marriage was supposed to be. And I just couldn't carry on living a lie any more.'

Megan nodded.

'So I understand that however much you may or may not have wanted the marriage to end, it's still a blow. You've suddenly got to navigate a life you thought you wouldn't lead.'

Megan wrapped her hands around her mug, drawing it close to her despite the warmth in the room. 'Yes, that's precisely it.'

'Did your ex cheat too?' Jay asked.

'No, he didn't cheat. Not that I know of, anyway. He worked too much to have the time to cheat.' She took a sip of her coffee. 'I found out he wasn't the man I thought he was. He'd changed too much.'

'Ah.' Jay picked up his mug and held it across the table towards her. 'Here's to new beginnings.'

Leaning forward, she gently clicked her mug against his and smiled. It was nice to be able to talk to someone who understood, who had been through something similar and really understood the mixed feelings. 'New beginnings.'

The bell above the door into the reception area tinkled and Flora's voice wafted into the kitchen. 'That's it. Careful! The last thing you need is to make it worse!'

Jay tilted his head and looked at Megan quizzically before leaning back in his chair and peering out of the open kitchen door. 'Everything okay?'

'Is that you, Jay?' Flora called.

'It is. Do you need a hand?'

'No, no. It's fine.' Percy's voice joined in.

'Yes, please, Jay,' Flora said, her voice tinged with concern. 'Percy's only gone and done his back in.'

Jumping up, Jay hurried out of the door.

Megan stood too, unsure whether she should go and help or if she wasn't needed. But before she could move, Jay and Flora appeared in the kitchen, both of them on either side of Percy, supporting him as he shuffled inside. Megan ran around the table to pull a chair out.

'Thanks, lovely.' Flora nodded to Jay, and they lowered Percy to the chair. 'I'll get you a hot water bottle.'

'I don't need any fussing. I'll be as right as rain once I've had a five-minute sit down.' Percy groaned as he shifted position.

'I told you, you were doing too much. The problem with you is you think you're still twenty years younger than you are.' Flora tutted as she pulled open a cupboard door and began rooting around.

'You're a fine one to talk.'

'Oi, Percy. I'm not the one trying to dig up a dried-out patch of mud, am I? I told you to take a break over an hour ago, but would you listen to me?' Flora shook her head as she freed a hot water bottle from beneath a pile of tea towels.

Shaking his head, Percy sighed. 'No, I wouldn't.'

Megan watched as Flora walked back around the table to Percy and placed her hand on his.

'I say it out of a place of love, Percy. You need to start looking after yourself. There's plenty of us here who can help. We've plenty of volunteers who would be happy to pitch in.'

'Absolutely. Tell me what you need doing and I'll do it.' Jay nodded as he sat back down.

'We've not got long, that's all. I need to get the groundwork done before I can lay the concrete.' Percy winced again.

'You're not doing that. As far as I'm concerned, you're off duty for the rest of today and as long as you need to get your back right again.'

Flora ran the hot tap, holding her hand beneath the running water before filling the hot water bottle.

'Ah no, don't say that, Flora, love. You know that I like to be busy. Can't stand the thought of sitting around.'

'You should have thought about that before you went and injured yourself then, shouldn't you?' Placing her hand on Percy's shoulder, she gently pushed him forward before slipping the hot water bottle down against the back of his chair.

'Aw, that's lovely. It feels much better already with that.' Percy relaxed back.

'Good. Now, do you want a coffee or a cold drink?'

'A nice coffee please, love.'

'Jay? Megan?' Flora made her way towards the kettle.

'No, you're all right, thanks. I'll go and carry on from where Percy left off.' Jay closed the lid of his lunchbox and stood up.

'Is there anything you want me to do?' Megan asked. 'I could do with a break from this lot, to be honest.' She indicated the pile of papers. 'I could walk a couple of the dogs or something?'

Flora paused, kettle in hand. 'Would you mind helping Jay please, lovely? All the dogs have been out already today, and we won't start the next round of walks until it's a bit cooler.'

'Yes, okay.' Megan nodded. Anything to get away from the thoughts whirring around in her mind. Besides, clearing the ground would be quite therapeutic. Just what she needed.

7

'I can see how Percy pulled his back.' With one foot on the shovel, Megan leaned as far back as she could in an attempt to lift the dirt.

'Mind yourself, you don't want to end up in the same predicament. I'll go and grab the hose and soak the ground a bit.' Jay leaned his shovel against the wheelbarrow.

As Megan watched him walk away, she smiled. Jay was a good man.

She released her shovel from the ground and stood it next to the one Jay had been using. Then she pulled her mobile from her back pocket, holding her breath as the screen illuminated. Nothing. No missed calls, not even a message from Lyle to acknowledge that he'd received the papers. She'd expected something. Probably an angry call, but nothing? Maybe he'd seen it coming. Maybe he'd been waiting for it. Or maybe he was just thankful she'd no longer be able to sabotage any of his dodgy building deals again.

She looked out across to the paddocks. Whatever the reason, she was relieved. Surprised, but relieved. Maybe she really could get on with building a new life for herself now. Yes, there was the financial agreement to get through – and that wasn't going to be easy or pleasant, she knew that – but for now, maybe she could try to start imagining how she wanted her future to look.

'Here we go,' she heard Jay say, who'd just returned. 'Once the ground is soaked, it'll be a lot easier to dig up.'

Turning back, Megan watched as he turned the hose on, the water flowing in a steady stream, the earth hungrily guzzling the cool liquid between its deep dry cracks.

'There.' After turning the hose off, Jay waited until the water had dribbled to a stop.

'Great, thanks.' After returning her phone to her pocket, Megan took hold of the shovel again and sunk it into the now-sodden earth. Sure enough, the blunt metal cut through the dirt easily and she was able to throw the loose earth to the side. She turned to Jay. 'You're volunteering here every day, then?'

'Yep, every day apart from Saturdays. I have my daughter on then, although Mia's desperate to come and meet all the pups I've been telling her about. I've promised her I'll check with Flora if it's okay to bring her in.' He bent down and picked up a clump of earth before throwing it across to the pile.

'I bet she'll love that.'

'Yes, she's always been a dog lover. Keeps begging me to get one. Apparently, Patrick is allergic, so her mum can't have one.'

'Ah, it's down to you then?' Megan smiled as she slipped the shovel into the ground again.

'It appears to be.' Jay chuckled. 'The only issue is I'm between jobs at the moment, so I won't be able to make a decision like that until I know where I'll be working and my hours and all that.'

'Is that why you're able to spend all this time here, then? Because you're between jobs?'

Megan paused and studied his face. A bead of sweat clung to

the side of his forehead. She smiled; Lyle would never have done anything like this. He might have trained as a builder, but she couldn't remember him ever getting his hands dirty and pitching in if his team were up against a tight deadline.

Pausing, Jay leaned against his shovel and looked at her. 'Yes. I didn't fancy spending all my time at home. I hate how quiet it is when Mia isn't there. Too quiet.'

Megan could see the sadness in his eyes. It must be even worse for him splitting from his ex, she couldn't imagine having children and living with them full-time one moment and not the next.

'That must be really difficult.'

Jay sighed. 'Yes, it is. But we make the most of our Fridays and Saturdays together.'

'I bet.'

'How about you then? Are you between jobs, too?'

Megan scrunched up her nose. Should she be honest?

'Kind of. I've not been employed for over ten years. I quit my job when me and my ex settled down.' She shrugged. 'I did a little of the bookkeeping for his company.'

'And now you've split up, you've lost your job too, then?'

'Yes.' She frowned.

Lyle had never really viewed her as an employee of his. He'd mostly just called on her when he'd needed her. And he definitely hadn't been honest regarding the company. He hadn't relinquished all of his financial information to her. That was for sure.

'We're both in a similar position, then?' Jay said.

'Yes, I guess we are.'

'How's it going?' Flora called from across the courtyard.

Jay waited until Flora had reached them before speaking. 'All good. I think we're making a dent.'

Flora smiled. 'It looks as though you're making more than a dent.'

'It's a slow job in this heat, but we'll get there.'

'How's Percy?' Megan asked.

'Oh, he's still in pain, not that he'd admit anything of the sort, of course. I've finally managed to convince him to let me drive him home.'

'That's good then. Hopefully, a good rest will help.'

'I hope so, yes.' Flora nodded. 'He's as stubborn as they come and a terribly lousy patient, so I know he'll be kicking himself for getting injured.' She glanced back towards the reception area. 'Will you two be okay if I take him home? I'll have to strike while the iron's still hot, so to speak, or he'll change his mind again and insist that he's okay.'

'Yes, of course.' Megan nodded. They were busy out here, so as long as no one came looking for a dog to adopt, they'd be fine.

'Okay, great. We're not expecting anyone, and Sally and Alex are in the paddocks. Plus, Ginny will probably be back from the suppliers soon enough.' Flora hitched her sleeve up and checked her watch.

'No worries. See you soon.' Jay picked up his shovel again.

Waving a goodbye, Flora turned and headed back towards the reception area.

Before he plunged his shovel back into the soil again, Jay paused and wiped his forehead with the back of his forearm.

'This is hard work in this heat, isn't it? We'd be done by now if it had been autumn or spring and the soil was softer, it's drying out so quickly after soaking it with the hose.'

'It sure is.' Megan watched him as he tilted his shovel back, loosening the soil. 'And Percy wouldn't have pulled his back, either.'

Jay nodded and slung the loosened soil onto the heap to the side. 'I'm not surprised he did.' He indicated behind him as Flora and Percy made their way across the courtyard towards Flora's car. 'They're a sweet couple, aren't they?'

Megan followed his gaze. Flora had one arm around Percy's middle, and was cupping his elbow with her other hand.

'I don't think they're together,' she said.

'Really?'

'No, not unless it's a recent thing.' She shrugged. She knew they hadn't been when she'd visited for Flora's party last year. She shuddered as she remembered that day; she'd come to see if the rumours had been true. One of the builders on the team Lyle had managed had come to her in confidence to say how uncomfortable he'd felt about Lyle's plan to buy the land Wagging Tails was on. He'd told her Lyle had even gone so far as to position a Portakabin right up against the fence of one of the paddocks. She'd had to see for herself. She'd known Lyle's last couple of developments had been shifty, but this had been a whole different level.

'What do you think?'

Megan blinked and looked from Flora and Percy to Jay. 'Sorry, I was miles away.'

'Shall we give it another ten minutes and then take a break?'

'Good idea.' She swallowed. She couldn't tell if her mouth was dry because she was thirsty or because she'd been thinking about that day. The day her fears had been confirmed, the day she'd realised she'd have to end her marriage.

She looked back across the courtyard as the hum of Flora's car starting hung in the still summer air. She was glad she'd found out who Lyle had become, glad she'd been able to stop Wagging Tails from being demolished, but it was still difficult. She'd still lost everything she'd once loved and treasured.

'Shall we go and grab a drink now?' Jay asked. 'You look as though you need one.'

Focusing once again on Jay, she nodded. 'I think that's a good plan.'

8

'I don't think I'm ever going to be able to get the dirt from under my fingernails.' Jay chuckled as he rubbed his hands together under the tap, the soap suds foaming on his skin.

'Oh, I must admit I gave up.' Megan smiled as she looked down at her own. Mud was engrained beneath her nails and the paper cut she'd given herself this morning had stained a murky brown. Before now, up until she'd walked out of the marital home, she'd have had a manicure once a week without fail. She kind of liked this, though. She liked how her hands looked after a decent morning's work. This was the new her. She didn't need to worry about whether her mascara had smudged or her nail varnish chipped. No one cared. The people at Wagging Tails were bothered about who she was, not what she looked like.

'Penny for them.' Jay passed her a large glass of water, the clear glass cloudy with the condensation of freezing water.

'Thanks. I was just thinking about how strange life is and how quickly things can change.'

'Oh, I hear you there.' Leaning against the work surface, he downed the glass of water before refilling it. 'In what way do you mean?'

After taking a sip of water, she placed the glass on the table and rubbed her fingers against the leg of her jeans before holding them up. 'A few months ago, I would never have left the house without my nails done and look at me now.'

Jay grinned, his blue eyes shining. 'There's something about a woman who's not afraid to get her hands dirty.'

Megan laughed. If Lyle had said something like that to her, she'd have immediately assumed he was putting her down, criticising her for not taking immaculate care of herself, but with Jay... She had a feeling he meant exactly what he said.

'I know this probably sounds daft, and please feel free to say no.' Jay held his hands up. 'But, I wondered if...'

The bell above the door to reception tinkled, and Megan glanced towards the open kitchen door.

'That was quick,' she said, as she waited for Flora to enter. 'I was expecting it to take a while to settle Percy at home.'

'Hello?' The voice was deep, and a scratching noise could be heard too.

'That's not her then.'

Megan stood up and headed out of the kitchen door, closely followed by Jay. A man and woman stood at the counter with a large greyhound pulling at her lead, sniffing the floor.

'Hello, can we help you?'

'I hope so.' The woman spoke first, leaning her handbag on top of the counter. 'We're hoping to speak to Flora.'

'I'm afraid Flora's just popped out. She won't be long, though. Would you like to wait?' Megan indicated the kitchen door behind her.

'No, we'd rather not.' The man lifted a large carrier bag onto the counter, dwarfing the woman's small handbag. 'We're sorry, but we're going to have to drop Cindy off. It's just not working out with her.'

'Cindy?' Jay frowned. 'Is she your dog?'

'That's right. We've tried all we can, but we just can't train her. It's ruining our lives.' The man sighed.

'She's ruining your lives?' Megan looked down at the dog again. Cindy's tail was wagging as she walked across to Megan and Jay.

'Hello, you.' Kneeling down, Jay fussed Cindy behind the ears.

'That's right.' The woman shifted position. 'Sorry, I don't recognise either of you. Are you new here?'

'Yes, we are,' Jay said, still kneeling down. He held his hand out as Cindy began licking his palm.

'I see. I suppose it would help if we explained the situation from the beginning, then.' The woman grasped the handles of her bag. 'We adopted Cindy a month ago. We knew she had some behavioural problems and that she couldn't be left alone, but we didn't quite realise how severe the problem was. We literally can't leave her alone. She cries when we pop to the bathroom even.'

'The neighbours are fed up with the noise,' the man continued. 'They're threatening to call Environmental Health if we don't do something.' He took a deep breath in.

'And she chewed through our brand-new sofa when we left to pop to the corner shop.'

The man breathed out heavily. 'That's two grand down the pan.'

'So you see, as much as we're fond of her—' the woman looked down at Cindy, her eyes sad '—we just don't have a choice but to bring her back.'

Standing up, Jay pushed his hands into the pockets of his jeans. 'Would you be able to wait for Flora or Ginny to get back?

That way you can explain everything to them, and they might be able to help.'

'Or Sally. She's the trainer,' Megan said. 'She'll be able to give you a few pointers, I'm sure.'

'I'm afraid not, no. We've got a plane to catch.' The man tapped his watch.

'You're going away?' Something wasn't right here. Megan bit down on her lip.

'That's right, we're treating ourselves after being effectively prisoners in our own home for the past month. We're going away.' The man wrapped his arm around his partner's waist.

'Yes, we're off to drink cocktails and lie in the sun.' The woman smiled and slid her handbag from the counter.

'You're dropping Cindy off and jetting away on holiday? You're not even willing to discuss anything? To give her another chance?' Jay's voice was laced with disbelief.

Megan could feel Jay tense up beside her, and she glanced at him quickly. His brow had furrowed, and his eyes were dark.

'As I said, we're on a tight schedule.'

And with that, they both left, the bell above the door tinkling to signal their departure, Cindy's lead loose on the floor.

'What was that?' Jay shook his head.

'I don't know.'

Sinking to the floor, Megan tapped her knees, waiting for Cindy to turn around from where she was staring at the closed door and walk across to her.

'Hello, Cindy. Aren't you a lovely girl?'

'I can't believe that.' Jay ran a hand through his hair. 'Why on earth would someone go to the trouble of adopting a dog and then abandon them after just a month?'

Megan stood back up and held her hand to his forearm. 'I don't know. It doesn't make any sense at all.'

Jay looked down at her hand and gave her a brief smile. 'No, I suppose we'll find out more when Flora gets back.'

Taking her hand away, Megan felt the hot flush of a blush flash across her face. Jay was right, though. They would find out.

Bending back down, she turned her attention to Cindy again. 'Shall we go into the kitchen and find you a little treat?'

'Good idea.'

Megan laughed. 'I was talking to Cindy, not you.'

She opened the kitchen door and waited until both Jay and Cindy had gone through before closing it again.

'So what do we do? Just wait until Flora gets back or Sally, Alex or Ginny come through?'

'I guess so.' Jay spun slowly around in the kitchen before picking up a dog bowl from the stack beside the sink. 'I'll get her some food to help her settle. Although it looks as though she's already making herself at home.'

Megan smiled as Cindy flopped to the floor at her feet, stretching her long legs out in front of her. 'I wonder if she realises she's just been abandoned.'

'Here you go.' Jay placed the bowl of kibble in front of her and watched as she pulled herself to sitting. Then he turned back to Megan. 'I'm not sure.'

'I might as well carry on with this lot while we wait.' She indicated the laptop and paperwork. 'It doesn't seem right to just leave her in here and go back to digging.'

'I'll go and get on then if you're okay with Cindy?'

'Yes, of course.' Megan looked towards the door as the bell tinkled, followed by the voices of Flora and Ginny.

As soon as the kitchen door opened and Flora and Ginny appeared, Cindy jumped up, all thoughts of food abandoned and rushed towards them, her tail wagging from side to side as quickly as physically possible.

'Cindy!' Ginny knelt on the floor and rubbed her hands across the greyhound's back and chest. 'Have you come for a visit?'

'Lovely to see you.' Bending down, Flora fussed Cindy behind the ears before looking around the kitchen. 'Where are Mr and Mrs Stevens?'

'Her owners? They've left.' Jay grimaced. 'They said they couldn't cope with her separation anxiety and are returning her.'

'What?' Flora slumped into a chair.

'Yes, we tried to tell them to wait and speak to one of you, that you'd be able to advise them or help them with training, but they didn't want to listen, did they?' Megan turned to Jay.

'Nope. Apparently, they've not been able to leave the house since they adopted her and when they did, she destroyed a brand-new sofa.' Jay shook his head. 'They had a plane to catch and were eager to leave as soon as they'd dropped her off.'

'A new sofa? Who buys a brand-new sofa when they've just adopted a dog?' Ginny shook her head and slipped into the seat next to Flora, Cindy following her close behind and lying over Ginny's feet beneath the table.

'They knew Cindy's problems with being left alone when they came to adopt her. We all told them, didn't we?' Flora glanced at Ginny.

'Yes, we all did. Sally even tried to encourage them to go to her training classes and when they refused, she offered to go to their house to help with training free of charge.' Ginny shook her head.

'That's right. And not to mention the fact they'd assured us they were experienced with dealing with dogs with extreme behavioural problems.' Flora tutted. 'They checked out, they ticked all the boxes. Their home was lovely, they worked from home.'

'That's a shame. It sounds as though they weren't as experienced as they made out they were then.' Jay took a sip of his drink.

'No, you're right.' Flora held her hand over her forehead. 'I do hate to see a failed adoption, although maybe in this case it's for the best. Cindy deserves a family who won't give up on her.'

'Too right.' Ginny looked down as Cindy laid her head on Ginny's knee. 'She's such a lovely character. So gentle.'

'She is, and it actually surprises me that she'd chew through a sofa. She never showed any signs that she was in the least bit destructive.'

'No, she didn't. There was never any mess in her kennels, no chewed beds. She even used to leave the soft toys we gave her.' Ginny laughed. 'Do you remember that little pink teddy she had? She used to carry it around in her mouth as though it were an egg or something equally fragile.'

Flora smiled and leaned over, fussing Cindy. 'Oh, lovely, we'll find you a happy home. Soon.'

'It's a shame they weren't at all willing to put any time into training her or anything.' Megan sighed.

'Yes, it is, but unfortunately, some folks are like that. They give all the talk and do very little action. I'm still shocked by the Stevens though. They came across as very experienced and dedicated.' Flora shook her head. 'And now we need to clear that cupboard out again and ask Susan to replace the gate.'

'Cupboard?' Jay placed his now empty glass on the work surface.

'That's right. When Cindy first came to us, we quickly discovered that she couldn't be left alone at all so Sally and Ginny here cleared out the storage cupboard off the reception area and Susan replaced the door with a gate so she could always see or hear someone.'

'Oh yes, and we'll have to make sure at least one of us is in the reception area or kitchen at all times or she'll start crying and set the other dogs off, too.' Ginny looked across at Megan. 'It's a good job we've got you here now doing the books. She'll have company. And if you wanted to work in here rather than at the counter, you could always bring her in – if that's okay with you, obviously?'

'Of course it is.' Megan grinned. 'It'll be nice to have the company.'

'That's decided then. We'll get that cupboard cleared out and get Susan on the case of the gate. Cindy can come over with me and Poppy to the cottage of an evening again. She and Dougal became the best of buddies by the time she was adopted.'

'Who's Dougal?' Megan asked.

'He's Poppy's little dog. Sweet little thing, he is.' Flora looked at Jay and Megan. 'Why don't you two go on your lunch break now? You must be done in after digging all morning.'

Ginny stood up as well. 'The chippy van is parked up in the village at the moment, too. I passed it on the way back from the suppliers.'

'Ooh, that's good timing.' Jay turned to Megan. 'Do you fancy chips on the beach?'

Megan glanced at the fridge where the pre-made sandwich she'd picked up from the corner shop was sitting and nodded. 'Sounds good.'

'This is nice.' Megan finished the last of her chips and leaned back on her elbows, looking up at the summer sun. With the sand beneath her and the gentle hush of the waves lapping at the water's edge, she might have been mistaken for thinking she was on some exotic holiday somewhere or other. She smiled. No, this was much better than a holiday. She had good company and after working on Wagging Tails' books and digging the ground, she actually felt as though she'd done a good morning's work. She felt as though she'd earned this lunch break.

'It is. You can't beat West Par beach. Especially during the height of the tourist season.' Jay sank against the sand next to her.

Sitting up on her elbows again, Megan glanced up and down the beach. It was desolate. 'It's empty,' she commented. Not another soul was even wandering across the sand.

'Exactly.' Jay grinned. 'That's how I like it. The peace and quiet.'

Megan laughed. 'I see. Yes, it is rather nice.'

It was definitely a stark contrast to the beaches she, Lyle and their friends would frequent in Mallorca. They'd often be lucky to carve enough space to stretch their legs, let alone to lounge and enjoy the tranquillity of being able to hear the ocean.

She looked down at Jay, suddenly realising that apart from the fact he was divorced, she knew very little about him despite having spent the last few days in each other's company at Wagging Tails.

'Do you live here?' she asked. 'In West Par?'

'I do. Just up the road from the village hall. How about you?'

'Oh no. I used to live up in Cumbria. I moved out when my soon-to-be ex-husband and I broke up.' She swallowed. After what Jay had said yesterday about Lyle and the proposed development, she was careful not to say his name.

Sitting up again, Jay shielded his eyes from the bright sun's rays with his hand and looked at her. 'You've got family down here?'

'No.' Megan shook her head.

'Friends then?'

'Nope.'

'How come you chose West Par, then, if you don't mind me asking? Have you been here before?'

'I have.' Megan nodded slowly. She could feel the prickle of heat tracing across her cheeks. 'I came here so I could volunteer at Wagging Tails.'

She looked across at the ocean, picking out a small ship on the horizon. Why had she said that? It was bound to raise more questions. Who would move hundreds of miles away to volunteer at a dogs' home when there were likely a few hundred, if not more, between there and here?

'You've lived here all your life?'

An awkward silence hung in the air before Jay shook his head ever so slightly. 'No, I moved down here with my ex-wife when we found out she was expecting our daughter. We were in London and wanted to get out of the rat race and Leanne had family this way, over in Gweek, so it was the natural thing to do. When we were looking, we both fell in love with this area and so when a small cottage came up for sale in West Par we jumped at the chance.'

Megan nodded. He'd bought another place in West Par when they'd divorced then. Likely to be close to his daughter. She couldn't think of anything worse than living in the same city, let alone the same tiny village as your ex. She shuddered. Even just the thought of running into Lyle in the shops or on the street made her feel sick.

'You decided to stay around here when you divorced then?'

'Leanne left to move in with Patrick, the bloke she had an affair with. They're over in Trestow so it's not far.'

'Ah. Sorry to hear that.'

Jay shrugged. 'It's nice to be able to stay in the same cottage where Mia grew up. It meant she had some sort of stability even when we were going through the break-up.' He shifted position on the sand and looked out to sea. 'Although of course when she's not there, all I'm left with are the memories of what was supposed to be our family home.'

Megan watched as he rubbed the palm of his hand across his face and looked across at her again. So he lived in his old marital home. She didn't think she could. Everything would have changed and yet nothing. The same house full of the same memories and yet not with the same people.

'Fancy a paddle?'

'A paddle?'

'Yes, in the sea.' He chuckled as he nodded towards the water.

'Umm, okay!'

'Great.'

Megan slipped her trainers off while Jay stood up, holding his hand out towards her.

His grip was firm but gentle, and Megan let herself be pulled to standing before following him towards the water's edge. She gingerly dipped her toes in, the water warm against her skin as she stepped forward, her feet sinking into the wet sand beneath the water. She grinned at Jay as he rolled the bottom of his jeans up and waded in up to his knees.

'Ah, that's lovely.'

'I was half expecting it to be cold. I'm not even sure why, being as it's so hot today.' Megan laughed. 'It's probably just memories of holidaying on the coast as a kid and my dad enticing me into the water only for me to discover it was absolutely freezing! I think it put me off getting into any British oceans since then.'

'Ah, you've not been to Cornwall in the summer before then?' Jay raised his eyebrows.

'Nope. I haven't.' She looked out across the ocean, the two cliffs on either side of them hugging the cove, the water a clear shade of blue. It really was picture postcard perfect here.

'Do you go abroad a lot then?'

Megan scrunched up her nose. She had. She and Lyle had always gone on a lot of holidays, four, five or even six a year, flying off to warmer climates, but all of that had stopped when he'd moved from building management to starting up his own company, or companies should she say? It had felt as though he'd started one company after the other in the last five years, one a year probably. Of course, she now guessed the new companies were to cover up some immoral thing or another, but at the time she'd believed him when he'd said he was merely experimenting with different business images and structures.

'I used to.'

'You don't like to talk much about yourself, do you?'

Megan looked out towards the horizon in the direction of the ship. It must have passed the opening to the cove now, leaving the waters still and empty.

'Honestly? It's not that I don't like talking about myself, it's just that I suppose everything about my adult life has included my ex, every holiday, everything really, and I guess I just don't want to dwell on that. It's in the past and I'm grateful it's in the past. This is my time to look to the future now.'

Jay nodded.

'Does that make sense?' She reached down and, copying Jay, rolled her jeans up before inching further into the water, the warmth a welcome distraction to the thoughts whirring in her mind.

'It does. It makes perfect sense.' Jay smiled, the lines around his eyes reflecting the kindness in them. 'In that case, where would you like to go on holiday? In the future. Anywhere you like?'

'Anywhere?'

'Anywhere.'

'Umm...' Megan smiled and dipped her hands into the warm sea. 'Scotland.'

'Scotland? Not Bali or the Bahamas or even Alaska? Scotland?'

'Yep. I've never been, and I've heard so much about it. About how stunning the countryside is, how beautiful Edinburgh is. I'd love to explore the history of Edinburgh too. Take a tour around that underground street, you know the one I mean?' Her eyes lit up as she spoke about it. 'Oh, and drive out into the middle of nowhere just to see the view.'

'That does sound wonderful.' Jay grinned. 'Scotland is a rather magical place.'

'Have you been? My parents went there on their honeymoon and I can't remember the number of times I looked through their old photo album, wishing they'd take me.' She tucked her hair behind her ears, little droplets of seawater dripping onto her cheeks from her hand as she did so.

They'd planned to go when she'd turned eighteen – a big birthday and a big holiday – only she'd gone and met Lyle three months before and he'd organised a party at his local pub instead. She'd been head over heels in love and so touched that he'd organise something like that for her that she'd insisted they postpone their Scottish holiday until her next birthday. By then, though, she and her parents hardly saw each other.

'Are you okay?' Jay walked towards her, the water splashing around his shins as he did so.

She smiled, a short, sad smile. 'I am. I was just thinking about my parents. They were going to take me for my eighteenth only plans got changed at the last minute.' She shook her head and focused on him again. 'How about you? Where would you go on holiday?'

'Oh, that's easy. I'd stay here.' Jay met her eyes.

Opening and closing her mouth, Megan then laughed. 'I don't know if that's allowed!'

'Ah, I guess it's cheating a little, isn't it?' Chuckling, he glanced around the cove. 'West Par just has all the ingredients for the perfect getaway, but okay, if I had to choose somewhere else, I'd probably choose somewhere like Lanzarote, I think. I've always wanted to see their rust-coloured beaches.'

'Fair enough. It's a good choice.' Lanzarote had been a firm favourite of Lyle's and hers, but Jay was right, West Par did have all the ingredients of the perfect holiday, and the bonus was there didn't seem to be many tourists.

'I suppose we should probably be getting back. Flora will be sending out a search party soon if we don't.' Jay made a face.

'Yes, you're probably right.' Megan checked her watch. 'We've been an hour and a half! Where did that time go?'

'It's a good job we're not employed, isn't it? Or else we'd likely be getting the sack.' He grinned.

'Ha ha, you're right. Not that I can imagine Flora sacking anyone.'

'No, we might be lucky. She does seem to be the perfect boss. In fact, Wagging Tails is likely one of the best places to work.' He stepped out of the water and rolled his trouser legs down. 'It seems like a little family rather than anything else.'

'Absolutely. I'm really enjoying volunteering there.'

As she walked back onto the sand, Megan brushed as much of it off her wet skin as she could before rolling down the legs of her jeans. She smoothed the fabric down just as Jay tripped beside her. Putting her arm out, she grabbed hold of his forearm to steady him and held it while he found his footing again.

'Thank you.' Jay chuckled. 'I'm not even sure what I tripped over. My own feet probably!'

Megan grinned. 'As long as you're okay. You can't break any bones, not when we've got to finish digging out the foundations.'

'Ha ha, you're right.' He looked down at his arm, where Megan's hand was still gripping it.

'Sorry.' As she drew her hand away, she could feel the tingle of embarrassment streak across her face.

'Hey, don't be sorry.' Jay looked at her, their eyes locking. 'You just about saved my life there.'

Megan snorted. 'As if.'

'Well, thank you again.'

And with that, the moment passed.

Megan tugged on her trainers; her face still tingling with heat. What had that been about? She glanced across at him quickly as he lowered himself to the sand, pulling on his own trainers. Had that been 'a moment'? The 'moment', the 'spark' which every single romance film she'd grown up with portrayed?

She shook her head. Of course, it hadn't. He was divorced and she soon would be too. Lyle hadn't even received the papers yet as far as she knew. She pulled her mobile from her back pocket and checked it quickly. Nope, nothing. Still no missed calls or angry messages to suggest he had.

She picked up their empty chip wrappers and looked towards the top of the beach. She was sure they'd passed a bin on their way on their way here.

10

———

Megan ran the brush through her hair again. What was it with that little bit at the front? She could never seem to get it to lie right. She sighed. It was probably because she hadn't had her hair cut recently. Perhaps it was her body's way of saying she should be taking more care of herself.

Drawing her hair up into a ponytail, she wrapped her hairband around it and sank onto the bed. She looked at her reflection in the mirror and smiled. There was a part of her who quite liked this low-maintenance version of herself. Without her every-five-week haircuts, her hair was longer than it had been in years and having left her straighteners behind, it was recovering from the frequent heat treatment.

After spending the day outside yesterday, her skin was glowing too, without the need for endless fake tans, the gloss of her youth having returned without the need for ten different daily serums. Maybe this life was agreeing with her. She furrowed her brow before relaxing again. Yep, life was certainly less stressful without Lyle and that huge house to take care of. Maybe finding out who Lyle really was had been the best thing. She hadn't felt this happy, this motivated or eager to start the day in a long time.

Memories of yesterday's trip to the beach with Jay suddenly replaced all thoughts of Lyle and she watched her reflection as her cheeks reddened. What was that about?

She looked down at the duvet and ran her forefinger across the floral design, drawing around the petals of the roses emblazoned upon it. Jay did seem lovely – kind, thoughtful, funny – and eager to get to know her, to listen to what she had to say, to *want* to listen to what she had to say. When had Lyle last been interested in what she thought? Or her dreams?

She couldn't remember.

She shook her head. She was being silly. Maybe this was what was meant by a rebound? Maybe these feelings she was beginning to feel towards Jay simply weren't real. They were a coping mechanism to help her get over her failed relationship.

Then why did they feel so real? Why did her lips involuntarily curl into a smile every time she thought about seeing him?

Gripping the edge of the bed, she looked down at the garishly patterned red carpet and took a deep breath in. Regardless of why she was feeling the way she was towards Jay, she knew he wouldn't be feeling the same. Not in a million years. He had his life together. He had a lovely home in West Par, a daughter, friends; he didn't need or wouldn't even want someone like her. What did she have to offer? Nothing. Her life lay in tatters around her feet.

Nope, she needed to push all thoughts of Jay away and get on with what she had come here to do – to try to make up in some small way for Lyle's actions towards Wagging Tails.

A quiet knock on the door broke the empty silence in the room, shortly followed by Lisa's voice. 'Are you in there, Megan?'

Pushing herself to standing, Megan pulled open the door as Lisa picked up her bucket full of cleaning products. 'Morning.'

'Oh sorry, I'll come back.'

'No, no, it's okay. I'm just on my way out.' She grabbed her canvas tote bag from the hook on the back of the door. 'I'll see you later.'

* * *

'Hi, just in time for coffee. Did you want one?' Percy nodded towards the kettle as he took a mug from the dishwasher and placed it next to his and Flora's.

'That'd be great, thanks.' Closing the kitchen door behind her, Megan pulled the sandwich she'd bought at the shop from her bag and opened the fridge, quickly realising yesterday's one was still sitting where she'd left it. 'Oops, I'd forgotten I had one in here already.'

'I bet the chips were worth it, though.' Flora finished scribbling in her notebook and smiled at Megan.

'Yes, definitely.'

The chips and *the company.* She swallowed. Why had she even thought that?

'Morning.' The kitchen door opened as Jay stepped inside, shortly followed by Ginny with Cindy.

'Morning.' Megan mumbled and turned back to the fridge, this time to get the milk for Percy.

'Hello, lovely.' Flora smiled at Jay. 'All ready for another day of volunteering?'

'Absolutely.' He grinned and looked over at Percy. 'How's your back now?'

'Good, good. Not a jot wrong with it today.'

Flora tutted. 'You might be able to think you can pull the wool over everyone else's eyes, but I saw the way you got out of that taxi.'

'There's nothing wrong with me.' Percy huffed as he placed Flora's mug down in front of her.

'Umm, and you could have rung me for a lift instead of wasting money. I said to you when I dropped you off yesterday that I'd give you a lift in today so you could collect your car.'

'Yes, well, I didn't want to put you out.' Percy lowered himself into his chair, wincing a little.

'Um, I rest my case.' Flora took a sip of coffee and looked across at him. 'You need to start thinking about yourself a little rather than everyone else.'

Frowning, Percy looked across the table. 'As I said yesterday, you're a fine one to talk.'

Standing up, Flora ignored his comment. 'I'm going to go and make a start on...' she said, picking up her mug and disappearing out of the door, leaving her sentence unfinished.

'She's just worried about you, that's all,' Ginny said, placing her hand on his shoulder. 'You gave her a scare yesterday when you hurt your back.'

'Umm.' Percy shook himself. 'Well, she's got nothing to worry about. I'll be just fine in a day or two.'

Megan watched as Percy took a sip of his drink and pulled the morning paper towards him, suddenly seemingly engrossed in what the *Trestow Telegraph* had to say about the proposal of a skatepark by the supermarket. She bit down on her lip. Maybe she should go and see if Flora was okay.

She picked up her mug and made her way into the reception area, careful to close the door behind her.

'Are you all right, lovely?' Flora looked up from a stack of letters she was opening on the counter.

'Yes, I just thought I'd come to see if you were?' Reaching the front of the counter, Megan lowered her mug to the surface.

Flora nodded. 'I am, thank you. I'm sorry about that. I just worry about him. He's been my closest friend for years now.'

Megan laid her hand on Flora's forearm for a moment. Flora obviously cared for him very much, that was obvious.

'I should go and apologise.' Flora pinched her nose. 'I just wish he'd take more care of himself, that's all.'

She took off her reading glasses and propped them on the pile of letters in front of her just as the kitchen door opened and Percy hobbled through. Her face softened, and she smiled at him.

'I was just going to come through and apologise to you,' she said. 'I'm sorry I spoke to you the way I did.'

Walking across to the counter, Percy gave her a warm smile. He took Flora's hands in his. 'No, I'm the one who should be apologising, love. I know you're only trying to look out for me.'

Deciding to give both Percy and Flora a little privacy, Megan walked back into the kitchen and closed the door quietly.

'All okay?' Jay looked up from Percy's newspaper.

'Yes, I think so.' She leaned against the counter. 'I just thought I'd give them a bit of space.'

'Oh, I'll nip out now before they get into one of their deep conversations. I need to take Rex out.' Ginny slipped out of the door.

'Look, I was wondering...' Leaning back in his chair, Jay rubbed the back of his neck. 'And don't worry if you want to say no...'

'But...?' Megan frowned.

'I thought the chips were really nice on the beach yesterday, so I wondered if you'd like to go out for dinner. If you're free, that is.'

Megan stifled a laugh and straightened her face. 'The chips were nice?'

'Aw no, you can tell I don't do this very often.' Leaning forward again, Jay ran his hand over his face, his skin blushing a pale crimson. 'I mean, the chips were good, but the company was even better.'

Megan grinned. 'I knew what you were trying to say.'

Chuckling, Jay shook his head. 'Sorry, I completely blew that one, didn't I? So much for trying to be charming.'

Megan laughed and slipped into the chair opposite him. 'I'd love to come for dinner with you.'

'Great! That's great.' The blush subsided. 'Maybe we could pop out after work today, then? And of course, by work, I mean our non-work day here.'

'I'd like that.' Megan took a sip of her drink in an attempt to calm the fluttering in her stomach.

'Great. Great.' Jay nodded and stood up, indicating to the door. 'I'd better go and make a start.'

As soon as the kitchen door had clicked shut, Megan grinned. He'd asked her out. That had been a date question, hadn't it? It wasn't the same as when he'd asked her for lunch yesterday. That had just been friends grabbing a bite to eat, but the dinner would be a date. She picked up her mug and took a sip, hardly noticing the cool temperature of the liquid.

11

Pausing just inside the door to reception, Megan smoothed her T-shirt down. Not that it made any difference. She'd popped to the launderette in Trestow just before meeting Jay for dinner yesterday evening and typically there had been a queue which meant she'd had to bundle her wet clothes in a bag and take them to the restaurant instead of dropping them off first and hanging them up. Of course, this had resulted in her entire wardrobe now being full of creased, slightly damp smelling clothes.

Never mind, Jay had seen her knee-deep in dirt. A few creases wouldn't put him off. Besides, if yesterday's dinner was anything to go by then it was her he was interested in, not what she was wearing. She stifled a giggle as she remembered the Bolognese sauce dribbling down her top after he'd made her laugh. After feeling briefly mortified, she'd shrugged it off. It hadn't bothered Jay, in fact he'd found it funny which was refreshing when she thought back to how Lyle would have reacted. Yes, she'd had fun last night. More fun than she'd had in a long while.

She smiled as she pushed open the kitchen door. 'Morning.'

'Morning, lovely.' Flora looked up from the notebook she was scribbling in.

'I've just put the kettle on,' Susan said, pulling out another mug from the cupboard. 'Would you like a coffee?'

'That'd be great, thanks.' Megan bent down as Cindy sauntered over to her, leaning against her leg as if waiting for the fussing she knew was to come. 'Hello, you.'

'Morning.' Jay grinned as he looked over from the line of dog bowls he was filling with kibble.

'Hi.' Glancing across at him, she smiled, her cheeks warming, before turning her attention to Cindy. Was she imagining things or could she feel the connection still from yesterday's date? Maybe she *was* imagining it, after all he'd made no move to kiss her or anything last night. Maybe their date hadn't gone quite as well as she'd believed, maybe he just saw her as a friend. She focused on Cindy. 'Has there been any interest in her yet?'

'No, nothing, but I'm just writing a little piece about her and then Darryl will feature her in the *Trestow Telegraph*.' Flora shrugged. 'I'm not holding out much hope because of the separation anxiety, but you never know, miracles do happen.'

'They do, and we managed to rehome little Dina, didn't we?' Susan waited until Megan had stood up again and then passed her a mug. 'She had really bad anxiety, do you remember?'

'Oh yes, she did, but it was a little more manageable because she was only tiny, so she wasn't quite so noisy and she eventually settled in a crate, didn't she?'

'She did. That's right, I'd forgotten about the crate training.' Susan took a biscuit from one of the bowls Jay was filling and held it out for Cindy. 'Still, we can't give up hope.'

'No, we can't. I'm sure there'll be someone out there.' Flora tapped her pen against her chin. 'I think I might actually include the fact that potential adopters can and probably should have a trial run with her before making their final decision. It might save a little heartache later down the line.'

'Good idea.' Susan slipped into the chair opposite Flora. 'And it might encourage people to come forward, knowing they have a few days of living with her and getting to know her antics before committing.'

'Exactly.'

Jay replaced the bag of kibble and stacked the bowls, ready to take to the kennels.

'I'll give you a hand if you like?' Megan put her mug down on the counter and walked across to him.

'Thanks. Ready?'

'Yep.' Holding her hands out, Megan took the bowls from him, his fingers brushing against hers as she did so.

'After you.' Jay smiled as he held the door open.

Once the kitchen door had clicked quietly shut behind them, she looked across at him. His brow was furrowed as he attempted to open the door that led to the kennels without dropping his stack of bowls.

'Thank you for dinner last night,' she said. 'I really enjoyed it.'

'You did?' He pushed down on the door handle with his elbow and kicked it open.

'You sound shocked?'

Megan slipped past him as he held the door open. Had she got the wrong impression here? Had he not enjoyed himself? He had seemed to. They'd spent the evening laughing and sharing details from their childhoods, she'd even told him about the time she'd taken the wrong train on the way to a job interview as a teenager and ended up in the middle of nowhere and three hours late.

Letting the door swing shut behind them, Jay waited for the

excited barking and whining to subside a little before looking her in the eyes.

'Oh, I did. I really enjoyed myself and thought we had a great time. I'm just not very good at these things and so I didn't want to presume that you felt the same way.'

Megan laughed, a wave of relief flooding through her. He did feel the same then. He had felt a connection.

'I did tell you after our meal.'

'I know you did.' Looking down, a slight blush crept up his neck. 'Like I said, I've always been rubbish at dating. In fact, that's not true. I haven't been rubbish because until I asked you out, I haven't been on a date since I met Mia's mum.'

Megan stared at him before shaking her head and looking away. He'd said he'd been divorced for two years, hadn't he? And he hadn't been on a date since? 'You haven't? How come?' After opening the door to Rex's kennel, Megan carefully lowered one of the bowls and quickly fussed him behind the ears before turning to the next one.

'I don't know. I suppose I just didn't feel ready. Besides, and I know this is going to sound self-pitying, and I can assure you it's not meant to, but my confidence with romance and relationships has well and truly been shattered since finding out about Leanne's affair.'

Megan sighed. 'I can understand that. It's difficult once you've been hurt to be able to trust again.'

'Exactly.' Jay passed Ralph his bowl of kibble. 'And I think it's the deceit too that has really had an effect on me. How do I trust someone else when I lived with Leanne whilst she was seeing someone behind my back?'

'I know what you mean by not being able to trust.' Megan opened the door to Angus's kennel and laughed as he bounded across the small enclosure towards his food faster than Megan had ever seen him move before. 'I didn't know you could move so fast, Angus!'

Jay glanced at her. 'I thought you said your ex didn't cheat?'

Closing the door quietly, Megan frowned. 'No, he didn't. He was busy with work. I don't think he'd have had the time to. The lies, though, I know about them. Even now, I'm not really sure what was real and what wasn't with him.'

'Sorry to hear that.' Jay paused outside Splash and Ocean's kennel. 'I suppose at least we both understand.'

'Exactly. We have to focus on the positives.' Megan smiled.

'Most definitely.' Grinning, Jay looked down as Splash pawed at the kennel door, his bowl already empty. 'That's it, all gone, Splash.'

'Aw, look at his face though. Anyone would think we'd starved him.' Megan laughed as she rummaged in her pocket for a treat.

'Ha ha, you're the same as me. Fill up with treats as soon as you walk through the door.' Jay patted his bulging pockets.

Megan looked around when she heard Flora walking into the corridor. Her face looked worried. 'Everything okay?'

'No, I've just had a call from the racetrack outside Trestow. They've asked us to take some of their dogs.' Flora began to walk up and down the corridor, peering into each kennel.

'How many?' Jay asked as he collected the empty bowls.

'Thirty.' Flora sighed.

'Thirty?' Megan's mouth dropped open.

'Yes. Thirty.' Flora shook her head, a flash of anger crossing her face. 'They do this. Every so often we'll get a call asking us to take some of their dogs, sometimes less, sometimes more. Of course, I can't just turn around and accept them all. We simply don't have the space. Plus, greyhounds are so difficult to find homes for, and I have to think about how many other dogs we can have and rehome in the time it would take to rehome one greyhound.'

'Why do they get rid of so many at the same time?' Jay asked.

'They retire them.' Flora shook her head. 'If they'd only learn and let them go in stages, but I suppose it's to do with the racing season or something. As much as I'd love to, we just don't have the capacity to take them all. Hopefully we can squeeze in one or two though.'

'What will happen to the rest? Do they ask anyone else to take them in?' Megan chewed down on her bottom lip. She wasn't sure if she really wanted to know the answer.

'Fortunately, Trestow racetrack won't just ask us, they'll ring around all the local rescue centres and the national greyhound ones too and try to find rehoming spaces, but of course with so many needing a safe space at a time...' Flora pinched the bridge of her nose. 'Not every racetrack will even bother to try.'

Megan blinked against the tears forming behind her eyes. She'd always had a soft spot for greyhounds. Of course, Lyle would never have agreed to open their home to a pet, not that he had been there much himself over the past few years.

'We'll be able to take two, I think.' Flora nodded. 'That's if they can share a kennel. Sonny is going to his new home tomorrow so they can have his kennel.'

'That's good then.' Jay held the door to the reception area open for them.

'Yes, it is. We seem to be on a good roll with rehoming at the moment.' Flora smiled a sad smile. 'There's always more needing our help though and I hate to let dogs down.'

'I'm sure you're not letting anyone down, Flora, love.' Percy walked into the reception area from the front entrance, the bell tinkling above the door.

'Greg from Trestow racetrack has just rung. Thirty of them

this time.' Flora walked behind the counter and picked up the phone.

'You can only do what you can. We can't take more dogs than there are kennels, love.'

'I know.' Flora nodded.

'I'll just pop these away and then make a start on the digging.' Jay held up the empty bowls.

'I'll help too. I can always carry on with the finances at home.' Megan shook her head.

Home? She was now calling the bed and breakfast home. She didn't know whether to laugh or cry.

'Don't do any such thing, lovely. There's no rush.'

'Ready?' Jay appeared again.

'Yep.' Megan nodded.

12

'I think we're almost there.' Megan launched a shovelful of dirt towards the ever-increasing mound at the side and nodded towards the ground. 'Surely it doesn't need to be much deeper than this?'

'Nope, I think you're right.' Jay leaned on his shovel and grinned. 'We should probably double-check with Percy once we've levelled this out. I've no clue about building or foundations at all.'

'Nor me.' Megan glanced across at him. 'Well, a little, but only what I picked up from visiting building sites.'

'You used to work for a building company?'

'No.'

Why had she mentioned building sites? It had just slipped out. Megan slid the metal of her shovel into the dirt again, pushing against the stones, slowing it.

'My ex works in the building industry,' she explained, 'and I did a little work for him. You know, accountancy-wise, so I've visited a few sites over the years.'

'You know more than me then.'

'What is it you do again? I mean, I know you're looking for work at the moment, but before that?' She should know this. She was sure he'd mentioned it on their date. Although had he? They'd been so busy chatting about growing up and everything and anything else, she couldn't quite remember if he'd explicitly said what line of work he was in.

'Well, I was working in marketing but I'm looking to change things up a little. I've been applying for conservation jobs.' Jay smiled shyly. 'Not that there's many around so I'll probably end up going back to marketing, but I have some redundancy pay I'm surviving off at the moment.'

'It makes sense you carrying on applying for your dream job, then.' Megan looked across at him. 'It must feel good choosing something you want to do and working towards it.'

'Yes, it does. I feel excited about finding a job and working again.'

Megan planted her foot on the shovel and leaned back, wriggling it in an attempt to dislodge it from the mud. She must have forced it in too deep. With her feet on either side, she pushed it forward and then back again, pushing her right foot back down on the metal. As the dirt shifted beneath her, the shovel fell back and she watched as a large lump of mud flew through the air towards Jay, hitting him square on the chin.

'Oops.'

Jay rubbed the back of his hand across his chin, smearing mud over his skin, and chuckled.

'Sorry!'

'Hey, don't be.' Grinning, he leaned down and took a handful of loose soil before throwing it at her.

Squealing, she jumped out of the way as the mud flew past her. 'Ha ha, you missed.'

Megan reached down and grabbed a clump of soil from the pile to her right, and launched it at him, watching as the dirt, drier than that from the ground where they had drenched it, dispersed in the air, leaving a cloud of fine dust to settle in Jay's hair.

Taking her lead, Jay grabbed a handful from the pile and propelled it towards her where a dusty trail landed across her cheek.

Megan clutched her stomach as she laughed. She couldn't remember the last time she'd had so much fun. Definitely not with Lyle, that was for sure. If she'd accidentally covered him in dirt, he'd have sulked for days rather than turn the mishap into a mudslinging event.

Straightening her back, she looked across at Jay and pointed to her cheek. 'You've got a bit...'

Jay walked towards her, grinning. 'Is this just a trick to get me to come closer? Are you going to rub mud in my hair or something? Because I think I probably have enough in there already.'

'Ha ha, nope.' Reaching out, she gently ran her finger down his cheek, wiping away the dirt. As she focused on wiping his cheek, she felt his finger across her own, his touch soft and gentle. Pausing, she looked into his eyes as he cupped her cheek.

'May I?' His voice was barely above a whisper.

Nodding, she leaned in towards him, and their lips met in a sweet kiss. Megan closed her eyes. Jay's hand was still against her skin as she stepped back and smiled.

'You still have a trail of mud down your cheek,' she said.

Jay grinned back at her, the fine laughter lines creasing around his eyes. 'And so do you.'

Reaching out again, he used the edge of his T-shirt to wipe her clean before kissing her once more.

Looking over Jay's shoulder, Megan stepped back.

'Percy is coming over now, so I guess we'll find out how much more needs to be dug.'

Jay glanced behind him before picking up his shovel again.

On reaching them, Percy shielded his eyes from the sun with his hand and surveyed their work before whistling under his breath. 'You've done a fine job. After levelling it, I think it'll be time for Susan to pour the concrete.'

'It's been tough work but satisfying.' Jay stuck his shovel upright in the ground and put his hands in his pockets.

'Indeed. At least we'll get it all prepared in time for installation day.' Percy stroked his beard. 'I'd have liked to have finished it off myself, but I don't think Flora would approve somehow.'

'We're happy finishing it off, aren't we?' Megan glanced at Jay as a warm glow swept across her face.

'Absolutely. We've got this far.'

'Good, good. Thank you, both of you. Come on in and take a break now, though. The sun's at its peak and I've just stuck the kettle on.'

'I wouldn't say no to a cuppa.'

Jay hung back, waiting for Megan to prop her shovel up against the mound of soil before joining her and Percy as they made their way across the courtyard.

As they reached the door, Megan took a moment to look back across at the foundations they'd been digging. She traced her forefinger over her lips. Jay had kissed her! Yesterday evening he hadn't made any move whatsoever. She'd all but given up on any idea that he might be interested in her romantically. Even after their chat earlier in the kennels she hadn't been overly convinced, but now... now she could begin to feel the excitement of a new relationship.

'After you.' Percy let Jay and Megan step through before

himself. 'Of course, with the weather being what it is, we'll have to be extra careful when mixing...'

The bell tinkled above the door as Percy shut it and Megan smiled at Flora, who was perching on the stool behind the counter.

'Oh, Megan, can I have a quick word, lovely?' Flora's voice was quiet as Jay and Percy continued to speak.

'Yes, of course.' Coming to stand in front of the counter, Megan frowned. Flora looked worried. Her eyes flitted towards the window and back towards Megan, deep lines etched across her forehead. 'Is everything okay?'

'Is that who I think it is?' Flora pointed her pen out of the window.

Following Flora's gaze, Megan froze. She could feel her heart beating faster, could hear it drumming in her ears.

'Lovely?' Flora placed her hand on Megan's forearm.

Glancing down at Flora's hand before steadying herself and taking a deep breath, Megan took a step towards the window, and looked out towards the gate across the lane, where the familiar BMW was parked and with it, the figure of a man standing there, watching.

'Yes, that's him.'

'What do you think he wants?'

'I... I don't know.' What could Lyle want? Why would he have travelled all this way to see her? He hadn't messaged or rung since he'd received the divorce papers, so what could have made him drive down here? Unless that was it, the divorce papers, unless he hadn't wanted to text or call but to speak face to face. But how had he known where to find her? West Par should have been the last place he'd expect her to be. 'He must have got the divorce papers. I'll go and talk to him.'

'Are you sure that's a good idea?'

Megan turned back to Flora. She could see the concern etched across her face and it took her a moment to realise she was nervous of Lyle. Another insight to the man he had become.

'I'll go and speak to him. Tell him to leave.'

Flora rolled her shoulders back, determination replacing the nerves. 'No, lovely. I'll go and tell him you don't want to speak to him.'

Megan smiled. It felt good to have someone who actually cared about her. Since moving away from her hometown and living with Lyle, she'd never had friends who would have gone out of their way to grab her a loaf of bread, let alone face her ex for her. She just couldn't imagine anyone from the social circle she and Lyle had shared would have cared enough to make any such effort.

'Thank you, but I'll go. He won't leave until I speak to him, anyway.'

'Well, I'll come with you then.' Flora walked towards the door as Megan's phone pinged to life.

Megan shook her head and held it up, the screen showing Lyle's message:

Need to speak to you. Lyle.

'I won't be long.'

'Right, well, give me a hand signal or something if you need me to come over.'

Nodding, Megan pulled the door open and stepped back into the humidity of the afternoon sun before closing it firmly behind her.

As she made her way across the courtyard towards Lyle, she

could feel his eyes boring into her. This wasn't going to be a pleasant conversation, but one she needed to have nonetheless.

When she was within a few steps of him, she stood still, leaving the gate between them. Lyle looked as though he'd aged about ten years since she'd last seen him, the day she'd walked out. His eyes were dull and dark grey circles clung to his skin underneath them.

'Hi,' she said.

'Megan.' Lyle nodded, pushing himself away from his car and straightening his back.

'What are you doing here?'

'I had a feeling you might ask that.' Turning, Lyle opened his car door, took something from the door pocket and held up an envelope. 'I received this yesterday.'

It was the divorce papers. 'You knew they were coming.'

'Umm, I suspected they might. I had hoped they wouldn't. I had hoped you'd have seen sense before speaking to a solicitor.'

'Seen sense?' Megan clasped her hands in front of her and rubbed at the callous on her thumb, likely caused by the amount of digging she'd been doing these last few days. 'This isn't some silly argument, Lyle. You knew I was leaving. You wanted this too.'

'Wanted this?'

'Yes, after all that happened here—' she waved her hand behind her encompassing Wagging Tails '—you said the same to me. You said you wanted a divorce.'

'What you did, going behind my back with Andy to jeopardise my career, was unforgivable, yes, but I never once said I didn't want our marriage to work.'

She narrowed her eyes.

'How could our marriage survive that? You've changed. You're not the man I married.' She shook her head, remembering the day she'd walked out. 'Besides, you made it clear you wouldn't change. You even said you didn't regret what you tried to do to this place. Sally could have been really hurt after falling down that hole you dug in the field.'

'The field was mine. Still is until I can sell it. She shouldn't have been trespassing.'

'She was rescuing a dog who had got through the fence that *you* sabotaged.' She curled her hands into fists. She could feel the anger coursing through her body. How could he still not see that it had been him in the wrong?

Lyle glanced down at his feet before looking up at her. 'Not my problem.'

'But...' It was no use. Megan was literally wasting her breath. She shook her head. 'Why are you here?'

'Ha, now that's the funny part.' Lyle shifted position, standing up straighter, his feet as wide as his hips. 'After receiving this beauty...' He waved the envelope in the air. 'I decided to come down to give you the chance to come home. To forget the bad blood and lost money between us, to give you a second chance.'

Megan held his gaze. Had he really thought that they could forget everything that had happened? That she could forget who he had become? The money-grabbing developer who wasn't afraid to use underhand tactics, paying off councils and trying to intimidate charity owners to leave their land, their rescue centres, as he had tried to do with Wagging Tails?

She opened her mouth to answer; the words fighting their way out.

But he held up his hand, palm forward. 'Although, you see, things have now changed.'

'I...'

He met her gaze again, locking her eyes with his, his stare intense, dark. 'It's been interesting standing here, waiting for you. And I've realised something.'

Megan blinked, suddenly needing to know his answer to the question that had been at the forefront of her mind since seeing him here. 'How did you know where I was?'

Lyle shook his head slowly. 'That's not the way it works. You see, I'm the one with the question, not you.'

What was he talking about?

'What question?'

Crossing his arms, the envelope held against his forearm, he tapped his fingers against his chin.

'I thought, stupidly, naively, that the reason you wanted a divorce was because you thought you were better than me. Because, although you were seemingly happy to live in the house that I bought, to spend the money that I earned, you've now decided you've reached a moral high ground and that you no longer want the luxuries that I can afford to give you.'

Megan stood her ground. 'I found out what you've been up to, how you've managed to get planning permission for these developments. You'd never have bribed people a few years ago, you'd never have threatened people, tried to coerce them out of their home.' She held out her arms. 'I don't know you any more.'

'I'm still the person I've always been.'

'No, no, you're not.' She shook her head. 'You've changed.'

'I can assure you I haven't. The only person in our marriage who has changed is you.'

'Me?'

'That's right. You.'

Megan paused, taking a deep breath in. She had so much to say, so much to get off her chest, so much she'd been bottling up inside.

'You might have been doing all this before, making corrupt business deals or whatever but I didn't know about it then. I believed your business was solid, was ethical. So yes, I'm walking away from you now rather than before, but that's because I've only recently discovered how you've been acting, how you've been running your business.'

'No,' Lyle said, rolling up his sleeves and taking a step towards her, a step closer to the gate. 'That's not why you've filed for divorce. You've filed for divorce because of *him*.'

He pointed behind her.

13

'What?'

Turning around, Megan saw Jay standing outside the reception area to Wagging Tails, Flora and Percy with him.

'I saw you... and him.' Lyle pointed his finger in Jay's direction again.

Megan could feel her cheeks reddening. He'd seen her and Jay. He must have seen them kissing. How though? She hadn't noticed his car here at the gate before Flora pointed it out. Had she just been completely oblivious?

'You've been spying on me.'

'Not spying, no. I came here to give you a second chance at coming home with me or, if not, then to give you the signed copy of the divorce paper and I happened to see you two together. I don't spy.'

Ha. He doesn't spy, instead lies, threatens and intimidates. Right. At least he'd signed the papers.

She held out her hand. 'Thank you for signing them.'

'Oh, I think you've misunderstood.' Looking down at the envelope, he slowly and methodically tore it into four pieces before letting it fall from his fingers.

She looked down at the pieces of paper on the dried dirt. 'What do you mean?'

'I'd been going to give you the choice: come home with me and I'll forgive you for foiling my plans to build over this place...' he signalled to Wagging Tails, his lips curling down in disgust '... or to take the divorce papers, the house and a fair percentage of the business profits. That's until I realised the only reason you want to divorce me is because of him.'

Again, he pointed towards Jay.

'He is not the reason I want a divorce. I want a divorce because I don't feel as though I know you any more.' She bit down on her bottom lip, forcing herself not to utter what she really wanted to, swallowing back the words telling him she didn't love him any more. That would only rile him further. She knew that.

'More like you want to get to know him better.' Lyle flared his nostrils.

'No, that's not the reason and you know it. We broke up months ago.'

'And I bet that was so you could come running down here and into his arms. How long has it been going on, Megan? Is he the real reason you didn't want me digging up this sorry place?'

'What? No. I've only just met him. He's only just started volunteering here. This has nothing to do with him. You know that.'

'Umm.' Lyle leaned forward, resting his elbows on the gate between them, and lowered his voice. 'Or do I? Or more to the point, does my solicitor?'

Megan opened and closed her mouth. So this was what all of this was about, then? He was planning to make it look as though she'd ended their marriage because she was having an affair.

Would she be entitled to less financial gains if she had been an adulterer? She wasn't sure, but she bet Lyle was hoping so. 'You know I haven't been. You know that.'

Lyle smiled slowly, a small, calculated movement, and turned around.

'You can't do this.'

Opening his car door, Lyle paused and looked back at her. 'Oh, but I can.'

'You've still not told me how you knew where to find me...'

It was too late, the car door was shut now, the engine rumbling to life.

Standing there, she watched him drive away, taking the corner at the end of the lane too sharply, the red brake lights pumping before he disappeared around the bend.

Great. So now he was going to make her life difficult. Now he'd make certain the divorce was long and drawn out, knowing that she wouldn't have the money to contest his arguments. She sighed. Who was she kidding? He would have done so anyway. He wouldn't have just handed over the divorce papers, come to a mutual agreement over their finances and gone their separate ways peacefully. No, this was just another of his games, another chance for him to get one over on her, to feel as though he'd won.

Megan walked towards the gate, then, bending down and slipping her arm through the metal bars, picked up the pieces of the torn envelope. It probably wasn't even the divorce papers. She separated the brown envelope from the paper and looked. Huh, it was. Had he really been going to give them to her? Signed?

She turned as she felt a hand on her shoulder.

'Are you okay, lovely?' Flora's voice was kind, worried.

Megan nodded and held up the scraps of the envelope. 'He was going to give me the divorce papers.'

'Oh, why did he rip them up then?' Flora frowned.

Megan looked from Flora to Jay, who was still standing in front of the reception area with Percy, and shook her head. She couldn't tell Flora why. She couldn't tell anyone. It was just one of Lyle's mind games. He would have found another reason besides Jay to have torn the envelope up. She was surprised the reason hadn't simply been because she was here, helping at Wagging Tails.

'I don't know.'

'Well, let's get you inside and get you a nice strong coffee, shall we?'

Megan nodded as Flora slipped her arm around her shoulder and began walking back across the courtyard. As they neared Percy and Jay, she noticed Jay say something to Percy before walking away.

Why had he just left instead of seeing if she was okay? Why hadn't he waited another two minutes until she'd reached him?

She turned back to Flora. 'A coffee sounds good, thanks.'

'All right, love?' Percy held the door open, letting the two of them through. 'Looks as though you sent him on his way. Good for you.'

She hadn't. He'd left on his own accord.

Megan glanced behind her back out into the courtyard. 'Where did Jay go?'

'Oh, he said he had to go and finish off levelling the ground for Susan.' Percy shrugged and shut the door. 'He could have waited a few minutes, if you ask me.'

'Right.' Sitting down at the kitchen table, Megan set the pieces of envelope and divorce papers in front of her.

'Here you go. Get that down you.' Flora placed a mug of steaming coffee in front of her. 'I'll just take this out to Jay and be right back.'

'I'll take it, love.' Percy took the mug from her.

Megan stood up and held her hand out. 'I'll take it. I could do with a bit of fresh air.'

Nodding, Percy passed her the mug.

She walked quickly through the kitchen and into the reception area, before stepping outside, the heat a barrier of warmth as it hit her. She needed to speak to Jay. She needed to know why he'd just walked away without even checking how she was.

As she walked across the courtyard towards him, she glanced back towards the gate and the lane beyond, half expecting to see Lyle still standing watching her.

Of course, he wasn't. But now he knew she was volunteering here nothing would stop him turning up as and when he wished. He didn't know where she was staying though. Did he? She took a deep, shuddering breath – this would be it now, she'd always be looking out for him, looking over her shoulder, searching the streets. West Par was no longer her safe haven, her new start.

Stopping a few feet away from Jay, she watched as he plunged his shovel into the ground, the dirt in front of him darker than the rest, the hose lying by his feet.

'Jay?'

He glanced at her before pulling the shovel back and throwing the loose mud to the side.

'Flora made you a coffee.'

'Thanks, just pop it down there, please?' He indicated to the slabs behind her.

After placing it down, she began to walk away before pausing and turning back. She couldn't work out if he just wanted to get the ground levelled or if he was being off with her. It certainly felt as though he was dismissing her. But why? Was it because of the kiss? Had it been a mistake? But he'd made the first move. He'd been the one to instigate it. No, it couldn't be the kiss. So was it Lyle?

'Jay?'

'Yes?' He turned and looked at her, his forehead creased, his eyes hooded.

'Why...? Have I done something wrong?'

After laying the shovel against the wheelbarrow to his right, he plunged his hand into his pocket. 'Percy told me that Lyle is your ex.'

'That's right.'

'The man who tried to demolish Wagging Tails in order to build a housing development.'

'Yes, he is. Percy is right.'

That's what it was. He thought she'd been involved.

She took a step towards him, flinching as he inched backwards. 'I didn't have anything to do with it, though. I didn't even know his plans, not at first, and when I realised what he was up to, what he'd done, I worked with Sally's partner, Andy, to stop him.'

He nodded.

'You've got to believe me. I'd never try to shut down a dogs' home, let alone threaten anyone. You must know that.'

She searched his face. He couldn't really think she was capable of something like that? Could he? Over the past week or so, they'd gotten to know each other. He knew her better than that.

'I believe you. I know you wouldn't do anything of the sort, and Percy told me your role in saving Wagging Tails.'

'Good.'

Great, that was great.

Jay turned back and picked up the shovel again.

'Jay...'

Looking back at her, he paused, shovel in hand. 'Yes?'

'Are we okay?' She gestured between them.

Sinking the shovel back into the soil, Jay shrugged. 'Why didn't you tell me who you were?'

'Who I am?' She frowned. Why did she have to be judged for the person she'd been, was, married to? She was an individual in her own right. She'd never hid the person she was from him. Yes, she hadn't told him Lyle was her ex, but that had been because she didn't want this. She hadn't wanted him to judge her against the man she'd spent her life with. Her marriage didn't define her.

'That Lyle is your ex.' Jay spoke quietly, his eyes fixed on hers.

'Because that's not who I am. Lyle is my ex, but I shouldn't be judged on that. I didn't know what he was up to like I said.'

'I'm not judging you on Lyle's actions. I'm judging you on your own. You should have told me.'

She bit down on her bottom lip. 'Why? What difference would it have made?'

She shook her head. That was it, wasn't it? He'd have never taken her for dinner, never kissed her if he'd known it had been Lyle who she'd recently split from. But that wasn't fair.

'It wouldn't have made any difference to how I felt about you.'

'Then what's the problem?' She didn't understand.

Her heart sank, he'd said 'felt'.

'You were there when I spoke about Lyle and his development in the kitchen. Do you remember?'

'Yes.' She nodded.

'And you didn't say anything. You didn't mention that he was your ex, you didn't even mention that you knew of him.'

'No, I didn't.'

'You hid that from me.' He pinched the bridge of his nose.

'You kept it from me and after Leanne hiding her affair and all the lies and secrets, I just can't do it. Not again.'

Megan's stomach lurched. 'I... I just didn't know what to say. I didn't want to be judged on his actions.'

Leaving the shovel stuck standing in the soil, Jay walked across to her and took her hands in his. 'I really thought we had a connection, but I can't walk into a relationship knowing that the person isn't being honest with me. I can't put myself through that. Not again. I'm sorry.'

Megan swallowed.

'If I'm going to open myself up to a relationship again,' Jay continued, 'I need it to be based on honesty.'

'I just didn't know how to tell you.'

She could feel the callouses on his skin caused by shovelling the dirt, could see the hurt in his eyes. She should have told him. She should have been honest instead of keeping it a secret. She hadn't meant to hurt him, but she understood. She understood he needed honesty after how Leanne treated him.

Jay closed his eyes for a moment before looking at her again. 'I'm sorry, I know it sounds over the top and I understand why you felt you couldn't tell me. I do. In a way anyway, but that's what I mean, we need to be able to trust each other.'

'I agree. Trust is everything, and the lack of trust ruined my marriage with Lyle. But you can trust me. I just...' She pulled her hands away. Maybe it wasn't the fact that she hadn't told him, maybe he was doing just what he said he wasn't. Maybe this lack of trust talk was to cover up the fact that he simply didn't want anything to do with her now that he knew she was Lyle's ex. 'I need to go.'

'Megan, wait. Please, let's talk.'

She turned around. He hadn't wanted to talk. He hadn't even cared enough to see how she was after speaking to her ex. He'd made his position clear; he didn't trust her. And that was fine. She shouldn't be getting into a relationship so soon after splitting with Lyle, anyway. She needed to give herself space. The few days when she and Jay had had a connection together had been lovely. It had shown her what was possible, what she might have in the future, but not now.

'Megan?'

Ignoring his voice, she hurried across the courtyard and back into the reception area, grateful that Percy had left to continue going about his day and Flora was on the phone behind the counter.

In the kitchen, sinking into a chair, she pulled Flora's laptop and the stack of paperwork towards her before leaning her elbows on the table and covering her eyes with her hands. She deserved this. She deserved all of it. She should have told Jay about Lyle when he first brought up the subject of him. And she shouldn't have spent time with Jay, gotten close to him, kissed him, not so soon after she and Lyle had broken up. She'd brought all this upon herself.

She shouldn't have even thought for a second that Jay would want her, not after he'd found out who she was, who her ex was. There must be a small part of everyone here who wondered if she'd had anything to do with his behaviour. A small part that must think she'd at least realised what Lyle had been up to. But she hadn't. She hadn't known he'd been capable of what he'd done. She hadn't even seen that he'd changed. Not that much.

As the laptop whirred into action, she let her thoughts drift back to when she and Lyle had married. He'd been so sweet, so kind with his time and money, always there to help others. What had happened to him? And when? Why had he turned into the man he was today? And now to refuse to sign the divorce papers, to threaten to lie about why their marriage had broken down...

She shook her head. He was going to throw everything at this divorce, wasn't he? She wouldn't stand a chance.

She clicked the folder on the screen, opening the spreadsheet. She'd have to book another appointment with her solicitor, make sure she was prepared for whatever he threw at her. Now, though, she needed to focus, needed to think about something else.

14

Megan poured herself another cup of tea from the small white teapot on the table before looking back at her mobile. She'd been researching about difficult divorces for the past half hour but she was none the wiser, not really.

Loud, raucous laughter sounded from behind her, and she glanced around. A group of women were chatting over their plates of Full English breakfasts, passing a phone around the table. Megan was sure she'd seen them leave the bed and breakfast when she'd come back yesterday. They'd been dressed up in tiaras and bright pink sashes, and the tall one had been wearing an equally bright pink T-shirt announcing she was the 'Bride-to-Be'.

Megan had heard them arrive back in the early hours, too. Yet after such a late night, they all appeared anything but hungover, all happy and ready for another day of celebrating, no doubt. Megan sighed. Hopefully, the girl would enjoy a long and happy marriage, which didn't end up in a divorce like hers.

She checked the time. It was gone nine now. She should be at Wagging Tails already. Not that Flora would mind what time she arrived, but she'd enjoyed having a schedule, enjoyed having a reason to get up and begin the day. Today, though, all she could think about was running into Jay again. She knew she couldn't avoid him forever, not if she wanted to continue to volunteer at Wagging Tails, which she did. But the mere thought of seeing him again reminded her how disappointed he'd looked when she'd spoken to him yesterday.

She put her phone down and picked up her teacup. After downing the now-tepid drink, she stood up. There was no time like the present.

'Have you finished?' The manager of the bed and breakfast, Tracey, walked over to her.

'Yes, thank you. It was lovely, as always.' Megan smiled. She'd pop back to the room, grab her bag and get going before she put it off any longer.

'Sorry, Megan. Can I have a quick word please?' Tracey's voice was low, her tone serious.

'Oh sorry. Yes, of course.' Megan turned back. Why did Tracey want to speak to her? She was friendly enough when Megan had booked in and whenever she saw her around the bed and breakfast, but Tracey had never pulled her aside for a chat before. She glanced back at the hen party. Was Tracey worried they'd been too noisy when they'd returned last night? She didn't need to apologise. Megan hadn't minded.

'Thank you. It's probably best if we take this in the office.' Tracey led the way through the breakfast tables and out into the foyer, towards the office behind the counter.

Following her, Megan had to sidestep as she narrowly avoided a toy car being propelled by a young boy. And once inside the office, she waited until Tracey had closed the door behind them before taking a seat in front of the immaculately organised desk.

'Is there something I can help you with?'

'Yes, yes, I won't keep you long. It's nothing to worry about, but your payment hasn't gone through this week, the direct debit has been declined so if you have another method of payment, I can get your account updated.' Tracey pulled a card reader into the middle of the desk.

'It's been declined? I'm so sorry.' Megan pulled her purse from her handbag and pulled out her card. 'Can we try it again, please? It shouldn't have.'

'Of course. It may be that there's a glitch in the system or something.' Tracey tapped away on her computer before nodding towards the machine. 'All ready for you.'

Megan pushed the card into the reader and tapped in her pin number, only to find the small screen blinked with the word 'declined'.

'Oh, that's strange.' Megan frowned. 'I'll try another one.'

'Maybe it's not an error on our end, then. It might be a problem with your bank.'

'Yes, maybe.' She turned the card over in her hand, checking that it was still in date, before shrugging and pulling out her credit card. 'Here, I'll pay with this one instead.'

Megan inserted her credit card and watched as the card reader flashed up with the word 'declined' once again. She frowned.

'I'm sorry, it looks as though that one's been declined as well.' Tracey tilted her head. 'Do you have another you could try?'

'I do.' What was going on? 'Ah, here we go. This one is with a different bank, so should work.' Megan pushed a different credit card into the machine and picked up the discarded cards. 'I'll have to give the bank a call and see what's going on.'

'Good idea.' Tracey smiled sympathetically before her shoulders drooped. 'Oh, I'm sorry, that payment isn't going through either.'

Taking the card back, Megan turned it over in her hand. 'Could it be a problem with your card reader, or the signal or something?'

'I'm afraid not, no. I've only just taken payment from someone else with this card reader.'

'Oh, right.' Megan slipped her cards back into her purse. 'They're with different banks though, they can't all have something wrong with the magnetic strip or something.'

Tracey shrugged her shoulders. 'It might be where you've been keeping them, maybe? They used to say not to keep your bank cards next to your mobile, didn't they? I don't know if that's still the case, but...'

Megan nodded. She kept her cards in a separate purse, though, not in the back of her phone case or anything. Admittedly, she used to when she went on a run on a Sunday morning, but she hadn't done that since she'd left Lyle, and her cards had been working perfectly fine up until today.

'Before you start panicking, why don't you give your banks a call? I'm sure there's a logical explanation.' Tracey stood up. 'You can use the office. I need to pop and check something with Layla on the front desk, anyway.'

Megan gave her thanks and watched as Tracey left the room.

Yes, she'd ring the bank. Or banks. That was the thing though, if it had just been her debit and credit card with her high street bank then that would make sense but her other credit card was completely separate. Lyle had taken it out with a different bank entirely to take advantage of the better interest rate.

Megan leaned back in her chair, her shoulders slumping. It had just hit her. She knew why this was happening.

Of course, Lyle. This stunt had Lyle written all over it. He'd cut her off.

She swallowed as bile rose to her mouth. He couldn't do that, though. Not legally. Surely? Taking her mobile from her handbag, she scrolled through to his name and stabbed the Call button, straightening her back, the fingers of her free hand tapping against the wooden desktop.

It rang once. It rang twice. She waited until it had rung ten times before pulling her phone away from her ear, ready to end the call.

'Megan. What a surprise to hear from you.'

She cringed at Lyle's voice, which sounded much smarmier than usual. 'Lyle. Have you closed our bank accounts?'

'Good morning to you too, Megan. I'm just fine, thank you. How are you?'

He had. She could hear the smugness in his voice. 'Have you?'

'Straight into the inquisition, I see. And to answer you bluntly, yes, I have. Although I've not exactly closed them, I've merely taken your name off of them.'

She breathed out forcefully, her nostrils flaring. 'You can't do that.'

'Oh, but I can. And I have.'

'Lyle, you can't just cut me off like that. That money is mine too.'

'Is it though? I think you'll find I was the one with the business, I was the one who worked throughout our marriage, and I was the one who earned the money.' His voice was clipped and short.

She gripped the phone tighter in her hand. 'You didn't want me to work. You wanted me at home, to look after the house. I quit work *because* of you.'

'Umm, I wonder if that argument will stand up in a court of law?'

'Of course it will. I looked after the house whilst you looked after the business. We were married, we're still married, you can't just cut me off like this, I legally own half of everything.'

How could he? How could he treat her with such disdain, such indifference? They'd been in love, they'd been happy, once.

'I think, Megan, my dearest wife, if you cast your mind back, you might just recall signing a prenup.'

As she opened her mouth to speak, all that escaped was a strange gurgle. The prenup. They had signed a prenup. It had been against her wishes. They'd been in love after all. What could go wrong? But she'd done it, scribbled her name on the stiff legal document.

'Goodbye.' His voice echoed in her ear, followed by silence. He'd hung up.

She could feel the blood rush from her face as she struggled to steady her breathing. She had nothing. Nothing. He would walk away with everything: the house, their savings, the business. Everything. And she'd be left with nothing.

When Tracey popped her head through the door, all Megan could do was force a smile and nod feebly when Tracey asked, 'All sorted?'

Megan tried to slow her breathing as Tracey slipped back behind the desk.

'Ready to try again?' she asked, taking the card reader and holding it out to Megan.

What should she do? Should she tell her the truth? That she couldn't pay the bill? That she had no money? That she'd been cut off? What would happen then? Would Tracey call the police? Or let her pay it off once she'd found a job?

She needed a job. That's what she needed. But how? Who would take her on? An accountant that hadn't practised in ten years? No one would. Things had probably changed, new policies, new software. They had – she knew that much from the research she'd done whilst making a start on the accounts for Flora. She was penniless and had been out of the workplace for long enough to be deemed unsuitably trained.

'Megan? Is everything okay? You look very pale.' Tracey frowned.

'I... I'm so sorry, but I'm not going to be able to pay my bill right now.' She clasped her hands in her lap, her knuckles turning white. 'My soon-to-be ex-husband has cut me off.'

'Cut you off? From everything?'

Megan nodded. 'From everything.'

'Oh dear.'

'I'm so embarrassed, but I'm going to have to ask you if I can pay the bill when I've found a job.' Megan rubbed her temple as a searing headache encompassed her. 'I don't know what else to offer.'

Tracey pursed her lips and shook her head.

'I'm so sorry.' Megan could hear her own voice wavering. What else was she supposed to say? How else could she make this right?

'Oh, love, I'm not angry at you. I'm angry *for* you.' Reaching across the desk, she patted Megan's shoulder before turning to her computer and clicking on the keyboard. 'It looks as though your previous payments went through just fine, so it's only this past week that you owe.'

'Okay.'

'Now let me see.' Tracey leaned her elbow on the desk, resting her head on her hand and looked up, thinking, before giving Megan a short smile. 'Let me make you a proposal. I'll pop the payment on hold and then when you've got yourself a job you start by paying it back to us in instalments. How does that sound?'

'That sounds amazing. I don't know what to say.' Megan relaxed her shoulders a little. 'You'd really let me do that?'

'Yes, I would. I've been through a difficult divorce myself and if my ex could have wangled it so I'd walked away with nothing, then he would have. We've got to stick together, us divorcees, haven't we?'

'Thank you.'

'The only thing is, I'm so sorry, but I'm going to have to ask you to leave. One week's missing payment I can live with, but the business just can't afford to rent rooms free of charge. Do you have someone you can stay with?'

Did she have someone to stay with? She had no one. Megan placed her hands on her knees and pressed down as her legs began to shake. She needed to keep it together.

'I understand, and you've done enough by allowing me to pay you back when I can. Thank you.' Megan leaned down and retrieved her phone from the floor before standing up and grabbing her bag. 'I'll go and pack up my room now. Thank you so much.'

Standing up, Tracey met her gaze. 'You do have somewhere to stay, don't you?'

'Yes, yes. I do. And thank you.' She pulled open the door and made her way to her room.

* * *

Hefting her holdall further up her shoulder, Megan gripped her handbag in one hand and the array of canvas bags brimming with clothes in the other and used her elbow to open the bedroom door. She kicked the door open and leaned back against it as she manoeuvred herself and her bags out into the corridor.

'Hold on, I'll get that for you, Megan.' Lisa ran towards her and held the door just as Megan fought herself and her bags free.

'Thanks.'

'Are you leaving today?'

'Yes, yes. I'm off now.' Megan looked down at the bags in her hands before automatically trying and failing to reach her pocket. She sighed. She couldn't tip her, even if she could reach the few coins she'd gathered from the room. That was all she had. 'Thank you so much for everything you've done throughout my stay.'

'My pleasure. It sure beats cleaning a room after a family of six have stayed, traipsing sand from the beach into the carpets and wiping food across the walls.' Lisa grinned. 'Hopefully, you'll pay us a visit again soon?'

'Hopefully.' Megan forced a smile before making her way down the corridor. As she walked past the doors to the other bedrooms, she heard the shrieking of excited children just beginning their summer holiday adventures, the raucous laughter and chatter from the hen do and the voices of families enjoying their stay.

At the lift, she laid her bags on the floor by her feet and rolled her shoulders back just as the lift door pinged open and revealed a family – a mum and dad holding hands, two children playing one of those clapping games. She picked her bags up again and waited patiently for them to walk out before stepping inside.

Looking at her reflection in the mirror along the back wall of the lift, Megan could see why Tracey had looked so worried. She did look pale. Leaning her forehead against the cool of the mirror, she closed her eyes, hoping the cold would help alleviate the headache.

No such luck.

The lift jolted to a halt as it reached the ground floor, jarring Megan's forehead against the mirror. Opening her eyes, she prepared herself to battle through the reception area, planning on keeping her head down and hoping she didn't run into Tracey again. She'd been so lovely, but she just couldn't cope with her pity – not now. If one other person so much as smiled at her or was kind she thought she'd just burst out crying. Not a good look in the middle of a bed and breakfast full of happy holidaymakers.

When she reached her car, she let her bags fall to a heap on the tarmac of the car park and opened the boot before shovelling them all inside. She pulled it closed and stood, palms on the top of the boot, the heat of the metal warmed by the morning sun piercing her skin. What was she going to do?

She took a deep breath. One thing she was sure of was that she wasn't going to let Lyle break her. She wasn't going to go running back to him. Not in a million years.

And she wasn't going to ring him again. She wouldn't plead or cry or beg. No, she wouldn't give him the satisfaction. She had her car and for that, she was thankful. She'd just have to sleep in it until she could find a job and a room to rent. At least the silver lining of her landing a job would be that she'd have an excuse to work on Flora's accounts away from Wagging Tails, away from Jay.

Yes, that was her plan. She'd continue with her volunteering at Wagging Tails, avoiding Jay whenever she could, and cram in as much job research as possible using her mobile at night. She'd get up to speed on the accountancy front. Perhaps take a course, and then she could start approaching local companies looking for work. And in the meantime, she'd try to pick up a few shifts in the local supermarket or somewhere. Maybe there was a temping agency in Trestow.

15

Experience needed.

Experience required.

Would suit a school leaver.

Megan leaned back in the chair and pushed her thumbs against her temples. What was the point? Every single company advertising a job in and around Trestow was asking for experience or looking to pay the least they could by asking for a school leaver. How was she going to compete with either of those scenarios? She wasn't, that's what.

She needed to think positively. And she needed to be proactive. Potential employers liked that, didn't they? Or they used to, when she'd last been in the job market. Sitting up straight, she tore a piece of paper from the notebook in front of her and began jotting down phone numbers. There'd be no harm in making a few calls and a few enquiries.

She blinked as the numbers she was scribbling began to merge into each other. If only she could shift this headache, then she'd be able to get on properly, be able to concentrate and make better sense of what was happening, of what Lyle had done.

'Hi, Megan. How are you?' Ginny walked into the kitchen and headed straight for the kettle. 'I didn't see you this morning.'

She held up the kettle as if to offer Megan a coffee.

'Yes, please. I've just got a bit of a headache, that's all.' She massaged her temples again. She hadn't been able to shift it since it had come on this morning when she'd discovered Lyle had cut her off from all of their money. Megan could feel her cheeks warm as Jay entered, followed quickly by Flora and Percy.

'Why don't you go back to your B and B for a lie down if you're not feeling well, lovely?' Flora spoke over her shoulder as she lifted mugs down from the cupboard.

'Oh, no. I'll be okay. It's nothing a paracetamol or two won't fix.' Megan quickly closed the laptop as Percy sat down, turning over the scrap of paper with the job vacancies and contact numbers scribbled on.

'Well, let one of us know if it gets worse and we'll drive you back. You don't want to be driving yourself around if it's too bad.' Flora pulled the bottle of milk from the fridge and passed it to Ginny.

'You're staying at a bed and breakfast?' Jay frowned as he slipped into the chair opposite.

Megan sighed. The tone in his voice suggested it was an incredulous place to stay for any length of time. Loads of people did though, contract workers, people who travelled regularly for work, anyone. Why couldn't she? Besides, it wasn't as though she was any more, anyway.

'Yes,' she replied.

'Oh right. Sorry, I assumed you were renting somewhere down here, that's all.' Jay shrugged.

Looking down at her paperwork, Megan pretended to jot something down, hoping he'd become quickly distracted. He had hardly spoken to her yesterday. Well, that wasn't true, she'd walked away from him, but that wasn't the point. It had been him who had basically told her he didn't see a future with them after she'd omitted to tell him about Lyle and yet here she was forced to lie to him again.

'You're staying at Honeysuckle Bed and Breakfast in Trestow, aren't you?' Flora asked. 'Nice place, that is. We had a couple come down from Norfolk to adopt one of our pups a couple of years back and after they'd explained to the owner what they were doing, she let them stay a couple of nights with their new addition.' Flora helped Ginny hand out the mugs. 'Hattie, her name was. A gorgeous little toy poodle.'

'Oh, I remember her. Had a bark on her as loud as a Great Dane, she did.' Percy took a sip of his drink.

'No, that was the terrier who came in with her, Teeny. Hattie was as quiet as a mouse, bless her.'

'That's right. I remember her now.' Percy smiled at Flora before turning to Megan. 'Must be nice having your breakfast cooked for you each morning, love.'

'Uh-huh.' Megan shifted in her seat. She needed to think of something to say that would change the conversation topic. She shuffled her papers together, her mind completely blank.

'Have you heard from *him* again?' Flora spat the word 'him' with venom.

Great, the focus was still on her, and the topic had worsened. She knew exactly who Flora was referring to. What was she supposed to say? Say no and downright lie, again, or tell the truth? She couldn't tell the truth.

'Only briefly to sort something out.'

'I hope he's not bothering you?' Flora frowned.

Megan crossed her legs, her knee hitting the underneath of the table, and wrapped her hands around her mug. 'He won't be.'

'Good, good.'

Ginny looked across at her and smiled sympathetically. 'Exes, hey? My ex was horrendous too. Even tried to sack Darryl. Well, technically he did, but then he was the one booted out and Darryl took over his job.'

Megan grimaced. 'Oh, that doesn't sound good.'

'No, it wasn't.' Ginny looked down into her mug before looking back up at Megan and grinning. 'But don't let Lyle put you off. If I had given up after Jason, then I wouldn't have what I have with Darryl now.'

Megan could almost feel Jay's eyes on her. Well, that bridge had well and truly burnt down, hadn't it?

'I agree,' Flora added. 'After my Arthur passed away, I threw myself into this place and the dogs I rescued, but I sometimes wonder how my life would have turned out if I'd let someone else in.' She frowned as she spoke, before shaking her head and looking into her mug. 'Of course, they'd have to have been as crazy for dogs as me, so I suppose that was always going to be limiting.'

'Yes, that's true.' Ginny looked directly at Percy and raised her eyebrows.

Shifting in his chair, Percy cleared his throat, and when he spoke, his voice was hoarse. 'I'm sure you could have had the pick of the bunch, still can.'

Shaking her head, Flora chuckled. 'I think that bus passed by a long time ago, don't you?'

'I don't think that bus ever has to pass, so to speak.' Percy picked up his mug and took a long gulp of coffee.

Megan looked from Percy to Flora and back again. Was there something going on there? That was the second time she'd picked up those sorts of vibes from the two of them.

'Right, well, we've got Greg dropping off the two greyhounds from the racetrack in half an hour, so I'm going to double-check their kennel is ready.' Flora stood up, mug in hand. 'Ginny, are you okay taking Cindy out please, lovely? I think it's probably for the best to let the two newbies settle into their kennel without her crying as soon as I take them through and leave her alone.'

'Oh, I've got that home visit for Splash. Sorry.'

'Of course you have. How could I forget?'

'I can take her out for a bit if you like?' Megan downed the dregs of her coffee. 'I could do with getting away from the computer screen for a while.'

'That would be lovely, thank you. I think both the paddocks are empty at the moment, so you have the choice of either.' Flora smiled.

'She quite likes playing with the agility equipment in the bottom paddock.' Ginny stood up and took her mug over to the dishwasher.

'Great, I'll take her there then.'

As she pushed herself to standing, Megan was grateful for the escape from the kitchen. It looked as though Jay was getting his lunch from the fridge and the last thing she needed right now was to be stuck in the room with him, trying to make polite conversation after yesterday.

* * *

'That's it, Cindy. Great job!' Megan cheered as Cindy made her way through the weave poles, her long body arching this way and that as she made it to the end.

She clapped before giving her a treat from her pocket.

'Do you want to go again?' Tapping her side, she walked to the start of the agility course and told Cindy to sit. 'Good girl. On your marks, get set, go!'

With the shade of the trees, the air was cooler here and

Megan felt as though she might be the only person for miles around. It was idyllic and she could see why Ginny, Sally and Alex enjoyed working here so much. And working with the dogs too, even from the little involvement she'd had with them, she could see how rewarding it would be.

She'd always wanted a dog. Something to keep her company on the long weeks Lyle was away. Though, of course, it had always been out of the question. Megan had long ago stopped suggesting the idea, had stopped trying to discuss the idea with Lyle. Too messy, too demanding, too dirty. That was his automatic response whenever she'd asked him.

She smiled. She didn't have to follow Lyle's rules any more. She was on her own. She could decide what she wanted and how she wanted her new stage of life to look. And maybe a dog would be perfect. They'd offer companionship, love and a purpose. Yes, maybe she would look into getting one. A rescue dog from Wagging Tails.

When she had a home for herself, of course, she had to remind herself.

She swallowed, the fear she'd felt this morning when she'd realised Lyle had cut her off, resurfacing. She was homeless. Penniless. And without a job or a way of earning money, she'd have to sleep in her car for the foreseeable.

She plunged her hands into her pockets, the meaty crumbs from the dog treats she'd filled her pockets with coarse against her skin. It wouldn't be so bad, would it? Loads of people ended up having no choice but to sleep in their cars. You heard about it on the news and on social media. With the enormous waiting lists for social housing, some had no choice but to sleep in tents or cars whilst they waited. If they could do it, so could she.

'Penny for them.'

Shaking herself from her thoughts, Megan turned and saw

Percy closing the gate behind him. She hadn't even heard him walk up.

'Oh, you know. Just watching Cindy, that's all. She's brilliant at making her way through this agility equipment.'

'Aye, she is. It always shocks me how easily she takes the tunnel. What with her long legs.' Percy chuckled.

'Yes.' Megan watched as Cindy sped towards her again, halting seconds before hurtling into her legs and sitting without being asked. Pulling another treat from her pocket, she held it out to her, waiting as the greyhound delicately took it from her palm. 'Good girl, Cindy.'

Percy grinned as Cindy lolloped towards him, her deep brown eyes staring at him until he gave her a treat. 'There you are, clever girl.' He turned to Megan. 'It's such a shame that Cindy's adoption failed. She's not one for life in a kennel.'

Megan nodded. Although everyone was careful not to leave Cindy alone or at least out of earshot, on the occasions when Megan had been working in the kitchen with the reception area empty, even the few minutes it took her to run to the toilet and back had instigated a meltdown for the poor dog.

'Do you think the separation anxiety will ever get better?' she asked.

'Oh, there's always hope. There is. We've had dogs before who have suffered and then we've heard back from their adopters how much better they've become. Sally's been working with Cindy, but, of course, it's difficult in the kennels. Even if she appears to make real progress, a home environment is completely different and a huge adjustment again, which might just set her back for a while.'

'Do you think that's what happened with the couple who adopted her?'

'I do, yes.' Percy fussed Cindy's ears before pointing to the agility course again and watching her bound off, her tongue lolling out to one side. 'Sally had made such a difference with her, but they'd been warned, this couple, and they'd assured us all that they'd had the experience of dealing with anxious dogs.'

'You think they were lying?'

'I don't know about lying, maybe they did, but I think they took on more than they could chew, so to speak, and when it dawned on them, returning her and jetting off on holiday was obviously the easier option.'

'Do you think she'll get rehomed again?' Megan watched as Cindy jumped over the hurdles, a huge grin plastered on the dog's face.

'Hopefully. We've had a few resident dogs over the time, dogs which we know can never be rehomed, but Cindy's not one of them. It might take a while but I'm positive there's someone out there for her, someone patient who works from home and can put the time in to train her.'

'Some dogs can't be rehomed? Like Ralph, you mean?'

'That's right. Some, like poor Ralph, are just so traumatised by what's happened in their past, the way they'd been mistreated, that they're reactive and it just wouldn't be safe for them to be rehomed. Not for them nor for the people who take them on, or anyone. It's safer to keep dogs like Ralph here, so they can be cared for by people they know and trust.'

'Is that why Ginny comes in early each morning to walk him?' She was sure she'd heard Flora tutting at Ginny for her getting in at five before or leaving late.

'That's right. Of course, it's easier in the winter, but when the days are long and the weather's like this, there are always people about and it's safer and less stressful for Ralph to be walked when it's unlikely he'll run into another dog.' Percy nodded.

'He seems such a sweetheart.'

'Oh, he is. He's just scared, poor soul.' Percy watched as Cindy looped around the course again. 'But he's safe here. He's taken to kennel life well thankfully, unlike some.'

'You mean Cindy?'

'Yep.'

Sticking his fingers in his mouth, Percy whistled and waited until Cindy had paused, tilted her head and ran towards him before leaning down and fussing over her.

'There'll be someone out there for you, won't there? You're such a gentle sweetheart.'

'She is.'

'You know what, I don't actually know if I believe all this talk about her having destroyed a brand-new sofa. She's never so much as touched the stuff in her makeshift kennel and I know she's rarely left alone, but on the occasions she is, we've always come back to a clean kennel.'

'You think that was a lie then?'

'I think they were trying to justify why they were returning her.' Percy frowned. 'We get that sometimes. People make out the dogs' behaviour was worse than it actually was, usually so they don't feel as guilty bringing their dogs in. All well and good for them, but then when it comes to adopting the poor dogs out, the guidelines are stricter to who we can and can't because we've been told this or that about them.'

Megan frowned. One lie or even embellishment of the truth could really affect a dog's life going forward then. She hadn't really thought about it like that. She looked across as Cindy ran to the end of the paddock and back, her long elegant legs giving her the look of a ballerina. Hopefully, what her previous owners had told Flora wouldn't have much of an effect on her chances going forward.

'Anyway, I wondered if I might have a little word?' Lowering his voice, Percy stepped closer to Megan.

'Oh right. Yes, of course.'

What did Percy want to talk to her about? Had she done something wrong?

'You're new here, so somewhat impartial, would you say?'

'Umm, I guess so.' Megan shrugged.

'Good, good. Now, you were there in the kitchen a few minutes ago. How did you take what was being said?'

What was being said? About Lyle? And Ginny's awful ex? She grimaced. The last person she wanted to talk about was Lyle. Again.

'About awful exes?'

Percy chuckled. 'No, the opposite, in fact. The talk about finding love again.' Looking down, Percy loosened a stone from the dry dirt at his feet. 'Of course, it's different for Flora. She and Arthur were the perfect couple. It was clear they loved each other, to anyone who knew them.'

'Okay.' Megan nodded. 'I think Ginny was saying that she was glad she gave Darryl a chance after her experience with her ex. I guess she meant that she could have turned her back on ever trying to find love again because of the way her ex had treated her.' Megan watched Cindy slow to a stop, drooping her head at the water bowl. Ginny had found love after Jason. Maybe there was hope for her, too. Although she knew she'd completely blown it with Jay. And she knew that had been her fault for not being open and honest. She sighed and shook her head. She just hoped they could at least get back to how things had been between them before they'd gone on that date, before they'd had that kiss. If all she could have with him was friendship, then she'd take it.

'And Flora?'

Megan chewed on her bottom lip as she tried to think back to the conversation. 'I think Flora was saying she regrets not letting someone else into her life again. I think. I might be wrong, though; I don't know her that well.'

'Thank you.' Percy nodded slowly; lost in his thoughts as he finally freed the stone with the toe of his boot.

'Can I ask why you're asking?' Megan looked at him. His ears were tinged red and his expression thoughtful.

'I've never heard her talk like that before. Hinting that she'd even think about courting again, I mean.' Percy shifted position, holding his hand above his eyes to shield the sun as he watched Cindy. When he spoke his voice was hoarse. 'It made me wonder whether she really would be open to being asked to step out. By me, I mean.'

Megan smiled. She had been right. Percy did have feelings for Flora. And by all accounts, Flora acted as though the feelings might be reciprocated, too.

'You can only ask.'

'Aye, I could, but we've been friends for years and I've been working here, helping her out with this place for over thirty-five now. I don't want to jeopardise any of that.' Percy shook his head.

'But if you don't ask, you'll never know.'

'No, I don't suppose I will.' Percy sighed. 'I suppose some things are best left unsaid though, aren't they?'

'Do you want me to try to speak to her? See if I can figure out if she feels the same way?' Megan grimaced as soon as the words left her mouth. How was she supposed to do that?

Percy turned to her, his face relaxing again. 'You'd do that?'

Taking a deep breath, Megan nodded. She'd offered now. She couldn't very well back out of it.

'Yes, why not?'

'Oh, love, that would be wonderful of you.' Percy drew her in for a hug. 'Thank you!'

'You're welcome.'

Megan watched as Percy made his way back through the gate and across the courtyard. Trying to become Wagging Tails' matchmaker would at least take her mind off her own dismal love life, or lack of it.

16

'Aw, you two really are beauties, aren't you?' Megan grinned at the two now-retired race greyhounds and fed them both another treat through the bars of their kennel.

'They sure are, aren't they?' Ginny closed Ralph's kennel door and joined her. 'I took them on a wander down to the cove when they were first brought in earlier and they're so good on the lead, too.'

'Are they? That's good. I would have expected them to be tugging and trying to run after anything they spotted.'

'No, I think they're so well trained in that respect. I suppose they have to be at the racetracks. All the ones we have in have always been super good on the lead.'

Ginny took two treats from her pocket and gave them to the pair.

'Hopefully, they'll be rehomed quickly then. Will they be rehomed together?'

'I don't know. We find greyhounds so tricky to rehome. The cute little dogs and the puppies are always snapped up but not many want a large dog like a greyhound, plus people see their long legs and hear they're ex-racers and think they need a ton of exercise and will be on the go all the time.' Ginny shrugged.

'And all they want is a comfy sofa or bed to lie on and short walks?'

'Exactly. They don't even need as long a walk as many other dog breeds. Greyhounds make the perfect companion; it's just not how they're perceived.' Ginny stroked each of them in turn through the bars of their door before turning and leading the way down the corridor. 'In a perfect world, they'd be rehomed together as they've been together their entire lives, sharing a kennel at the racetracks, but two perfect homes are better than none.'

'That's true. At least it sounds as though they'll be easier to rehome than Cindy.'

'Oh yes.' Ginny nodded as she pulled the door into the reception area open, and Cindy tilted her head, looking at them from the makeshift kennel in the cupboard as though she realised they were talking about her. Laughing, Ginny went across to her and slipped her a treat. 'Don't worry, you're gorgeous too, Cindy.'

Megan smiled as she fussed over the large greyhound. 'She really is, isn't she?'

'You just need to learn how to be left on your own for even a millisecond and you'd make someone a wonderful companion too, wouldn't you?' Ginny fussed over her before pulling her car keys from her pocket. 'Right, I'd better be off. I promised Darryl I'd meet him half an hour ago.'

'Oops.'

Ginny laughed. 'It's a good job he knows what I'm like. See you in the morning.'

'Yes, bye. Have a nice evening.'

'You too.'

The bell above the door tinkled as Ginny left.

'Is that you, Megan?' Flora called through from the kitchen.

Aha. That was why Cindy hadn't been crying when she and Ginny had been in the kennels then; she must have heard Flora in the kitchen.

Following Flora's voice, Megan called out and made her way to the kitchen, where she paused at the end of the table.

Flora placed two mugs on the table before sitting down in her chair. 'Here, come and have a cuppa if you've got time?'

'Thanks.' Megan sat down and pulled the mug towards her.

'I thought we could have a catch up. How are things going with you?'

'Oh, okay, thanks. I'm still working my way through the receipts and invoices and documenting the expenditure.'

'Good, good. I didn't mean about the books, though. I meant how are things going with *you*, lovely? You've been through a fair bit recently and it can't be easy having left your home and everyone you know to come down here and live in a B and B.'

Megan squirmed in her chair. 'It's okay, thanks.'

'Are you sure? You're holding up, okay? It's a huge transition.'

Megan looked down at her drink. Tiny bubbles of milky coffee floated on the top. She gently swirled the mug around, watching them disappear as they dispersed.

'It's not been easy, but then staying in the house with Lyle, after knowing what he's capable of, wasn't either. I don't regret making the decision to move out.' Even if she would be spending her first night sleeping in her car, it would be easier than living with him.

'No, I can imagine that wasn't easy. I can imagine it wasn't a very nice atmosphere in that house.' Flora took a sip of her drink.

Megan shuddered. 'It's strange. I know I was with him for so long, but now, being on my own, life is so much easier. I haven't got to second guess what he means when he says something, always wondering if he's telling me the truth or not. Even before I discovered what he was up to with this place, I mean. It seems he's been lying to me for such a long time, and I hadn't even realised he was doing it.'

Flora nodded quietly.

'It's a relief our marriage is over now.' Megan smiled sadly. She'd never get back the years she'd dedicated to him, but she was glad she'd now seen him for who he really was.

'Well, as long as you're holding up okay.' Flora patted Megan's hand.

'Yes, I am, thanks.'

Or she had been. It had almost felt like an extended holiday of sorts living at the bed and breakfast. Now, though, she knew things were going to be different, but she'd cope. If she could walk away from Lyle after the years they'd spent together and brave coming down here not knowing what welcome she'd receive then she knew she'd be okay sleeping in her car for a few nights, or weeks, or however long it took her to find a job.

'I know I've said it before, but I'm always here if you need an ear. We all are. We've all been through our share of difficult times, and we understand.'

'Thank you, that means a lot.' Megan smiled. 'And I know I've said it before too, but thank you again for accepting me and letting me volunteer here.'

'Oh, lovely, it was never you who wasn't welcome here.'

'I know, but thanks.' Megan took another sip of her drink before standing up. 'I'll see you in the morning.'

'Yep, see you. Have a good night.'

* * *

'Okay, thank you anyway.' Megan clutched her mobile closer to her ear and stared out of the windscreen as a van pulled into the lay-by in front of her. 'But you'll let me know if anything else comes up? Anything which doesn't require experience?'

'You're on the list.' The voice at the other end of the phone sounded irritated. Probably eager to get her off the line so they could go home.

'Thank you.' Ending the call, she placed her mobile down on the dashboard. Thanks for nothing. And what had they meant by 'the list'? Did that mean they had a lot of people looking for a job or was 'the list' code word for 'the bin'?

Picking up the scrap of paper she'd jotted the numbers down on, she crossed off the last number. That was it. No more. She sighed. She'd contacted all the potential employers who had advertised for jobs in the *Trestow Telegraph*, but that didn't mean there weren't other businesses out there looking for new employees. There were probably loads. It was the height of the tourist season, after all. There must be companies looking to recruit temporary staff at least.

Yes, she just needed to take a look. If she'd had the energy, she'd have looked online now but after all of the rejections she just couldn't bring herself to. Besides, it was getting late, most places would be closed or closing. She'd find something. She would.

Despite what she was trying to tell herself, she couldn't ignore that little niggle inside her mind, telling her that all summer vacancies would have already been filled, telling her that with university students back home and the colleges having broken up for summer any temporary spikes in the need for employees will have already been accounted for. If she acknowledged that niggle, that nagging doubt, what then? How was she supposed to survive on no money?

And who could she turn to? Not her parents, that was for sure. They'd hated Lyle when she'd introduced them and when she'd announced their engagement they'd all but disowned her, told her they wouldn't be picking up the pieces when the marriage fell apart. She pinched the bridge of her nose. What had they seen in him then that she hadn't? What had everyone else seen in him that she hadn't?

Andy, Sally's partner, had trusted him, though. He'd trusted him enough to go into business with him. She shook her head. Andy hadn't known him for as long as she had. And their shared friends – or should she say Lyle's friends – had been the same as him, ambitious without a conscience. Maybe she had been the only one gullible enough to see him for who she wanted him to be.

No, that wasn't true. He *had* been nice, he *had* been kind, but maybe only to her. Maybe he had acted differently towards others, towards her parents, whilst putting on a show for her? That would explain why they'd been so against her marrying him. And that would explain how easily he'd turned against her when she'd scuppered his plans to demolish Wagging Tails.

There was nothing she could do now. She couldn't change the past.

Shaking her head, she tore open a bag of crisps before pushing the rest of the multipack across the passenger seat. She looked down into the packet. When had portions become so meagre? This wasn't going to fill her up, but now she'd used the last of her change on the crisps and a bottle of water it would have to do. She'd need the other five in the pack for her upcoming meals.

She crunched down on the first one. If Lyle had even given her a little notice before he'd cut any ties to the money, then she'd have got some cash out, but there'd been nothing to suggest his plans. No signs, no mumblings from him. Although he had been fixated on having seen her and Jay together when he'd turned up the other day. Maybe she should have guessed.

She should have remembered about the prenup, she should have figured out what his next move was going to be. But that had been years ago. They'd been married fourteen years now, together even longer. Would it even stand up in court now?

When she finished the crisps, she crumpled up the packet and shoved it in the pocket of the car door. She picked up her mobile. Still nothing from the solicitor. She'd rung and left a message earlier, but he hadn't got back to her yet. Hopefully, that meant he was looking into it. She tapped the steering wheel. She wasn't going to hold her breath. The articles she'd read online about prenups didn't give her much hope.

It was 6.05 p.m. She had the whole evening ahead of her, the whole night stretching out. Leaning down, she pulled up the small lever beneath her seat, sliding it backwards, away from the steering wheel. What was she supposed to do with all this time? Just sit here? Research, she guessed. Yes, she'd take this opportunity to research some accountancy refresher courses. There might even be a free one she could begin right now.

* * *

Megan blinked, the tiny screen of her mobile bright in the dim evening light. The lay-by was empty again now; the van having moved on. She could hear the odd car zooming past on the road beyond the thin line of trees screening the lay-by from the road. Apart from that, she was alone. The world around her silent.

Turning the ignition on for a moment, she held the button down and watched the window close. It was still warm, and she knew the temperature in the car would only rise without the tiny breeze coming in from the open window, but she felt uneasy going to sleep with it open.

Huh, she felt uneasy full stop. She tried to calm her breathing. It would be okay. There was no one about and it wasn't as though she was parked up in the middle of a town centre or somewhere. There likely wouldn't be another car joining her in the lay-by until the morning. She'd be fine. It would be all be fine.

Moving across to the passenger seat, she leaned her chair back as far as it would go, and drew her coat up to her chin once more. Staring into the darkness outside, she curled her fingers against the collar of her coat, willing sleep to come.

17

Megan pulled her mobile towards her and checked the time. It was 2 a.m., and she still hadn't fallen asleep. What had she been expecting? To be able to get to sleep as easily as she had at the bed and breakfast? Even there, it had taken her a few nights to get used to the unfamiliar sounds and creaks of the building. Out here there was just a thin piece of glass or some metal or fibreglass or whatever cars were made of between her and the outside world.

It would take time. That was all. Just time to get used to her new reality. She swallowed as the sting of tears caught in the back of her throat. She wasn't going to cry, she wouldn't give Lyle the satisfaction – whether he found out or not, she'd still know. No, she was going to prove to him and to herself that she could fend for herself, that she could do this. She was going to build a new life for herself. Life after divorce – it had a special ring to it, didn't it?

Yes, a new life, or at least a new chapter in her life. She had this. And if it took a few weeks of living in her car before she could start, then that's what it took.

She turned over and wriggled her toes, hoping the pins and needles that were creeping up her calves from trying to sleep with her legs bent would disperse.

Nope. Sighing, she sat up and stamped her feet on the floor, catching a glimpse of her reflection in the window as she did so. She stifled a scream. Why was she so jumpy? The lay-by was on a quiet road, hidden from the view of the very few drivers travelling past. She wasn't usually a nervous person. She didn't usually have anything to be nervous about. Not when sleeping in her big detached house, knowing the only thing the CCTV cameras Lyle had installed would catch would be a neighbour's cat meandering across their vast lawn.

Here, though, all she had was darkness and the field beyond. If someone did pull into the lay-by and want to carjack her or anything, then what would she do? Who would hear her screams?

She pulled the lever to the side of the seat, letting it angle upwards again. There wasn't any point lying here trying to sleep, she wasn't going to. She'd look for jobs instead, while the hours away by searching for a way to get out of this mess she'd found herself in. That's what she'd do.

Waking up, Megan looked out of the window, the images from her nightmare mixing into reality. As she blinked, she let her eyes focus. It was morning. The sun was rising and the chill of the night air quickly warming.

She must have fallen asleep after all. Rubbing the back of her neck, she winced as a sharp pain shot through her muscles and she rolled her shoulders back. How long had she slept for? It certainly didn't feel like long enough, that was for sure. She searched the footwell for her mobile and looked at the screen. It was quarter to eight; the last time she'd noted had been half four. She must have had about three hours. That wasn't so bad. Not for her first night, anyway.

She unlocked the car, opened the door and stepped outside, reaching her arms above her and drawing in a deep breath of the fresh country air. Now what she needed was to get to Wagging Tails whilst it was only Flora and Ginny there and to slip into the toilet without either of them noticing. If she could do that, she could freshen up and change her clothes before anyone noticed.

Yes, that's what she'd do. And she needed to hurry. As she walked quickly around to the driver's side, something cold splashed up against the leg of her jeans. Her heart sank. It must have rained in those few hours she'd been asleep and now she'd gone and stepped in a puddle, leaving a large muddy brown stain up her leg.

She sighed. She'd just have to sneak her jeans into the washing machine when the dogs' bedding was washed. That was all. It was doable. She nodded. There'd be a solution for everything. Although the one thing she really needed at the moment was the toilet and she didn't fancy jumping the ditch to go in the field. She just hoped she could get to Wagging Tails quickly and there wasn't going to be any traffic.

Just as she'd turned the ignition on and the car purred to life, her phone rang, cutting through the soothing sounds of the early morning radio. Answering it on her hands-free, she pulled out of the lay-by and onto the road.

'Hello?'

'Megan.' Lyle's voice filled the car, his tone cold, unnerving.

She fought the urge to yawn and instead tried to fill her voice with optimism. 'Lyle. How can I help you today?'

'Ha, it's more what I can do for you. I see your payment at the

Honeysuckle Bed and Breakfast in Trestow was declined yesterday.'

She hesitated. He'd been looking through the bank statements, seeing what she'd been spending money on. That's how he'd known to find her at Wagging Tails then. He'd traced the payments to where she was staying in Trestow and put two and two together. She shuddered. It hadn't even occurred to her that he'd have been spying on her spending, working out what she was doing.

'Three times, in fact. Once on the debit card, and once on each of your credit cards.' His voice was full of smarm, the self-assured smarm of a person who knows they've got the other one right where they want them to be.

'That's right.' She tapped on the steering wheel as the car in front of her slowed, approaching a roundabout.

'I can hear you're in the car, is that right? What a shame it will be when you run out of fuel and your insurance payments bounce.'

'You can't do that! I need my car!'

Damn, why had she said that? Why had she let him know he was getting to her? Because he was, that's why. If she couldn't use her car, she wouldn't have anywhere to go, anywhere to sleep.

'Oh, but I can. Correct me if I'm mistaken, but I don't recall the prenup mentioning anything about me being legally obliged to pay for you to run a car.'

'Lyle...'

'And once my solicitor serves you with the divorce papers stating adultery as the cause of our marriage breakdown, well, I don't think any judge will rule in your favour.'

She hit the steering wheel. 'I was not having an affair. You know that. You know why our marriage broke down. You know it was your actions that caused it.'

'It's very rare for an adulterer to admit their misdemeanours. I do believe, however, it's quite common for the one in the wrong to try to deflect the blame.'

'You know—'

Too late, the call had gone silent, music from the radio filling the car once again.

He couldn't do that, could he? She'd served him the divorce papers. Could he really overwrite that by filing for one himself? And when was her insurance due? The payments came out once a month; she knew that, but when, what date? It was the end of the month; she was sure of it, which meant she had just under two weeks to secure a job and get her first wage.

She bit down on her bottom lip, the taste of blood filling her mouth. It felt impossible. Heck, it probably was impossible. Most places paid monthly, didn't they?

As she turned down the lane leading to Wagging Tails, she took a deep breath. She had to act normally. She couldn't let herself be riled by Lyle. That's what he wanted.

After she'd drawn into a parking spot and turned the ignition off, she leaned her forehead on the steering wheel. Why did Lyle have to ring? All she could think about was him stalking her every move now. All this time she'd thought she'd been free of him and yet she hadn't. He'd been there, spying on her, watching her every move through the bank statements.

Megan forced herself to sit back up and grab her bag from the passenger seat. She'd wanted to get here early so she'd be able to freshen up without drawing any attention to herself. If she continued to sit in the car and mope that wasn't going to happen.

She got out, turned back to the car and reached in, pulling her mobile from the passenger seat.

'Megan.'

She straightened, banging her head against the ceiling. 'Jay? Hi.'

'Sorry, I didn't mean to startle you.' He grimaced. 'Are you okay?'

'I don't think I'll have any lasting damage.' She forced a smile.

'That's a relief.'

'Is everything okay?' she asked as they walked towards Wagging Tails. She looked down at the bulging canvas bag in her hand and swapped it to the other side.

'Yes, I just wanted to catch you to clear the air. I'm sorry I reacted the way I did when I realised that Lyle was your ex.'

'Don't be. I should have told you.'

'No, it was none of my business and after the way I'd spoken about him, I can understand why you didn't tell me. I should have apologised yesterday...'

'Honestly, it's no bother. Anyway, I can understand why it felt as though I was deceiving you, especially after what you've told me about your ex-wife. I wasn't though, I just didn't think it mattered and then after you'd made it clear what you thought of him, I guess I just didn't know how to tell you.'

She pulled the reception door open. The area was empty, Cindy wasn't even in her makeshift kennel, Flora must have taken her for a walk or something.

'Well, I'm sorry for the way I reacted.' They headed into the kitchen and Jay lifted up the kettle. 'Coffee?'

'Oh, what I wouldn't do for a coffee!'

Megan smiled. Maybe things were getting better after all. Yes, hopefully, she and Jay could become friends again, could be comfortable in each other's company once more. That's all she could ask for right now. Besides, it was probably for the best now that Lyle was trying to steer the divorce in his favour by accusing her of having an affair.

She glanced behind her towards the reception area. She could really do with freshening up before everyone else got here, but now Jay had seen her in these clothes, she wasn't really sure how she'd get away with changing without it raising questions. She could clean her teeth and put some deodorant on, though.

'Everything all right?'

'Yes, yes.' Megan pointed behind her. 'I'm just going to pop to the loo, but I'll definitely be back in time for that coffee.'

Jay nodded.

Turning, she rushed out into the reception area and the small bathroom.

18

Megan closed the bathroom door behind her and made her way back to the kitchen. She could hear Flora and Alex talking, perhaps Sally too. Yes, Sally had definitely arrived.

Lifting her arm above her head, she sniffed her armpit tentatively. She might not have changed her clothes since yesterday morning, but at least the deodorant seemed to be working.

When she pushed open the kitchen door, Cindy trotted towards her to greet her.

'Morning, Megan.' Alex grinned.

'Hi.' After fussing Cindy, Megan sat down next to Ginny and opposite Jay.

'Here's your coffee.' Jay smiled at her as he slid the mug across the table.

'Great, thanks.' As she took a sip of the warm drink, she noticed a plate of biscuits in the middle of the table, and her stomach growled as if to remind her it wasn't satisfied with her dismal dinner of crisps yesterday and no breakfast today.

'Is that your stomach?' Alex looked at her and laughed.

'Yep.' She grinned. 'I didn't have time for breakfast this morning.'

'Ouch, I don't know how you do that, skip breakfast. I need my breakfast in the morning or I'm super grouchy.' Alex passed her the plate of biscuits.

'And don't we know it?' Ginny raised her eyebrows.

'Oi! I'm not that bad!' Alex swatted away the accusation.

'Now, now, you two.' Flora chuckled and looked towards the door as Percy came in.

'Have I missed something?' he asked, glancing around the room and frowning.

'No, no, just Alex and Ginny bickering as usual.' Flora stood up. 'Coffee?'

'Oh, nothing out of the ordinary, then.' Percy walked across the room towards Flora. 'I'll get it, love. Anyone else?'

A chorus of 'no thank you's filled the room.

Swallowing the last of her biscuit, Megan looked at the plate again, trying to decide whether it would appear rude if she took another. She hadn't actually asked if she was supposed to be giving Flora any money towards the coffee and biscuits or not. She should have.

Looking away from the biscuits, instead, she took another sip of coffee. She couldn't ask now – what would she do if the answer was yes? – but she'd ask when she received her first wage. If she ever did get a job, that was.

'What do you think, Megan?'

Focusing on the conversation in the room again, Megan looked across at Ginny, who had spoken.

'Sorry, I was miles away. What do I think about what?'

'Coming on a walk with the two new greyhounds? I thought we could take them around the village, see how they interact with people and other dogs.'

'Yes, that sounds good. I should really get on with the books, though.'

'Oh, that can wait,' Flora said. 'Get out and enjoy the sunshine while you can. Summer won't last forever.' She lowered her mug and stood up. 'Right, where's Cindy got to?'

Everyone looked under the table and laughed as they spotted the large greyhound flopped out across the kitchen tiles, the length of her almost filling the spot beneath the table.

'Aw, she's so lovely.' Megan smiled and Cindy lifted her gaze, looking at the faces peering at her before flopping her head against her front paws again.

Ginny stood up. 'We can take her along for a walk too, if that's easier, Flora?'

'Oh, yes, it would be actually as I've got some bits and pieces to see to so I don't think anyone will be about for a while and you know how she is when left alone.'

'Come on then, Cindy, let's go for a walk.' Megan tapped the side of her leg. Cindy stood up and stretched before ambling towards her.

* * *

'Did Flora tell you? We have a family coming today to take a look at Ocean,' Ginny said as she tied the poop bag together before starting to walk again.

'Oh, that's great news. So that's both Splash and Ocean who will have found a new home then? Has there been any interest in little Angus?' Megan gently guided Cindy to the side of the pavement as a man walked past them.

'I'm sure Flora said there have been a few enquiries, but no one's come in to meet him yet.' Ginny crossed the road to the bin before jogging back to Megan, the two greyhounds enjoying the increase in the pace.

'The enquiries sound hopeful, then?'

'Yes, yes, they do. I think Flora will be a bit happier when she has an empty kennel, just in case there's an emergency or anything. Although, we'll soon have the four new ones too.'

'Ah yes, that's the end of the week, isn't it?' Megan gave Cindy a treat from her pocket before they began walking again.

'That's right. I can't wait. I know it's going to be more work with four extra dogs in our care, but it's going to be so great to be able to rescue more from the pound.' Ginny shuddered. 'I hate thinking about the ones we can't fit into Wagging Tails when other rescues are full too.'

Megan nodded. The four kennels would have a huge impact and literally be the difference between life and death for so many dogs.

'Anyway, let's talk about something else before I get super angry.' Ginny visibly shook herself before pointing down a narrow lane leading off the main street through the village. 'That's where I live down there. My cottage is the third one on the right.'

Following Ginny's gaze, Megan smiled. Traditional thatched cottages lined the road, all with wrought-iron gates and lavender growing in the front gardens, just as Megan would have imagined a seaside cottage in a small village. 'It's beautiful.'

Ginny grinned. 'Thanks. I feel very lucky to live down here. What with the cove just a few minutes down the road and Wagging Tails a few minutes in the opposite direction, I couldn't really ask for more.'

'I don't blame you. I think anyone would feel lucky to live in a place like this.'

'Where do you think you'll move to? When your old house is

sold, and the divorce goes through, I mean.' Ginny looked across at Megan. 'Have you thought about relocating down here full-time?'

Megan laughed, her voice catching in her throat. She'd only discounted West Par a few days ago as there were too many memories of what Lyle had been planning to do, but with every day she spent at Wagging Tails, the more it felt like somewhere she might want to put roots down in. West Par felt like home.

'I don't know. I think the dream would be to live somewhere like this, yes, but unfortunately, I think it's more likely just a dream. At this rate, I won't be able to afford to buy a tent let alone a house.'

Ginny frowned. 'Really? How come? I would have thought you'd be able to get a place after the divorce, surely?'

Megan shook her head and fixed her eyes ahead. 'Nope. It turns out I stupidly signed a prenup before we got married, so Lyle will probably walk away with everything. I can't believe I'd forgotten about it.'

Ginny paused. 'That's awful. Will it actually stand up in court, though? Surely he wouldn't do that?'

Megan looked up at Ginny and raised her eyebrows.

'Umm, yes, I suppose this is Lyle.'

'Exactly.' Megan shrugged. 'It's fine. I'll sort it. I can rebuild my life.'

'Of course you can. It just seems so unfair.'

Megan shrugged. 'I know, but life sometimes is, isn't it? I mean, you all didn't ask for all the drama he brought to your doorstep last year, did you?'

'No, but this is different. This is your life, your future.'

'I just need to find a job, that's all.'

'I'm sure you'll get one easily enough.'

'I'm not sure about that. Everyone wants experience these

days, but I'm hoping to take a refresher course in accountancy and then I can start doing that again. For money, I mean.'

'That's a good idea. You could even start up your own business.' Ginny grinned. 'Be your own boss.'

'Umm, now I like the sound of that.'

She did. She quite fancied being in control, balancing work and life herself, making her own business decisions.

'Careful!'

Megan heard Ginny call out just as her foot slipped, and her ankle gave way. Shooting her arms out, she landed in a heap on the ground and winced as the sharp pain shot through her ankle. As she gripped her foot, she looked up and realised she must have dropped the lead because Cindy was trotting on ahead of them.

'Ginny, quick, look!'

Ginny began to run after Cindy, the two smaller greyhounds following at her heels.

'Cindy! Cindy, come!' Pushing herself to standing, Megan held her breath as the pain seared up her leg. 'Cindy!'

Pausing, Cindy looked around, her ears pinned back as if only just realising that Megan wasn't still holding her lead.

'That's it, Cindy. Good girl, come on.'

Megan breathed a sigh of relief as Cindy jogged back, her lead dragging on the ground behind her. Bending down, Megan gave her some fuss and grabbed her lead again.

'Wow, what a good girl you are, Cindy,' Ginny said as she made her way back to them. Holding Petal and Willow's leads in one hand, she fished in her pocket for treats before giving them one each in turn. 'Are you okay, Megan? Are you hurt? You took quite a tumble.'

'I'll be all right. I just can't believe I let go of her lead.'

As they began walking again, Megan tried to put the least amount of weight on her injured ankle as possible.

Ginny turned and frowned at her. 'You're not okay. You're hurt. Have you twisted your ankle?'

'A little I think.' Megan shrugged. 'I'll live.'

'You might live, but it looks painful. We need to head back, and you need to rest up. Maybe put a cold compress on it.'

Megan nodded. She wasn't going to argue about heading back – even the thought of making the fifteen or so minute walk back to Wagging Tails worried her. Would she even make it that far?

She forced a smile and began to limp back with Ginny's help.

'Hold on, why don't you go and sit on that bench over there and I'll go and get my car? I can drive you back.' Ginny pointed across the lane to a wooden bench flanked by flowerbeds.

'Nope, I'll be okay. It's going to take more than a slightly twisted ankle to stop me.'

She grimaced. It definitely felt more than slightly twisted, but after a few minutes of resting it up, she'd be fine.

* * *

Megan hobbled into the courtyard and paused as Ginny closed the gate behind them before jogging up to her and taking her elbow. With every step she took she could feel it swelling.

'Almost there now.' Ginny smiled sympathetically.

'Thanks.' Megan looked towards the reception area as the door opened and Jay came running across the courtyard towards them.

'What's happened? Are you okay?' He stopped in front of Megan, looking her up and down.

'I'm fine. Just a bit of a twisted ankle, that's all.'

'Here, let me help you.' Moving next to her, he wrapped his arm around her waist and took her forearm in his hand, supporting her weight.

'I'll be okay. It's not that bad.' Megan could feel the warmth from his body next to hers. He was wearing the same aftershave as when he'd kissed her. 'I stupidly fell and let go of the lead, but this one here was amazing and came trotting straight back to me.'

'I don't think she even noticed you weren't holding it any more.' Ginny laughed, looking down at Cindy. 'You're right though, she was perfect at coming back as soon as you called her name.'

'Aw, clever girl, Cindy.' Jay smiled. 'How did you fall? Are you hurt anywhere else?'

'No, no, just my stupid ankle.' Megan tried and failed to cover a wince as she attempted to put weight on it. 'I don't really know what I did. I think I just tripped over my own foot.' She shrugged, the red tinge of embarrassment flushing across her cheeks.

'We've all done it.' Jay shook his head.

'We sure have.' Ginny held out her hand. 'Here, give me Cindy's lead and I'll take these three in while you put your foot up.'

'Thanks.' Megan passed it to her and watched as Ginny walked on ahead.

Jay frowned. 'Are you sure you're not hurt anywhere else?'

'No, I really am okay. Just a little embarrassed that I've managed to injure myself by stupidly tripping over my own foot.' She waited as he opened the door before taking hold of her by the waist again and helping her up the step. 'Thank you.'

Flora rushed out from behind the counter as soon as she saw them. 'Oh, what have you done, lovely?' she asked. 'Ginny said you were hurt.'

Megan shook her head. She really didn't need all this fuss. It was just a twisted ankle.

'I've just sprained my ankle. It's only a little sprain.'

'Oh dear.' Flora pulled out the stool from behind the counter and indicated it to her. 'Why don't you go back to the bed and breakfast and rest it for the day?'

Back to the B and B? Megan bit down on her bottom lip as Jay helped her to the stool.

'No, no, I'll rest it here.'

'That's a good idea. I'll go and get my car. I can drive you.' Jay, seemingly ignoring her refusal, made his way towards the door.

'I said no. I don't want to go back. I'll be perfectly fine here.' Her tone was harsher than she'd intended and she shook her head. 'Sorry, I didn't mean to snap, but I'll stay here all the same. I can get on with the paperwork and I have everything I need. It makes more sense.'

'Well, I don't know. Won't it be best back in your room? You'll be more comfortable.' Jay furrowed his brow, concern flooding his features.

'I'll be more than comfortable here, but thank you.' Gripping the edge of the counter, Megan stood up, forcing a smile, trying desperately to downplay how much it really hurt. She couldn't have Jay insisting on taking her back to the B and B. If he did, then they'd all find out she didn't actually have anywhere to go.

'Okay, sorry. I didn't mean to try to tell you what to do.' Jay ran his hand across the back of his neck.

'Hey, don't apologise. Thank you for looking out for me.'

Briefly touching his forearm, she hobbled into the kitchen. All she wanted to do was to curl up in a comfy bed and with the thought of having to spend another sleepless night trying to fall asleep in her car at the forefront of her mind, it was all she could do to keep the tears at bay.

19

Shoving the car into first, Megan flicked the windscreen wipers on and watched as they smudged last night's excuse for a rain shower from the glass. It hadn't so much as rained as sprinkled. And she'd been awake the whole time. She gritted her teeth as she lowered her foot to the accelerator. If anything, the sprain felt worse today, probably due to the fact she hadn't been able to lift it up all night, but she was coping. Just about anyway, and she certainly couldn't let anyone back at Wagging Tails see how much pain she was in. She couldn't face sitting in her car all day if Flora told her to have the day off. And even worse, she couldn't have one of them insisting on driving her back to the B and B. No, she'd cope. She had to.

Before pulling out of the lay-by, she glanced at the backseat. She might try to sleep there tonight instead of scrunching herself in the front passenger seat, she just didn't like the thought of not being able to drive off quickly if something happened or even to sit up and pretend she was just resting if another car pulled in.

But she couldn't carry on like this. She was doubtful if she'd even got two hours of sleep last night because of her throbbing ankle – and five hours every two nights wasn't sustainable. She had to try something. Tonight, she'd try the backseat, and failing that, by the end of the week she'd likely become so tired that she'd be able to sleep standing up, anyway.

Megan turned into Wagging Tails, relieved to see only Ginny's car parked. Even the Wagging Tails van had gone, meaning that either Flora or both Flora and Ginny were out. And even if Ginny hadn't gone with Flora, she'd be walking Ralph. Great, she'd be able to actually go and get cleaned up.

She smiled. A fresh pair of clothes would be perfect, and she'd shove her dirty stuff in the washing machine too.

* * *

Scraping her hair back into a ponytail, Megan grimaced at herself in the mirror before running her fingers across her hair, pulling out wispy strands. That was better. The grease was a little more disguised now. She looked behind her at the shower they used to wash the dogs. If only she'd arrived a little earlier, she may have been brave enough to wash her hair under that without the fear someone would come in and see what she was doing.

She packed her make-up bag back into her tote bag and picked up her dirty clothes, wrapping them in a towel. Never mind, she felt a million times better after a wash and a freshen up, plus she'd be able to pop her dirty stuff into the washing machine.

It wouldn't be forever. One of the potential employers she'd contacted yesterday might call her back and offer her an interview despite her lack of experience. She opened the door to the reception area just as her mobile rang, punctuating the silence in the room.

Holding the phone between her ear and her shoulder as she

made her way into the kitchen towards the washing machine, she answered the call. 'Hello?'

'How are you coping with your current situation, Megan?'

Her shoulders slumped as she shoved her clothes into the machine. That'd teach her for not looking at the screen properly before accepting the call.

'Lyle.'

'Did you hear my question?'

'I heard. It's fine. Everything's fine.' She pushed a pile of dog blankets into the drum, covering her clothes.

'Is it, though? Really?' The smarm was back, the overly soothing tone mocking her. 'That's funny, because it doesn't look as though you've tried to charge anything to the card again.'

'It is.'

What did he want from her? Wasn't it enough to know that he'd cut her off from all their money, or his money according to him? Why did he feel the need to contact her and gloat?

'I suppose that could only mean one of two things. You're either shacking up with your fancy man or you're... what? Sleeping in your car?' Lyle scoffed. 'Of course, I should have known you would go running to him. After all, it's anyone's guess how long you've been seeing him behind my back.'

Megan closed her eyes, trying to keep her voice steady, to qualm her anger. 'You know I didn't have an affair and, no, I have not moved in with him.'

The line was silent.

Pulling the phone away from her ear, Megan looked at the screen. He was still there, on the other end.

Just as she was about to end the call, a low rumbling of a laugh echoed down the line.

'You're sleeping in your car then.' He spluttered the words

through his laughter. 'I do apologise, just give me a moment to compose myself...'

After stabbing her finger on the End Call button, Megan threw her phone onto the kitchen table, listening to it skid across the tabletop before she slammed the washing machine door shut. How dare he? How dare he laugh at her situation? She should have told him she'd moved in with Jay, anything would have been better than him realising where she was actually sleeping. How could he possibly think it was funny? He knew she hadn't cheated. He knew she was the one who hadn't done anything wrong. She wasn't the reason they were on the path to divorce. He was. And yet now it was her suffering, not him.

A cough sounded from behind her, and she spun around, her lips pursed. She felt herself instantly relax as she spotted Jay standing in the doorway.

'Sorry, I wasn't eavesdropping or anything. I've only just arrived.' He picked up her phone and held it out towards her. 'Are you okay?'

Megan sighed as she took her phone. 'Thanks. Not really, no. It was my ex and he, well, I'm quickly learning that he has even fewer morals than I thought he did.'

'Lyle?'

'That's right.' She slumped into a chair at the table. 'And I know everyone else knew how awful he was, but I didn't see it. Not until everything that happened with this place, so when he pulls a stunt like this.' She held up her phone. 'It still comes as a bit of a shock.'

'Can I ask what he's done?' Sitting in the chair opposite, Jay leaned his elbows on the table, clasping his hands together.

Megan looked down at the tabletop and moved a biscuit crumb in a circle beneath the pad of her middle finger. She couldn't tell him. Not the truth. Not why Lyle was so ecstatic with his actions. Instead, she shrugged. 'Just being his true self, that's all.'

Jay pulled a face. 'Sorry to hear that. I hope it all works out.'

She nodded.

'Not that you get back with him. That's not what I meant. Just that the divorce runs smoothly for you.' Jay frowned. 'Or as smoothly as a divorce can run.'

'I knew what you meant. Thanks.' Megan smiled.

'How's your ankle holding up today?' Jay nodded towards her foot. 'Did you manage to put it up last night?'

'It's okay, thanks. A lot better than yesterday.'

It wasn't. If anything, it felt worse than yesterday, but she wasn't about to admit that.

She looked towards the kitchen door as Flora walked in, Cindy rushing ahead of her and beelining for Megan.

'Oh, hello, Cindy,' she said as the dog rubbed her nose against Megan's arm, asking for a fuss. 'Lovely to see you too.'

'As soon as we'd stepped foot in the door, she knew you were here.' Flora chuckled as she closed the door again. 'Her tail was wagging that hard, I was worried she'd snap it off.'

'Aw, is that true, Cindy?' Megan patted her knees, waiting until Cindy had placed her front paws on her lap before fussing her behind the ears. 'Well, you know what? I love you too.'

'You're not looking to rehome a large needy greyhound with separation anxiety, are you?' Flora raised her eyebrows as she placed a newspaper and a bottle of milk on the table.

'I would love to.' Megan grinned. 'Sadly, though, not at this moment in time.'

'Well, let me know if you change your mind when you're all settled in your own place. I think she'd move in with you in a heartbeat.' Flora grinned and tapped Megan on the shoulder as she walked past her to the fridge with the milk.

Leaning down, Megan kissed the top of Cindy's head. Getting her own place was a pipe dream which was likely going to take about fifty years to accomplish with the luck she was having.

'I've got some good news,' Flora said as she closed the fridge door. 'We may have found a home for little Angus.'

'Really?' Megan thought back to her first day at Wagging Tails when Angus, Splash, and Ocean had been brought in. Little Angus was almost a different dog now. His confidence had grown that much.

'Yep, I'm popping to do the home visit this morning.' Flora glanced at the clock. 'In fact, I'll have to leave in a few minutes.'

'I'll keep my fingers crossed for you then.' Jay held his hand up, crossing his fingers.

'Yes, please do.' Flora smiled as she gave both Megan and Jay a mug brimming with coffee. 'Can I leave that little one with you, Megan? Or should I say not so little one?'

'Yes, of course.' Megan turned towards Cindy again. 'You can help me with my paperwork today, can't you?'

Megan yawned and deleted the number she'd just entered into the spreadsheet for the seventh time, then checked the receipt once more before inputting it again. She glanced beneath the table at Cindy, sprawled out across the floor, legs in the air and her tongue hanging out as she snored. If only Megan could sleep as easily anywhere.

Rolling her shoulders back and filling her lungs, she forced her eyes to stay open and instead of admitting defeat and lowering her head to the table, she reached for another biscuit. She wasn't sure how long she could keep this up – the lack of sleep mixed with the lack of food wasn't a great combination, and she was struggling.

After finishing the biscuit, she wiped the crumbs from the keyboard and pushed the laptop away. Maybe she *would* just shut her eyes, have a ten-minute rest. It was probably all she needed to get through the rest of the day and then hopefully she'd be too exhausted to worry about anything and would actually fall asleep tonight. Ten minutes, that's all she needed.

As she folded her arms across the table and lowered her head, the kitchen door opened again and she jerked her head up.

'I didn't just catch you trying to take forty winks, did I?' Jay said as he walked in, feigning an air of shock, looking behind him dramatically.

'Ha ha, of course not.' Megan shook her head. 'I was just... resting my eyes.'

Jay indicated the door behind him. 'Seriously, though, I can come back if you do want a nap.'

'No, no. Don't be daft.' She waved him in and stood up. 'Do you fancy a coffee?'

'Yes, please. A mug of caffeine sounds good to me. I had Mia over last night and she woke about five in the morning full of beans.'

'Ouch.' Megan filled the kettle with water and flicked it on.

'Ouch indeed.' Jay chuckled as he picked up the laundry basket and began emptying the washing machine. 'I don't think her teacher will be thanking me this afternoon when she's falling asleep at her desk, though. Still, it was lovely to have her over for an extra night. I'd trade my sleep in a heartbeat to have her wake me in the morning.'

'Ah, she might be okay?' Megan shrugged as she spooned coffee granules into the mugs, two heaped ones for herself, one level for Jay. 'I take it she's a morning person and you're a night owl then?'

'Ha ha, yes, that's right. Something she definitely gets from her mother. I like my evenings too much to go to bed early.'

Megan began pouring the hot water and watched with satisfaction as the coffee granules dissolved. 'I don't blame you. I'm the same.'

'Whose are these, then?' Jay suddenly sounded baffled.

'What are they?' Megan turned and realised he was holding up her wet top. She jumped as the boiling water splashed across her knuckles. 'Drat.'

'You okay?'

'Yes, just caught myself with the hot water, that's all.' She lunged forward and grabbed her top. 'I can sort that.'

Standing back, Jay frowned, his face etched with confusion. 'Are these your clothes?'

Megan nodded, wracking her brain for a simple explanation. 'I didn't get time to pop into the laundrette yesterday, and I didn't think anyone would mind me washing a few bits here.'

After emptying the rest of the laundry from the machine, Megan pulled out her jeans and underwear and put them in a small pile on the work surface before rolling them and squashing them into her tote bag. She'd pop out and place them in the car later. It wouldn't take long for them to dry in this weather.

'I shouldn't think anyone would mind if you didn't want to wash them with the dog bedding.' Taking over the coffee making, Jay poured in the milk before handing her a mug.

'I know.' She wrapped her hands around the mug and breathed in the strong, bitter aroma. 'I was just embarrassed, I guess.'

'Nothing to be embarrassed about.'

Sitting back down, Megan looked under the table. Cindy was still fast asleep, oblivious to any drama.

'I wonder how Flora is getting on with the home visit,' Jay said as he bent down and took his lunch from the fridge.

'I don't know. Hopefully it'll be good news. She's been there a while.'

'Yes, that's got be a good sign, hasn't it?' He nodded towards her. 'Are you not having your lunch?'

Megan shook her head. 'I've already had mine.'

It wasn't a lie, she'd had all the lunch she was going to have.

The door opened again, and Susan walked in, followed shortly by Percy.

Percy made his way to his chair and sat down, rubbing his hands together. 'All done. The concrete is laid and the foundations will be ready for the new kennels.'

'Yes, no thanks to Percy here, who ended up walking in it.' Susan laughed.

Percy chuckled, took a handkerchief from his pocket, and began wiping flecks of grey concrete from his boots. 'I may have had a momentary lapse of concentration.'

'Or two you mean.' Shaking her head, Susan threw him a packet of antibacterial wipes. 'Here, try these. At least they'll be wet.'

'Thanks.' Percy folded his handkerchief and slipped it back into his pocket before taking a wipe. 'Much better, thanks.'

While Susan began speaking to Jay, Percy turned to Megan and lowered his voice. 'Have you managed to speak to Flora yet?'

'Flora?' Megan frowned.

'Yes, about what we spoke about in the paddock.' Percy glanced across at Susan, who was still speaking to Jay and lowered his voice even further. 'About dating.'

'Oh, yes. Of course.' Megan grimaced. She'd completely

forgotten, what with everything going on between her and Lyle, it had slipped her mind. 'Umm, no, not yet. Sorry, I'll try to have a word with her today.'

'Thank you.' Percy grinned.

'What are you two whispering about over here?' Susan asked.

'Oh, you know. Just this and that.' Percy winked at Megan. 'Just discussing the perfect process of laying concrete, that's all.'

'Pouring concrete, you mean?' Susan raised her eyebrow.

'Yes, yes, pouring concrete.' Percy folded up the used wipe and laid it on the table before reaching across and taking a biscuit. 'These look good, don't they?'

'They're the same biscuits we have here all the time.' Smiling, Susan shook her head and sat down.

20

Megan pulled a notebook stuffed with yet more receipts from the shelf above the counter and tucked it under her arm, looking down at Cindy who had followed her through to the reception area and was now sitting patiently, wagging her tail and watching Megan's every move.

'I take it you want a treat, hey?'

Cindy held a paw up, her head tilting to one side.

Megan laughed. 'After that performance, I think you deserve one, too.'

'Deserve what?' Jay stepped through the door from the kennels.

'A treat. She has such cute puppy dog eyes. I don't know how anyone can resist her.' Taking a treat from the tub on the counter, Megan held it out and waited until Cindy had gently taken it from her hand before wiping the crumbs down the front of her jeans.

'She is a gorgeous pup.' Jay grinned and slung the pieces of a half-chewed tennis ball in the bin. 'There goes another tennis ball chewed by the one and only Petal.'

'Ah, she does like to destroy them.' Megan grinned.

'She sure does.' Jay turned to the courtyard, seeing Flora pulled up in the van. 'Looks like we'll find out if Angus will be going to his new home or not.'

'I hope so. He's such a sweet little thing and does seem to be struggling to settle into his kennel.'

The bell above the door tinkled as Flora stepped inside, a large smile covering her face.

'Good news?' Jay leaned against the counter and crossed his arms.

'Good news.' Flora gave them both a thumbs-up. 'He's going to be so happy there too. And she's had a rescue pup before, so knows what she's getting into.'

'That's fantastic news.' Megan took the notebook from under her arm and held it in her hand. 'So, she'll be aware of what to expect of the settling-in period and everything?'

Flora nodded. 'Yes, which makes things easier. She mentioned she knew you, actually. Lisa? She works at Honeysuckle Bed and Breakfast?'

'Yes, I know Lisa.' Megan nodded. 'She's really lovely.'

'She mentioned you'd moved on. Have you found somewhere to rent? You're still local, I hope.' Flora smiled kindly. 'You're one of us now.'

Megan glanced down at the notebook in her hands, her knuckles turning white as she gripped it tightly to her. 'Still local.'

'Good, good. Whereabouts are you now?' Squeezing behind her, Flora hung the keys to the van up on the hook behind the counter.

Megan swallowed and shifted on her feet. She hated lying, but what else was she supposed to do?

'Oh, not far.'

'Right.' Flora frowned before shaking her head and touching

Megan's forearm. 'I'm glad you've found somewhere more permanent.'

'Me too.' She tried to relax her grip of the notebook. She could feel Jay's eyes upon her. 'So, when will Angus be going to his new home?'

'At the end of the week. Lisa has next week off work to help settle him into a routine before she goes back, so she'll be picking him up on Saturday morning.' Flora fussed over Cindy before looking across to Jay. 'Do you mind helping Susan pack away the tools please, lovely?'

'No problem.' Jay nodded.

'Thanks. Percy's out there too, so if you could try to guide him towards the lighter stuff, that'd be great, please? He assures me his back is better, but I'd hate to see him injure himself again.'

'I will.' Jay grinned before pulling the door open and disappearing outside.

'And how about you, lovely? How are you bearing up with that ankle of yours?' Flora asked as she held the kitchen door open for Megan and Cindy. 'I hope you've been resting it?'

'It's much better, thanks. I don't think it'll be long until it's completely healed now.'

Megan sat down, placing the notebook next to her, and looked across at Flora, who had begun to fold dry towels from the tumble dryer. She knew she'd promised Percy she'd talk to Flora, but she wasn't sure how to bring up the topic of dating. Not whilst keeping the conversation natural.

'How are things between you and Lyle?' Flora asked, folding the last of the towels. 'I hope he's not making life too difficult for you?'

'Not too difficult, no.' Megan shrugged. 'I'll be glad when I can close the book on that part of my life, if I'm honest.'

Flora nodded. 'I can imagine. Still, you must have been happy together once.'

Megan looked ahead. She had been. She'd been very happy when they'd first met. She hadn't believed her luck – how could someone confident and ambitious like Lyle have fallen for her? She'd always been the quiet, shy one at school and college and now this man who was the complete opposite of her – outgoing, popular – had chosen her to spend the rest of his life with. He'd promised her a future full of holidays and fancy restaurants. And once his business had taken off, he'd given that future to her. All of it. She'd never felt so special. In the beginning, that was.

'Yes, we were once.'

Flora sighed. 'Life can be cruel, can't it?'

Megan nodded. It certainly could. The more successful Lyle had been, the less he'd needed her, the less time they'd spent together and even when he'd been home, she'd felt like a nuisance. He hadn't wanted to listen to *her* dreams, *her* ambitions. There had only been room for one person's dreams in their marriage, and that had been his. At the expense of hers.

'You'll find someone else.' Flora leaned across the table and patted her forearm. 'Someone who sees you for who you are and treats you right.'

'Umm, I'm not so sure about that.'

There was a time she'd thought Jay might have been the one to show her how love was supposed feel, but thanks to Lyle, he'd run a mile from that idea.

'You will,' Flora said. 'I'm a firm believer in true love and you'll get another chance at it.'

Megan bit down on her lip. This was her chance. This was the opening in the conversation where she could bring up what she'd promised Percy.

'How about you? Do you think you'll find love again?'

Flora smiled sadly. 'I think my second chance at love has sadly passed me by.'

Megan frowned. 'Why do you think that?'

Sighing, Flora shook her head. 'Who would take on someone like me? Devoted to this place, to the dogs we rescue? Only someone as mad as me would even contemplate sharing my lifestyle.'

'There's a lot of people who share your passion for this place, though. Susan, Ginny, Alex, Sally, to name a few.' Megan met Flora's eyes. 'Percy.'

Flora nodded slowly, thinking. 'I suppose you're right.'

Megan opened the notebook and began to make a small pile of the receipts held inside.

'So, you think everyone has a second chance at love, then?'

Flora frowned. 'Yes, maybe I do.'

Megan nodded. Without actually asking her out for Percy, she couldn't really say much else, but at least she could report back that Flora might well be open to dating. She glanced across at Flora quickly, who was still seemingly busy thinking. Maybe it was Percy she had on her mind?

21

'Right, Cindy. We'd better get you across to the cottage now and settled with Poppy and Dougal before I come over and lock up.' Flora stood up and tapped her side as Cindy opened her eyes and stretched. 'And you'd best get home too, lovely.'

Megan nodded and began to pull her papers into a pile.

'I'm sure I heard on the radio that we're expecting a bit of a storm tonight, so I don't want anyone staying late and getting caught up in it on the way home.'

Megan scrunched her nose up. There went any hope of a decent night's sleep tonight then. If she couldn't sleep when it was quiet and the weather relatively calm, she'd have no chance when the rain was lashing down around her and the wind was bombarding the car. She stifled a yawn. Still, she was tired, so maybe it wouldn't affect her as much as she thought.

'You look as though you need an early night too.' Flora smiled kindly.

Megan covered her mouth as she yawned again. 'Sorry. Yes, I think I do.'

'Don't worry about tidying up, it'll only be there in the morning. You get off now.'

'Okay, thanks.' After closing the laptop down, Megan waited until Flora had left before stacking up the biscuits left over on the plate in the middle of the table and wrapping them in a sheet of kitchen roll. She then took her water bottle from her tote bag and refilled it, looking out of the window as she did so. If those dark clouds were anything to go by, then Flora was right, a storm was brewing.

The cheerful ringtone of her mobile filled the room, and she picked it up to see who it was. Lyle. Nope, she would just ignore him. She didn't need to speak to him. She waited until the call had rung out and put it down again.

Almost instantly, the landline rang in the reception area, but the rings stopped quickly. Megan breathed a sigh of relief and slipped the small parcel of biscuits into her bag. Biting her thumbnail, she stared at the little tissue-covered parcel and tried to squash the feeling that she was doing something wrong, that she was stealing. It was stealing, wasn't it? Taking those biscuits, and from a charity too. And washing her clothes here. She pinched the bridge of her nose, trying to block out the thoughts.

'Megan! Phone for you,' Susan's voice called from the reception area.

'Coming.'

Taking the parcel out of her bag again, Megan began to empty the biscuits back onto the plate. She couldn't do it. She couldn't take from Wagging Tails, from Flora, who had been nothing but kind and accepting. She had a bag of crisps left in the car and she'd eaten enough biscuits for lunch. She'd be fine.

Walking into the reception area, she took the phone from Susan and, covering the mouthpiece, said, 'Thanks.'

'No worries. I'm off now, so I'll see you tomorrow.' Susan waved as she walked out of the door.

Megan knew who it was before she lifted the receiver to her ear. Lyle, and she knew there was no point in just putting the phone down, ending the call before speaking to him. He'd only ring again. And again. And again. He'd keep calling until she spoke to him.

'Lyle.'

'Ah, you were expecting me. I hope you weren't just ignoring my call to your mobile. We have options to discuss. Options which may just prevent you from camping out in your car again tonight.'

Huh, yep, she believed him. Not. He was having far too much fun knowing what her life had become to change anything. And if she knew one thing about him, it was his inability – no, his down-right refusal – to change his opinion about things, especially when it came to money, which this did.

'What do you want?'

'I want to give you a chance, say a Get Out of Jail Free card if you please?'

She sighed. She didn't have any option but to go along with his games. 'What would that be, then?'

'Come home and we can forget all of this. You've had time to mull things over, think about your decisions, now it's time to come home.'

'Come home?' Was he being serious? He wanted her back?

'Yes, you'll have a roof over your head again. I'll reinstate your cards.'

Megan closed her eyes before opening them again and looking out of the window she could see Jay and Flora talking in the courtyard, Rex circling their legs. How did he even have the gall to ring the Wagging Tails' landline? He was lucky Susan didn't recognise his voice; Flora would have.

'We can tell all our friends that you've been on an extended holiday. They know we've not been away for years due to my work; we can spin it. No one will ever have to know.'

Megan laughed, a loud snort coming from her nose. This was what it was about then. He didn't want her back. He wanted to save face with their friends. But she'd left him months ago. She'd told him she wanted a divorce soon after she'd helped Andy scupper his plan to knock down this place.

'You haven't told them we've separated, have you?'

She could hear noises down the line before his voice boomed back at her. 'Of course not, why would I bother our friends about a little tiff? You don't hear any of them discussing the difficulties in *their* marriages.'

She rolled her eyes. 'Lyle, this is not a little tiff. I've left you. I've applied for a divorce, and you've retaliated by cutting me off from our money. I've left you.'

'On this occasion, just this once, I'm prepared to forgive you. Mind you, this is it, there won't be a third chance.'

Megan turned and leaned her back against the counter, staring at the noticeboard on the wall.

'I'm not the one who needs to be forgiven. I'm sorry, Lyle, but we're over. I'm not coming back to you.'

Was that clear enough? How had he even thought there was a chance she'd go back? Even a slight chance that she'd get in her car, drive home and walk through the door pretending as though nothing had happened? She'd seen who he really was. When he had threatened Flora and the team right up to blocking her from accessing their money. How could she live with him, knowing what he was capable of? How could she even pretend to love him again?

'I'm glad.' Lyle's tone had changed, his voice clipped and cold once more. 'I'll see you in court.'

She stood there, holding the phone to her ear, the silence of the now abandoned line encompassing her. Had he really thought she'd go back to him? She shook her head and lowered the phone to its cradle, her mind whirring with questions.

At that moment, Jay pulled the door open and entered the reception area, Rex scurrying through in front of him. 'Flora said there's a storm coming.'

Megan nodded, trying to push all thoughts of Lyle to the back of her mind. 'Yes, she said that to me, too.'

Jay glanced out of the window before looking at her again. The clouds were even darker than they had been a few minutes earlier and a light sheen of rain had begun.

'It looks as though it won't be long before it gets here, either.'

'Nope.' She watched as Sally walked across the courtyard, gripping the agility tunnel in one hand as it blew out to the side, Percy just behind her, carrying the hurdles. If this was what it was like when the wind was already picking up, what was it going to be like when the storm actually hit? The lay-by she'd been parking in at night was lined with trees. Should she go somewhere else, or would the trees protect her a little? And if she parked somewhere else, then where?

'Your new place isn't too far, is it?' Turning, Jay looked at her.

'Oh, no, not far at all.' That was the truth, at least. The lay-by was only just down the road.

'That's something then. You don't want to be driving far if this gets any worse.'

'No.' Megan shifted on her feet.

'Whereabouts is it? I missed where you said you were staying.' Jay bent to fuss over Rex whilst keeping his eyes on her.

Megan shrugged. What was with all the questions? She

picked up a clipboard from the counter and stared at it, pretending to be engrossed in whatever was written on the page. 'Not far. A little drive in that direction.' She blindly pointed to the right.

After a moment's silence, Jay cleared his throat and spoke. 'The dogs have already been fed. Ginny and I fed them about half an hour ago.'

'What?' Looking over at him, Megan frowned. What had the dogs being fed got to do with where she was staying?

'The dinner list.' Jay indicated the clipboard in her hand.

'Oh, right.' Megan focused on the scrawled handwriting. He was right, it was the dinner list, noting any allergies the dogs had and their preferred food.

'Is everything okay? You seem distracted.' Jay stood up again, Rex pawing at his leg for more fuss.

Megan smiled. 'Yes, all good, thanks. Just a bit tired, that's all.'

Jay nodded slowly before looking down at Rex. 'Okay. I'd better get this one in his kennel. See you in the morning.'

'See you.'

As the door leading to the kennels swung shut behind him, Megan rolled her shoulders back. Why was he suddenly so interested in where she was staying? It didn't affect him. It wasn't as though they were seeing each other any more. Not that going on one date and sharing one kiss could actually be described as 'seeing each other', but still, why would she give her address to him anyway?

She looked out of the window. Flora was hurrying across the courtyard holding a plastic bag over her head in an attempt to dodge the rain. She'd have to go or else Flora would only tell her to leave, to go home in the warm and out of the way of the storm. If only.

The bell above the door tinkled as Flora rushed in before

shaking the rainwater off the bag and shutting the door. 'You still here, lovely?'

'Just getting my bits together.' Megan smiled and walked into the kitchen to grab her bag.

'Okay, well take care on your journey, won't you?'

'I will. See you tomorrow.' Pulling her tote bag onto her shoulder, Megan walked back through the reception area and braced herself for the storm outside.

22

Megan pulled the handbrake up and looked across the lay-by towards the row of trees that shielded her from the road. In the few minutes it had taken her to drive here, the sky had unleashed the storm. Sheets of rain covered the windscreen and could be heard hammering against the roof of the car, and the wind had picked up, bombarding the trees she'd hoped would protect her from the worst of it.

Leaning forward, she put the windscreen wipers on, her visibility only improving for a millisecond before rainwater flooded the windscreen again. She could hear the low rumble of commuters as they inched forward along the road beyond, their vision as obscured as hers.

She jumped as a particularly strong gust tore twigs from the trees, throwing them against her car. Would she be safe here? There was a branch just ahead of her, a large gnarly branch that was swinging dramatically as the wind pummelled it, which was worrying her. Would it hold or would it be torn off the trunk? If it did come down, then it would be thrown this way, and she didn't much like the chances of driving her car away unscathed.

Megan reversed a little, backing up further down the lay-by. She was closer to the road now, still over enough so not to prevent other vehicles from driving into the lay-by, but further away from the tree with the dodgy branch. She glanced behind her. Her car was likely visible from the road but at least she'd feel a little safer.

* * *

With the evening drawing in and further darkening the sky, Megan checked the clock on the dashboard once again before turning the ignition off. It was only half past seven. She'd tried to stay at Wagging Tails for as long as she possibly could, but with Flora worrying about people driving in the storm, she hadn't been able to stay indefinitely. Never mind, she was here now, and the storm wouldn't last forever.

Crossing her arms over the steering wheel, she fixated on the branch dancing in the wind. With each gust, she could hear the wood creak and splinter from the trunk. Should she move from the lay-by? Try to find somewhere safer? But where was there? She couldn't park up in a car park due to parking restrictions.

She closed her eyes, letting her forehead dip to her arms. She could feel the tiredness creeping in and if she'd still been at the bed and breakfast she knew she'd have been asleep within minutes of her head hitting the pillow. But here, with the wind and the rain battering the car? She kept her eyes squeezed shut. She might just be able to fall asleep. Even a nap would be better than nothing at all.

* * *

A loud bang echoed, visions of a giant yellow vehicle, a bulldozer hitting the side of a building. Another bang, louder this time, encroached on her dream. A version of herself watching as the old marital home was razed to the ground. Lyle was there. Grinning from ear to ear, telling her that if he couldn't have the house, then no one would. He was happy. She wasn't.

Again, the giant iron ball smacked into the brickwork, the house falling like a pack of cards around her.

'Megan!'

Who was calling her? She turned and looked at Lyle, his eyes still fixated on the house as the glass from the window smashed around them, a million little pieces snowing down on them.

'Megan! Wake up!'

Jolting to consciousness, Megan blinked and stared out of the windscreen. The branch had fallen, missing the bonnet by half a metre.

Another bang, a loud tap this time, to her right. She turned and jumped as Jay's face came into focus. Winding the window down, she spoke, her voice thick with sleep.

'Jay? What are you doing here?'

'I could ask you the same question. It's dangerous out here. Why have you pulled up?' He held the hood of his coat over his head, the wind trying to tug it from his grasp.

'I...' She looked in the rear-view mirror. He'd parked behind her, the orange of his hazard lights flickering on and off.

Peering through the window, the muscles in his cheek twitched. 'Follow me to my place.'

'What? Why?' She started the ignition. 'I'll just get back to the bed and breakfast, that's all. See you tomorrow.'

She wound the window up again, the sheet of glass obscuring his words.

Jay tapped on the window again, waiting for her to open it once more.

'You're sleeping in your car, aren't you?'

'No. Of course, I'm not. Why would I be?'

How did he know? She'd have to get going somewhere else, anywhere but here, pretend everything was fine.

'Megan, please?' His voice was almost lost as a huge gust tore past them. 'Just come back to mine and we can talk. Or I can take you to Flora's if you don't want to come to mine. You can't stay out here. The road is flooding and there's already been one tree down and that's just between Wagging Tails and here. It's only going to get worse.'

Megan looked out of the windscreen. He was right, from the little she could see through the sheets of rain cascading down from the sky, the wind was relentless. He was right, she couldn't stay here. If she did and the car became damaged, she'd have nothing.

She nodded.

'Follow me back.' He indicated his car before running towards it.

Megan waited until Jay had reversed out of the lay-by before doing the same. She couldn't pull forward, not with the huge branch lying across the ground. Back on the road, she gripped the steering wheel as she followed him, keeping the speed low and the windscreen wipers on high. Not that it was making much difference. She could barely see the red glow from his back lights, let alone anything else.

As they approached West Par, Jay's car stopped suddenly and Megan slammed on the brakes, her bag on the passenger seat falling to the floor, her clean, damp clothes spilling across the footwell. She wound her window down as she watched Jay running towards her.

'Another tree has just come down; we'll have to turn around and go the other way.' His voice was laced with urgency.

'Okay.' She nodded before he retraced his steps back to his car.

What had she done? If anything happened to Jay on their way back to his... She shook her head, turning her thoughts instead to focusing on the road, to turning around down the narrow lane, to following his car.

She hadn't asked for him to come and find her. In fact, she'd done the exact opposite. She hadn't told anyone where she was sleeping. She hadn't mentioned Lyle cutting her off. She'd tried desperately to keep attention away from her situation.

Although what was she thinking? He'd probably just spotted her car on his way home. He might not have driven out to look for her. She took a deep breath. It didn't make any sense. How had he known where she was? He couldn't have followed her back from Wagging Tails, if he had he would have got to the lay-by when she had and yet he couldn't have spotted her on his way home either as Flora would have ensured he'd left with everyone else. That only left the scenario, that he'd come looking for her. But would he have? Why?

She gripped the steering wheel tighter and leaned forward. She needed to focus on driving instead of thinking about how Jay had found her. She'd find out soon enough.

As they inched towards the 'Welcome to West Par' road sign, she took a deep breath in. They'd made it. She watched Jay pull into a driveway next to a whitewashed thatched cottage and drew her car in behind him, hearing the unmistakable crunch of gravel beneath the tyres.

They were safe. She reached down and squashed her clothes back into her tote bag before opening the door, clutching the door handle as the wind tried to rip it from its hinges, and stepping out.

She ran across the driveway and reached the porch just as Jay swung the front door open.

After letting Megan through first, Jay shut the heavy wooden door and slipped out of his rain-drenched coat.

'That's crazy weather,' he said.

'It sure is.' Megan took her trainers off and then just stood there awkwardly.

'Come on through, I'll get the kettle on.' Jay indicated the door behind her.

Nodding, she stepped into the living room. The whitewashed walls here were hung with photographs, and the back of the door decorated with paintings and drawings stuck haphazardly onto the wood. A pink play kitchen stood in the corner of the room, plastic bricks overflowing from a nearby tub, and a small child's tent had been erected beneath the window overlooking the front garden, a line of teddies positioned in a group by its entrance.

'Excuse the mess. Mia has made me promise not to touch a thing.' Jay grinned. 'She was in the middle of a game when her mum picked her up the other day and, believe me when I tell you that she knows exactly how she's left everything and if I so much as move one of the teddies a millimetre to the left, she'll spot it as soon as she walks through the door.'

Megan smiled.

'What would you like? Tea, coffee, squash?' Jay began to walk towards the back of the room where Megan could see another door open leading through to the kitchen.

Clutching her tote bag in her hands, she tucked her hair behind her ear. She closed her eyes momentarily, adjusting to the quiet of the room, the wind muffled by the glass. Opening her eyes, she glanced out of the window, rain was still drumming against the glass and the storm still raged but in here it was warm and dry and for the first time since she began sleeping in her car she felt safe.

She looked around the kitchen as Jay filled the kettle with water before switching it on. Everything was so clean, so tidy. She looked down at her hands, her fingers were greasy from the last packet of crisps she'd eaten for dinner and she dreaded to think how her hair looked – she could feel how dirty it was. She felt out of place as it was here, knowing that he was now privy to her secret, but even more so because of how dirty she felt. The last thing she wanted to do was to put him out further but if she didn't ask him she might not have another chance for a while. 'I know this sounds really cheeky, but could I have a quick shower, please?'

'Umm, yes, of course. I'll get you a towel.' Jay indicated the door.

'Thank you.'

* * *

Her hair now wrapped in a towel, Megan used her palm to wipe condensation from the mirror and looked at the reflection staring back at her. She looked awful. The dark circles under her eyes had only increased and her skin was paler than ever. She took the towel off, shaking her hair out and using her fingers to comb it through. She might look a mess, but she felt better than she had since she'd begun sleeping in her car. She felt clean, refreshed.

She folded the towel before placing it in the dirty laundry basket in the corner of the room. Taking a quick glance around the bathroom, she ensured she'd left everything as it had been, before opening the door and as she made her way along the landing and down the stairs, she took a deep breath in. Jay was cooking. The aroma of tomatoes and onions hit the back of her throat, and her stomach began to growl with hunger.

She pushed open the door into the living room, where the smell of food was stronger. The radio was on and Jay was singing along to a cheesy eighties song, his voice cracking as he attempted the high notes of the chorus. Unsure whether she should announce her arrival or not, she walked slowly into the kitchen and stood in the doorway.

The song ended, and the DJ began talking, his soft tone filling the kitchen.

Shifting position in the doorway, Megan cleared her throat. 'Thanks for that.'

Jay turned around, the tinge of embarrassment reaching his ears. 'How long have you been standing there?'

Megan laughed. 'Long enough.'

'Ah.' Jay looked down at the ladle in his hand as a splodge of red sauce dripped onto the glass hob. 'Then I apologise.'

Megan grinned and shook her head. 'You've got a nice voice.'

Jay chuckled. 'You're only being polite because I'm cooking dinner.'

'Ha ha, maybe.' She walked towards him and leaned awkwardly against the counter as he stirred the sauce into a pan of pasta. Keeping her eyes fixed on a framed picture of Mia on the opposite wall, she spoke quietly, her voice catching in her throat. 'How did you know?'

Jay filled two bowls and passed her one before indicating the pine table in the corner of the room. Sitting down, he poured them both a glass of juice and set the carton down.

'The clothes in the washing machine, you not wanting anyone to drive you home after you sprained your ankle, trying to change the subject when Flora began talking about visiting Lisa from the bed and breakfast...'

Megan grimaced and stabbed a pasta shell with her fork. 'It was that obvious?'

Jay shook his head. 'No. Not to everyone.'

'But to you?' She took a mouthful of pasta, the tangy flavour of tomato filling her mouth. She'd missed this. She'd missed home-cooked food. Heck, she'd missed food other than crisps and biscuits full stop.

Jay took a sip of orange juice and shrugged.

'Are you sure nobody else realised?' she asked.

Jay smiled. 'I'm sure. Don't you think Flora would have had something to say about it if she had?'

'That's true.' Megan nodded. Flora would have. 'And you won't tell them?'

'I won't. But I think you should.'

'What? No. No, I can't do that.' She shifted in her chair.

Why would she tell them? Anyone? She hadn't even wanted Jay to know.

'Why not?'

'Why? Because...' Wasn't it obvious? 'I don't want to. I just don't want their pity.'

Jay frowned. 'They wouldn't pity you.'

'Of course they would. A few months ago, I was living in a huge five-bedroom detached house and now, now I have nowhere. I have nothing. Of course, they'd pity me.' She swiped a tear that had slid down her cheek. 'I'm supposed to be doing this on my own. I'm supposed to be able to.'

'And you are.' Jay gently touched her hand. 'You are doing this on your own, but sometimes people need to take a bit of help from others.'

'No, I'm not. And that's final.' She laid her cutlery down across her plate and pushed her chair back, standing up. 'Thank you for the shower, but I'm going to get going now.'

'Megan.' Standing up, Jay looked at her. 'Don't go. The weather's awful. Anything could happen.'

Slumping back in her chair, Megan covered her eyes with her hands. 'I just can't do this. I left him and he's still trying to control my life. He's still there.'

'Lyle?' Moving his chair closer, Jay wrapped his arm around her shoulders.

'Yes, Lyle. All these years I've stuck by him, I've done what he wanted to, when he wanted to and now, now I'm left with nothing.' She leaned her head against his shoulder, allowing the tears to run, her body wracked with sobs.

'It'll be okay. This won't be forever. When the divorce has gone through and the financial agreement has been finalised, this will just be a blip in your memory.'

Megan looked up at him and wiped her eyes with the back of her cardigan sleeve. She knew she looked a mess, even more so now she'd been crying. 'It won't. This is it. This is my life. I signed a prenup. I won't get a penny from him.'

Jay opened and closed his mouth, seemingly looking for something to say.

'See what I mean? He's still playing with my life. I'm being punished by trying to do the right thing, but what else could I do? I couldn't stay with him, not after everything he put everyone at Wagging Tails through. I saw him for who he'd become. He wasn't who I married, he wasn't who I wanted to stay with for the rest of my life. I had to leave him. But now, now what?'

'Megan, I'm so sorry you're going through this.' Jay swallowed. 'Things will get easier, though.'

She nodded. His words were empty, but she knew he spoke the truth. They would. If this was rock bottom, then there was only one way left to go.

'I can only go up, right?'

'Exactly. I know it probably feels impossible, but you'll get through it. You'll be able to carve a life for yourself again. One that you want this time.'

'I suppose so.' She leaned back in her chair and looked at him. 'I'm so sorry.'

'What for?'

'For everything. For not telling you about Lyle to begin with, for risking your life out there.' She indicated the window, the storm still raging outside 'For using your hot water, for eating your food, for crying at you.'

He chuckled. 'You've nothing to be sorry for. I should be apologising for the awful food. I'm not trying to poison you, I promise.'

She smiled, her eyes sad. 'The cooking is good.'

'Why don't you get some sleep? I can't imagine you've had much over the past few days?'

Megan nodded. At the mere mention of the word, she could feel her eyes wanting to close. Sleep would be good.

23

'Thank you for last night, but now the storm's over, I'll be fine back in my car.' Megan looked out of the kitchen at Wagging Tails. Both she and Jay had arrived early and no one else was to be seen.

'No, you can't do that.' Jay ran his fingers through his hair. 'Have the spare room again.'

'Thanks, but no. Putting me up last night was amazing of you, but you have your daughter tonight and there's no chance I'm going to intrude on your time with her.'

As the kettle boiled, Megan spooned coffee into two mugs. She felt a million dollars after having a shower and a good night's rest. She smiled as she caught sight of Flora and Percy chatting by the gate to the bottom paddock. She watched as Flora let Cindy loose into the paddock before leaning against the fence next to Percy.

Megan groaned. She hadn't told Percy what Flora had said when she spoke to her about dating again. She'd been so wrapped up in Lyle's games and trying to survive the nights in the car that she'd clean forgotten to report back to him.

'Have you forgotten something?'

Glancing over her shoulder, Megan smiled at Jay. 'Just something I was meant to tell Percy. I'll speak to him today.'

'You're going to tell him and Flora about Lyle having blocked your cards?'

'No, not that. Something else entirely.' She shook her head. 'Like I said, I'll be fine back in my car.'

'And what about the small matter of food? You're going to carry on filling up on biscuits from here?' Jay indicated a plate of Bourbons sitting in the middle of the table.

Megan turned back to the kettle, filling the mugs with boiling water. 'I don't want to tell Flora. I don't want to tell anyone. Heck, I didn't even want you to find out.'

If she was being honest, Jay was the last person she'd have wanted to know about her situation. She felt the warmth of embarrassment mixed with shame sweep across her.

'I know you didn't. But I'm glad you told me, and Flora will be too.'

'I didn't tell you. You guessed and came looking for me.' Megan placed a mug in front of Jay before slipping into the chair opposite him. He'd admitted it last night, eventually.

'Yes, well. I'm glad I did. Anything could have happened to you in that storm. Anything could happen to you any night, sleeping in a lay-by.' He locked eyes with her.

'No, it won't. This is West Par, not Las Vegas or somewhere.' She laughed, trying to make light of the conversation.

Jay lowered his mug. 'Megan, please? Tell Flora. Someone will have a spare room you can stay in. Besides, she might even give you a job here.'

'There's no way I'd accept a job here, I'm a volunteer.' Her whole trip down to Cornwall would be rendered pointless if she were to be given a job at Wagging Tails. She was here to make up in some small way for what Lyle had done and the only way she could do that was by volunteering.

'Okay, well, she might know someone who would give you a job then.'

'Please, drop it.' Megan spoke quietly. She knew he was right. She knew she should ask for help. But she couldn't. That wasn't who she was, who she wanted to be.

Sighing, Jay shook his head. 'Then you can sleep at mine again tonight.'

'We've already been through this. You've got your daughter tonight.'

Jay shrugged. 'I'll think of something to tell her.'

'No.' Megan sat a little straighter. 'And I mean that. I'm not imposing.'

'You—'

Jay stopped as the kitchen door swung open and Cindy bounded in, followed shortly by Flora and then Percy.

'Hello, you.' Megan fussed over Cindy, grateful for the excuse to drop the conversation.

When Flora sat down at the table, she looked from Megan to Jay and back again. 'Are we interrupting something?'

'Nope.' Megan spoke quietly, but firmly.

'Are you sure?' Percy asked. 'Not being rude, but it feels as though I could cut the atmosphere in here with a knife.' He picked up a teaspoon from the counter before flicking he kettle on.

Jay cleared his throat. 'So, we have the new kennels being constructed today, then?'

Percy smiled. 'We certainly do.'

'Great. How's the concrete holding up?' Jay asked as he finished the last of his coffee.

'Come and take a look if you like? I can grab a coffee after.'

'Okay, sounds good.' Jay stood up.

'Are you coming, Megan?' Percy asked. 'You put a lot of work into it too.'

Megan nodded, pushing her chair back and standing up.

'Megan, hold on a moment, would you?' Flora held her hand up and indicated the chair Megan had just vacated. 'Take a seat a moment, lovely.'

Sitting back down, Megan automatically wrapped her hands around her empty mug. 'Is everything all right?'

'I couldn't help but overhear a little of the conversation you were having with Jay. I'm sorry, I promise I wasn't eavesdropping, and I wouldn't usually butt into a conversation I wasn't privy to, but I heard Jay saying that you could sleep at his again tonight. Are you having problems finding another bed and breakfast?'

Megan looked down into her mug. There was a faint tide line around the edge of the ceramic indicating where her coffee had been filled up to.

'I can imagine it's a little tricky finding somewhere at the last minute.' Flora looked across at her. 'Especially with it being the summer holidays.'

Megan nodded. What was she supposed to say?

'I have a friend who works at a bed and breakfast just outside Trestow. I could have a word with her and see if they have any rooms available?'

Megan bit down on her lip.

'Or is there something else going on? Is there another reason you left Honeysuckle Bed and Breakfast?' Leaning forward, Flora briefly touched the back of Megan's hand.

She didn't have a choice, did she? She couldn't lie. Flora would only find out one way or another, and then what would she think of her? Besides, things weren't going to change anytime soon. Lyle wasn't going to suddenly backtrack and give her what she deserved, and she was pretty certain there wasn't a queue of prospective employers ready to offer her a job. All she had was the truth.

'Lyle has cut me off from any money.'

Flora leaned back in her chair, visibly shocked.

Megan steadied her voice. 'I have nothing.'

'Oh, lovely.'

'It's fine though,' Megan continued, despite her voice cracking. 'I'm looking for jobs and as soon as I get one, I'll be able to find somewhere to live. And I have my car in the meantime.'

'Please don't tell me you've been sleeping in your car?'

Megan shrugged. 'I didn't last night. Jay somehow guessed what I was doing and insisted I stay over at his.'

'That horrible, horrible man.' Flora pursed her lips and narrowed her eyes. 'Lyle, of course, not Jay. He's one of the good ones. Why on earth didn't you say anything? Why didn't you ask for help?'

Megan could feel the sting of tears behind her eyes. 'I... I don't want to be a burden to anyone. I should be able to do this myself. I should be able to cope by myself, provide for myself. Everyone else does.'

'Everyone else doesn't have a Lyle in the background pulling the strings, do they?' Flora patted Megan's hand. 'Everyone needs help at some point.'

'No, they don't. Look at Jay. He's coping after his divorce. Ginny had a bad experience with her ex and she's just fine.' Megan wiped her eyes, pressing against her eyelids, willing the tears to stop.

'Jay's ex-wife moved out, leaving him to live in the marital home, I believe. And Ginny. Well, has she told you how she got this job? She rang me from Trestow train station after she'd left her ex, Jason. She saw a poster I'd popped up asking for volunteers and arrived here with only the clothes on her back. I gave her a room and eventually a job.'

'Really? You did?'

'I did.' Flora shook her head. 'So, you see, everyone needs a little bit of support every so often. And I'll tell you what we're going to do, you're going to come and stay over at the cottage with Poppy and me and I'll see if I can give you a little for all the work you're doing with the books.'

Megan held up her hands. 'No, I'm not taking any money from the charity.'

'You wouldn't be taking money, lovely. You'd be working for it, and besides, it'll be out of my own money, not the charity's.'

'Definitely not.' Megan shook her head. 'Thank you, but I really won't be taking any money from you.' She had to learn how to stand on her own two feet. And she most definitely would not be taking any handouts.

Flora nodded slowly. 'Okay, well, in that case, you come and stay, and we'll pop some cards up in the local shops, see if anywhere has any job vacancies. I know it's unlikely in West Par but one of the village residents might just be able to pass your name on to their boss in Trestow or wherever they work and let you know about any upcoming work.'

'I don't know.' Megan turned her cold mug on the tabletop so the picture was facing her; a yellow teddy, the huge smile cracked from being washed so often.

'I'll help you search for jobs online, too. You'll be earning in no time.' Flora raised her eyebrows at her. 'And I won't take no for an answer to you staying at the cottage. No one from my team sleeps in a car.'

Megan sighed. 'Are you sure?'

'As sure as I know that we could both do with another cuppa.'

Standing up, Flora picked up her and Megan's mugs and turned to the kettle. 'Everything passes and this will too.'

Megan looked down at her hands. Would it? The future looked pretty bleak from where she was sitting, and it could get worse if Lyle wanted it to. She wasn't quite sure what he was capable of.

* * *

With her tote bag hanging from her shoulder, Megan gripped her other bags in her hand and rang the doorbell to Flora's cottage. She smiled as she heard the scurrying and excited barking from the other side of the door. She could tell which bark was Cindy's and which must be Dougal's, Poppy's little dog.

As soon as the front door opened, Cindy bolted out, standing on her hind legs and leaning her front paws on Megan's stomach while little Dougal circled her legs, reminding her of an old friend's cat.

'Hi, come on in, welcome to the madhouse.' Poppy grinned. 'Aunt Flora's just burning dinner.'

Just on cue, the fire alarm sounded from the back of the cottage and Poppy grimaced.

Megan laughed and stepped inside. 'Are you sure you don't mind me invading your space?'

'Of course not! The more the merrier.' Poppy held out her hands for some of Megan's bags. 'I'll take those. I'll show you to your bedroom in a bit, but first, we'd best check Aunt Flora isn't actually burning down the house.'

Megan copied Poppy in piling her bags at the foot of the stairs before following her through the living room to the kitchen at the back of the cottage. Sure enough, Flora was in there, wafting a tea towel towards the alarm on the ceiling.

Eventually, the piercing beep-beep of the alarm slowed and stopped.

'Sorry about that, lovelies.' Flora now waved the tea towel in the air, dispersing the smoke. 'I hope you're not a fussy eater, Megan.'

'Nope, I'll eat anything.' Megan smiled and looked across to the oven where two pizzas and a garlic baguette stood lightly singed.

'I wouldn't say that if I were you,' Poppy stage-whispered, holding her hand in front of her mouth.

'Oi.' Flora flung the tea towel at Poppy, who caught it deftly and glanced at the pizzas. 'Takeout it is then.'

'Now you're talking.' Poppy laughed.

'Why don't you show Megan her room whilst I order?' Flora said, taking the tea towel back from Poppy.

'Okay.' Poppy nodded and turned towards the door again. 'This way.'

'Thanks.'

As Poppy led Megan back through to the hallway again, Cindy followed, almost leaning her long body against Megan's legs with every step, as if glued to her side.

'She sure does like you, doesn't she?' Poppy laughed as they gathered Megan's bags and headed up the stairs.

'Aw, she's such a sweetheart. I know she has her problems, but she more than makes up for them with her lovely nature. She's such a gentle character.'

'She sure is. Dougal loves her. He waits on the doormat for Flora to bring her over. I don't know what he'll do when she's rehomed.' Poppy shook her head and opened a door on the landing. 'Here's your room.'

'Great. Thank you.' Stepping inside, Megan lowered her bags onto the floor and looked around. Three walls of the room were painted a pale yellow, the fourth, behind the pine headboard was wallpapered, large sunflowers the size of dinner plates emblazoned across a deep royal blue background. 'It's lovely.'

'I'll leave you to settle in. Come on down when you're ready.' Poppy smiled as she lowered the bags she was holding. 'Come on, Cindy. Let's give Megan a bit of peace and quiet.'

Instead of following her, Cindy sat next to the bed, her eyes fixed on Megan.

'Don't worry,' Megan said, as Poppy tapped her leg, to encourage the dog to come with her. 'She's okay.'

Poppy nodded and closed the door whilst Cindy jumped onto a pale blue crocheted blanket which was draped across the duvet.

'Well, you've certainly made yourself at home here, haven't you, Cindy?'

Megan looked down at her bags heaped by the doorway. She should probably unpack, but she was drained. Not tired – she'd had the best night's sleep in a long time at Jay's last night – but she was most definitely emotionally drained. She perched on the bed next to Cindy before lying back and staring at the ceiling. How could she ever thank Flora for taking her in? And Poppy for making her feel so welcome?

24

'Thank you.' Megan smiled at the shopkeeper as he took the small A5-sized postcard from her. She'd made sure to write her contact details and a couple of lines about herself and the type of work she was looking for, which was basically anything, in her neatest handwriting. Now all she could do was hope and continue to look and apply for jobs online.

'No worries. I'll pop it up.' He walked around the counter and pinned it to the noticeboard next to the tills.

As she left the shop, she took Cindy's lead back from Jay.

'All done?' He clicked his fingers, signalling to Petal and Willow that they were on the move again.

'Yep. All done. That's a card up in there as well as in the ice-cream parlour, plus the village noticeboard. Not that I'm expecting anything to come of them, but Flora thought it would be a good idea.' She paused as Cindy sniffed a tuft of grass at the side of the path.

'You never know.' Jay glanced down at the ground. 'I hope you don't think I was trying to meddle when I encouraged you to tell Flora about the car and everything?'

'No, not at all.' She had at the time, but she knew why he had. She'd have done the same. 'Flora overheard the end of our conversation in the kitchen, anyway.'

'Ah, so it wasn't my brilliant advice that has resulted in you staying at Flora's, then?' Catching her eye, he grinned, the dimple deepening in his cheek.

'Ha ha, no I'm afraid not.' She laughed. 'But, hey, I should have listened to you. Both Flora and Poppy have made me feel really welcome.'

It was true. She might have only stayed there for one night so far, but to have a room, a bed again, a place to call her own, it meant more to her than either Flora or Poppy probably realised.

'Well, I'm glad it's all worked out for the best.'

'Yes, me too. I don't know why I was so adamant not to ask for help earlier. I just...' She shrugged. She couldn't really explain it. It hadn't been that she was too proud to admit what path her life was taking her down. It hadn't been that. More that she just hadn't wanted to be anyone's burden, but over at the cottage, she didn't feel as though she was. She felt welcome, accepted. 'I don't know.'

'It's okay. I think I know what you mean.' Jay paused and looked at her, running his fingers through his hair. 'Now that you've got a place to stay, did you fancy celebrating?'

'Celebrating the fact I'm not sleeping in my car any more?' Megan grinned and raised her eyebrows.

'Exactly. Why not?'

'Umm, I guess so. You think I should shout it from the clifftops or something to celebrate?'

'I was thinking more along the lines of going to a theme park?'

'A theme park?' She frowned. 'I've not been to one in years.' Theme parks really weren't Lyle's thing. At all.

Jay grinned and carried on walking. 'Maybe that's even more of a reason to go?'

'Is there even one around here?' She automatically looked around herself at the beautiful, quaint little cottages and narrow lanes.

'Well, not here, no. But there's a good one just over an hour away. Flambards. Mia is desperate for me to take her, so I thought perhaps you and I could go and check it out first? I haven't taken her in while and have forgotten what rides will be suitable. It could be a celebration trip and a reccy all in one.'

'Like a risk assessment?' Megan laughed. Her mum had been a teacher, and Megan remembered going on day trips with her, usually to museums, to check places out before she would commit to taking her class.

Jay shrugged. 'Yes, I guess so.'

'Okay.' Megan narrowed her eyes at him. 'You do know they probably have a website, right? Which will list the rides they have?'

Jay glanced towards the other side of the lane before catching her eye again. 'You've got me. I was asking you out.'

Megan bit down on her bottom lip. 'You were?'

'Yes.' He chuckled. 'Remember, I did tell you I was terrible at these things.'

'Ha ha, you did.' She nodded.

'It was just a suggestion. We don't have to.' He shook his head. 'Of course, you don't have to. That was a daft thing to say.'

'You're cute when you get tongue-tied.'

She covered her mouth quickly. Had she really said that out loud? She could feel the prickling of a blush creeping across her face. Why had she said that?

'Oh. Umm... thank you.' Jay chuckled.

'I can't believe I actually said that.' She laughed.

'So, what do you think? Would you like to come?'

She looked down at Cindy, who was walking perfectly at her heel. She would. She'd love to go with him and enjoy a day at the theme park. A day without a care in the world. But she couldn't.

'I can't. I just don't have the money. When I have a job, though, I'd love to come.'

'You don't need any money.'

She held her hand up. Jay had done enough putting her up for the night during the storm, cooking her dinner and just generally being there. 'Thank you, but there's no way I'm taking money from you.'

'You don't need to.' He reached into his back pocket and pulled out two vouchers. 'I have vouchers.'

'You have vouchers?'

'Yep. An old colleague of mine was given them by their marketing team after some work he did over there and he's not going to use them, so he passed them on to me.' He slipped them back. 'What do you say? Shall we go and spend the day at Flambards Theme Park?'

Megan grinned. 'Yes, in that case, I'd love to.'

'Brilliant.'

As they carried on walking, Megan glanced at Jay out of the corner of her eye. It would be nice to spend more time with him. More than nice. Yes, they both spent most days at Wagging Tails together, but it would be good to meet up outside of their work environment. It would be good to get to know him a little better.

She touched the pad of her index finger against her lip. Would this be a date or just a day out with friends? Whatever it was, she was looking forward to it.

* * *

'You look happy today.' Percy slipped into his chair at the table before sliding a mug towards Megan.

'Thank you.' She took a sip of the coffee, strong with a teaspoon of sugar. 'I am.'

'Good, good. It's nice that you're over in the cottage with Flora and Poppy now.' He nodded at Cindy, who was lying in her usual position under the kitchen table, almost on top of Megan's feet. 'I bet this one is happy to have you over there too?'

'Ha ha, yes. She's a proper little, or should I say big, Velcro dog. Wherever I go she's always there right next to me, just as though she's stuck to me with Velcro.' Megan grinned.

Cindy had insisted on sleeping in her room last night. After her whining at the door for half an hour, Megan had relented and let her in, and she'd sprawled across the foot of the bed, stretching out from one side to the other.

Percy nodded and took a sip of his drink before glancing at the door and lowering his voice. 'I don't suppose you've had a chance to speak to Flora, have you? Don't worry if you haven't. I know you've had a lot going on and all.'

Megan pushed the laptop away a little and wrapped her hands around her mug. 'I have actually. Sorry, I completely forgot to tell you what she said.'

'Don't worry, love. I know it's been a tricky time for you recently.' Percy clasped his hands on the tabletop. 'What did she say?'

What had she said? The conversation she'd had with Flora felt as though it had been ages ago. A lot had just happened between then and now.

'From what I could understand, she *would* be interested in dating. She said she thought she'd left it too late, and that anyone who would want to be with her would have to be as crazy about dogs as her.'

Leaning forward, Percy nodded. 'And?'

Megan shrugged. What else had she said? 'That they'd need to share her love of this place.'

'Right. Anything else?'

'I don't think so. Not that I can remember, anyway.' Megan nodded. 'Yes, I think that was the general gist of the conversation.'

'She definitely said she'd be open to dating then?'

'Yes, well, I think so.' She looked at Percy as he frowned. 'I'm sure of it – as much as I can be, of course.'

'Okay, okay. So, what now?'

'What do you mean?'

'What do you think I should do now?' Percy furrowed his brow.

Megan looked at him. She knew he wanted her to tell him to ask her, but she couldn't. Although she felt as though she knew him and Flora well enough, and from what she'd picked up on, she definitely felt there was a connection between them both, this was too big. Percy and Flora had known each other for over thirty-five years. If Megan was wrong, then who knew how it might alter the friendship they had?

'What do *you* want to do?'

Wringing his hands, Percy glanced over his shoulder towards the kitchen door. 'I want nothing more than to ask her, but if she says no...'

'What would you say to me or Alex or Ginny? What would your advice be for us?' Megan sipped her coffee.

'Well, that would be easy, wouldn't it?' Percy shifted in his chair. 'I'd have told you not to be so daft and to ask her to dinner.'

Megan looked at him. 'Why aren't you following your own advice, then?'

'Because I'm a coward, that's why.' Percy rubbed his chin, his beard shifting beneath his hand. 'I love her. I only want the best for her and if that means being her friend for the rest of my life, then that's what I'll do.'

Megan gazed into her coffee before looking across at Percy. His eyes were shining with tears. From an outside perspective, he and Flora were perfect for each other and definitely appeared to have a connection, to have more than a friendship, but she was new here. Maybe she'd got it wrong. Maybe she was picking up on things which just weren't there. She didn't know their history. Percy did.

'Why don't you have a think about it?'

Percy nodded sadly. 'I've been thinking about it for the past thirty or so years.'

Megan glanced at Cindy, who had left her favourite spot beneath the table and was now standing in front of the kitchen door, her left front paw held against the door frame.

Percy followed her line of sight. 'It looks as though she needs to go out, love. You go, I'll be okay.'

'Are you sure?'

'Aye.' Nodding, Percy pulled the daily paper towards him, apparently immediately engrossed with the goings-on in Trestow.

'Okay.' Standing up, Megan picked up Cindy's lead from where it was hanging over the back of her chair. 'Come on then, Cindy. Let's go out for a wander.'

Clipping her lead on, Megan took another look at Percy, who was still seemingly reading the paper. Had she said the right thing to him? Should she have encouraged him to ask Flora to dinner? Maybe she wasn't cut out to be a matchmaker after all.

Stepping outside into the courtyard, Megan loosened Cindy's lead and she matched her pace as they made their way towards the grass. The air was cooler today, still warm, but the storm had cleared the humidity a little.

As she walked towards the bottom paddock, she noticed that Ginny was in there with Rex.

'Hey,' Ginny called across to her when she saw Megan approach.

'Hi.' Megan joined Ginny on the other side of the gate and lengthened Cindy's lead in her hand.

'You look deep in thought.' Ginny threw a tennis ball she'd been holding and little Rex ran across the paddock chasing it.

'Oh, I am. I'm not sure if I've said the right thing to someone who asked for advice.'

'Ah, do you want to share?'

Megan looked down at her trainers. 'I'm not sure if I should.' She glanced towards the reception area. The last thing she wanted was for Percy to step outside and see her chatting with Ginny after speaking to her in confidence. 'But I'm honestly not sure if I said the right thing to them or not.'

'You're welcome to tell me. I won't mention it to anyone else and you don't have to use names.' Ginny bent down and retrieved the ball from Rex's mouth before throwing it again.

Looking up at Ginny, Megan nodded. It couldn't hurt to get someone else's perspective, could it?

'Thanks. Well, in that case, someone asked me to try to find out if the person he liked... loved... fancied...' None of those words seemed appropriate, not when she was talking about Percy and Flora. 'Whether they would be open to dating or not.'

Crossing her arms, Ginny leaned on the gate. 'Open to dating them or in general?'

'Just in general. Anyway, they basically said they would but think their time has passed for starting another relationship, so I relayed the conversation back to him, and he asked if I thought he should ask her out.' Megan frowned. 'I just said they should do what they think is right, but I'm pretty certain there's a connection between the two of them and I'm pretty sure he's never going to act on it because he hasn't for years. So, yes, I don't know if I should have told him to go for it.'

'Umm...' Ginny frowned.

'Sorry, that was a big old waffle, wasn't it?' Megan shook her head.

'No, it's not that. I understand what happened. It's just I have a feeling I know who you're talking about.' Ginny grinned. 'It's not Percy and Flora, is it?'

Megan nodded.

'Well, you're right on both accounts. There is a connection between the two of them. We all see it. I even assumed they were a couple when I first arrived here and I'm pretty sure everyone who meets them for the first time thinks so, too. And you're right about Percy never plucking up the courage to ask her out. If he hasn't after all this time, then why would he now, right?'

'That's just what I was thinking.' Megan leaned against the gate next to Ginny, Cindy circling the grass to her right. 'What do we do then?'

'Let me have a ponder, but I think we need to come up with a plan. If we leave those two to their own devices, then they'll never do anything about it. It reminds me of Elsie and Ian over at the bakery in Penworth Bay. They didn't get together until a few years ago and I'm pretty sure they were in a similar situation too, both having feelings for each other for years.'

'If it worked out for them, it might just do for Flora and Percy.'

'Exactly.' Ginny grinned and tapped the top of the gate. 'Let me have a think. I can feel a plan brewing.'

Megan laughed. 'I'm glad I told you now.'

'I'm glad you did, too. This toing and froing between them has been going on for far too long now.'

Megan watched as Ginny threw the ball again before pulling a poop bag from her pocket and walking across to Cindy. 'Come on, you. Let's go and check on Percy.'

25

'Ready?' Jay held his hand out, indicating for Megan to go first.

In front of them stood a café, a gift shop and an ice-cream parlour. Stepping through the gates into Flambards Theme Park, Megan took in the sounds of excited shouting and laughter from children and adults alike mixed with loud fairground music. She grinned, memories of her teenage years coming back to her.

'Where would you like to go first?' Jay looked up from the map he was holding. 'We could check out the roller coaster, the log flume if you don't mind getting soaked, or maybe something more leisurely, such as the swings, to ease us in gently?'

'Why don't we jump straight in and head for the log flume?' Megan grinned, the buzz in the air rubbing off on her.

Jay chuckled and pointed to their left. 'Okay, getting soaked it is then.'

'Great.' As they fell in step with each other, Megan glanced across at Jay. 'You're not afraid of heights, are you?'

'No. Not usually, anyway. I'm quite happy climbing a ladder or going on a plane. I'm more worried about getting covered in water.'

Megan grinned. 'We might get a bit splashed.'

'A bit? I think I remember getting completely drenched last time I went on the log flume here, but it has to be done when at a theme park, doesn't it?'

'I guess so. I've not been to one since I was about sixteen, I don't think.' She took the map from him and pointed them in the right direction.

He whistled under his breath. 'That's a long time ago, then.'

'Oi!' Laughing, she swiped the map at him.

'Ha ha, I didn't mean it that way! I used to go to theme parks quite a bit. I must have been to this one at least three times.'

'Really?' She frowned. 'Why did you need to come again to check it out then?'

He smiled. 'It's been a couple of years, so things have bound to have changed. Besides, I thought it'd be nice to hang out with you.'

'Aw, thanks.'

'Here we go.' Jay pointed ahead, and they joined a short queue that had formed at the base of the tall log flume. 'I guess there's no turning back now, then.'

'We can turn back.' Megan indicated behind her.

'No chance.' Grinning, Jay stepped up onto the platform surrounding the entrance to the log flume as the queue surged forward, and taking his hand, Megan stepped up onto the platform beside him.

'Thanks.'

His hand felt warm in hers. She could still feel the callouses on his skin from the work he'd been doing at Wagging Tails.

Still with her hand in his, she kept her eyes focused on the person in front as the queue steadily inched forward. What would Lyle say if he could see her now? He'd certainly be disgusted that she was at a theme park. And he'd probably be equally disgusted that she was here with Jay. She laughed. Which would he hate more? What she was doing or who she was doing it with?

A man wearing a blue baseball cap waited until they'd taken their seats before checking the safety bars. 'Morning! Are you all set to ride on the Colorado River Log Flume?'

'Absolutely!'

As the log flume lurched upwards, the theme park opened up beneath them and Megan could see for miles around. It was bigger than she'd first thought it was.

'Oops, I always forget about this bit,' Jay said as the cart came to an abrupt halt as it neared the top of the track, throwing them forward a little. He glanced down beneath them before looking at Megan. 'It's this bit I hate when it slows right down, and we know what's coming.'

'Ha ha, I used to love this bit! The anticipation.'

'Umm, that's one way to think about it.'

Just as she turned back to face the front, the cart inched over the cusp of the track and began its descent. She could feel her hair flying out behind her and her cheeks being pushed back by the wind as they plummeted down towards the pool of water at the bottom.

In no time at all, the cart plunged into the pool, spraying water upwards and over them both before slowing down and meandering around a curve. 'That was brilliant!'

Jay chuckled. 'It was. I'm soaked now though.'

'Yes, same here.'

Jay seemed to have come off the worst. He really was soaked. His light blue T-shirt had been turned navy with the water, and on his jeans it had fashioned huge wet patches.

Megan grinned, holding in her laughter. 'Are you feeling refreshed?'

Shaking his head, Jay reached out to her, drawing her into a hug.

As she laughed against his shoulder, Megan could feel the water dripping from his hair onto hers and the liquid from his T-shirt soaking hers too. Pulling away and holding his hands at arm's length, she said, 'I can't believe you've just done that!'

Jay shrugged, his lips twitching as he tried to stop himself from laughing. 'I was being nice. Refreshing you too.'

Megan smiled. There was something about Jay – he made her feel comfortable, made her feel as though she could just be herself. She didn't feel the need to put on an act or try to behave in a certain way as she thought he'd expect her to. She hadn't felt that way with Lyle, or with the people they'd used to spend time with. She'd always felt as though she wasn't enough. Wasn't enough for Lyle, wasn't enough for their friends. That she didn't fit in. But with Jay, here, at Wagging Tails, even at his house, she was able to be herself. No airs or graces or second-guessing her actions and words.

Jay tilted his head. 'You look as though you're thinking about something deep.'

Shaking herself from her thoughts, she took hold of his hands again and met his gaze. 'I was just thinking that I can be me around you.'

Jay frowned. 'Of course you can.'

'I couldn't always be me, be just me, but with you I can.' She wasn't explaining herself very well, she knew that, but she hoped he knew what she was trying to say.

'Well, I'm glad to hear that.' He smiled, his dimple deepening in his cheek.

With her hands still in his, she leaned forward and touched his lips with hers. What was she doing? Leaning back again quickly, she dropped his hands and held her palms against her cheeks, trying to cool the hot rush across her skin. 'I'm so sorry. I don't know what I was thinking.'

Jay looked into her eyes again, the lines around his creased with kindness. 'Don't be sorry.' He leaned forward, pausing a mere inch away from her. 'Is this okay?'

Megan nodded. It was more than okay. It was what she'd been hoping for since he'd kissed her that day at Wagging Tails. She leaned forward, meeting his lips as he wrapped his arms around her.

* * *

'This looks nice. Just what I need after all those rides.' Jay lowered the tray of sandwiches and drinks to the table and sat down.

'Me too! Although I felt that sick after going on the Sky Force ride I didn't think I'd be able to stomach lunch.' Megan laughed as she took the plates and mugs from the tray before slipping it onto a spare chair next to her.

'Ooh yes, that one was brutal. I think I might be a little old for rides like that.' Jay chuckled.

'You're not too old, you just don't have an iron stomach any more.' Megan bit into her sandwich and then held it up slightly. 'Thank you for this.'

'You're very welcome.'

'I'll pay you back when I have a job. If anyone ever wants to employ someone with zero experience in the last ten years, that is.' Shifting in her chair, she pulled her mobile from her back pocket and looked at the screen. Still nothing. 'They don't seem to be in a hurry to contact me.'

'You'll get one. Just you wait and see.'

Megan smiled and nodded. She wished she had his confidence.

'You will.' He took her hand and grinned at her. 'So, are we like official now then?'

Bursting out laughing, Megan wiped her mouth with a napkin. 'Official? What are we, teenagers?'

Jay shrugged as he chuckled at himself. 'I'll say it again, but I did warn you I'm not used to this sort of stuff.'

'Yes, you did.' She met his eyes. 'I'm not either though, remember?'

'True.' He nodded.

'But, yes, I'd like that. Let's call ourselves official.' She grinned. It felt right, here with him. It had felt right before too, but hopefully this time Lyle wouldn't get in the way.

'Great.'

Standing up slightly, Jay leaned across the table and kissed her.

Megan kissed him back, laughing as he sat back down, causing Jay to hold his hand against his chest, his eyebrows raised, and pull a face of mock-shock.

'Charmed.'

'Ha ha, no, I was just thinking how much my life has changed in the past few months. Before this whole thing with Wagging Tails, I'd never have imagined, dreamed, that I'd be in this position. Here, at a theme park, with you, someone I really care about. For once, I'm excited about the future.'

She was. When she'd been with Lyle, her future had been laid out in front of her. She had known what to expect – dinner parties, silent evenings, rambling around that big house alone. Now, she felt as though she didn't really know what her future held. She hadn't foreseen falling into another relationship – she hadn't even thought about it – but it was exciting.

'Cheers to Wagging Tails then.' Raising his mug, he waited for Megan to do the same before they clinked ceramic to ceramic.

'To Wagging Tails.'

As she lowered her mug again, she accidentally knocked it against her plate and watched as a splash of coffee covered the table. 'Oops.'

Jay stood up. 'I'll go and get some napkins.'

'No, don't worry. I'll go. I want to grab some mayo for my sandwich anyway.' Pushing her chair back, Megan got up, turned and headed towards the corner of the till where the cutlery, condiments and napkins were displayed. As she stood in the short queue, Megan glanced back at Jay, who was eating his sandwich and looking out of the large window. He was a good man, kind. And cute too. Even though they'd only just started their relationship, there was no denying that she'd grown close to him. They had a real connection and, hopefully, a future, too.

Megan picked up the napkins and mayo before heading back to the table.

'You had a message ping through.' Jay nodded towards her mobile and lowered his sandwich.

'Thanks.' She sat down and wiped up the spilt drink before bunching the napkins into a ball and picking up her mobile.

> Hope you're happy being skint. Your fault. If you hadn't been with HIM I would never have stopped your cards. My solicitor will be in touch. Lyle.

She sighed. Really? Did he really have to text that? Now? Today, whilst she was trying to enjoy herself and forget about everything? Of course, he didn't know that.

She automatically glanced around the café, half expecting to see him. She wouldn't put anything past him after the way he'd tracked her down through her bank statements.

'I... umm...' Jay indicated Megan's phone.

Looking up, she frowned. 'What?'

'I didn't mean to, but when it pinged up, I saw the message.' He squirmed in his chair. 'Is it my fault your ex cut you out of the money?'

Megan picked up the wet napkin ball, gently pulling it from its scrunched-up state and smoothing it over the tabletop.

She shook her head. 'No, it's not your fault. It was me that signed a prenup before we married. And if he hadn't spotted us kissing at Wagging Tails, he would have found another reason. He would have thought of something else I'd seemingly done wrong in order to justify his actions.'

'He saw us kissing? When we were digging up the foundations?'

She nodded. 'Yep. He tracked me down here using the bank statements from my card and put two and two together.'

'That's how he knew where you'd gone? From your bank statements?'

'Yep.' Megan shook her head. 'You couldn't make it up, could you?'

'Ha, no, you couldn't. I'm sorry, I feel awful that he's using me against you and I'm sorry about seeing your message.' Leaning back in his chair, he rubbed the back of his neck.

'Don't be. Lyle is just being Lyle. I filed for divorce, but he's ripped up the papers and is adamant he's going to file for it instead.' She shrugged. 'Is that even possible? For someone to counter file? Is that the right word? I was going to check on the internet if what he's done is legal but completely forgot.' She grimaced. There had just been so much going on, what with the sleeping in the car, then moving into Flora's, it had slipped her mind.

'Really? Why?'

'Because he wants me to be the reason the marriage is over,

not him.' She shrugged. 'It doesn't matter, anyway. Not really. As long as I get a divorce, that's all that really matters. It's not as though I stand to gain anything from the years I was with him, not with the prenup anyway.'

'That's awful. Are you going to contest it?'

'Maybe. Probably.'

She should do, shouldn't she? Although part of her wanted to make this new part of her life her own, she wanted to start over and would she be able to do that if she had court hearings and meetings with the solicitor which, knowing Lyle, would go on for years?

'I don't know. I'm trying to focus on building my life again and if I eventually receive anything from the divorce, then great, but if I don't, then at least I'll have my new life.'

'That sounds sensible.'

'Yes, the only thing I can rely on Lyle for is that he'll make it as difficult as possible for me to get my share of anything.' She looked up from where she was playing with the napkin. 'Although it feels almost just as impossible to find a job as it is.'

'Don't say that. Any employee will be lucky to have you onboard.' He reached out and took her hand.

'Yep, they'll be lucky to have someone clueless who hasn't worked for a decade.' She scrunched up her nose and shook herself. 'Nope, you're right. I need to think positively about this. As soon as I find a job which pays me enough to pay Flora something for rent and food, then I'll invest the rest of my wages in an accountancy course and refresh my skills.'

'That's more like it.' Jay squeezed her hand.

She nodded and squeezed his back. 'Then I can become a freelance accountant, build my own hours, work from home and still have enough time to help out at Wagging Tails. I can dream, right?'

'I think that's more than a dream.' Jay smiled. 'That's a plan.'

'Yes, maybe you're right. Okay, that's my plan.' She smiled at him. 'How about you? Any luck on the job front yet?'

'Maybe.' He grinned. 'I got a letter this morning asking me for an interview over at the nature reserve by Penworth Bay.'

'Really? Why didn't you say anything?' She'd been so engrossed in her own problems that she hadn't thought to ask him.

He shrugged. 'I didn't want to jinx it.'

'But you're telling me now?'

He shrugged. 'I just thought I'd take my own advice.'

'Turn your dreams into a plan?'

'Exactly and so, now that I've told you, hopefully, it'll be a plan rather than a dream.'

'I like your way of thinking.' Megan rubbed the pad of her thumb across the top of his hand. 'Good luck with your interview.'

Jay glanced out of the window. 'Where do you want to go now? Do you fancy another ride? Or we could take a look around the Victorian Village?'

'Umm, maybe the Victorian Village? Let our lunch go down first before we venture back onto the rides?'

'Sounds sensible.' Jay piled their empty crockery and used napkins onto the tray.

Pushing her chair back, Megan stood up and pocketed her phone. She wasn't even going to give Lyle the satisfaction of replying. He was trying to bait her into a conversation. Well, he could wait.

26

'Megan, are you okay coming in here for a moment?' Standing at the door into the reception area, Ginny indicated to Megan to join her.

'Yep, okay.' Megan held her hand next to Cindy and waited until she'd dropped the tennis ball she'd been carrying into her hand before leading her towards Ginny. 'Is everything all right?'

'Yes. I hope so, anyway.' Ginny lowered her voice. 'I had a think about what you were saying about Percy and ended up speaking to Susan and Alex, and, well, we've decided an intervention is needed.'

'An intervention?' Shutting the door, Megan unclipped the lead from Cindy's collar.

'That's right. This has been going on for years. Percy being too nervous to ask Flora out. Certainly before I came and Susan, who's been here the longest, even remembers when she started volunteering that she thought they were a couple. If Percy doesn't ask her now, I don't think he ever will.'

Megan reached into the jar of treats on the counter and

passed one to Cindy. 'I guess you're right. But what if it goes wrong? What if Flora says no?'

'I don't think that will happen.' Ginny walked across to the kitchen door. 'They'd make a great couple, but even if it did go wrong, Flora's so lovely. I think she'd go out of her way to make him feel less awkward about the whole thing.'

'Their friendship still wouldn't be the same though, would it?'

Were they doing the right thing by interfering?

'But if he never speaks to her about how he feels, then they will definitely never get together.' Ginny shrugged.

'True.' Megan nodded as Ginny opened the kitchen door. Percy was sitting reading the newspaper in his usual spot at the end of the table, opposite Flora's chair, and Susan and Alex were chatting between themselves. As they walked in, the room fell silent.

Looking up from his paper, Percy frowned. 'What's all this then?'

'We wanted to speak to you,' Susan spoke first.

'You want to speak to me?'

'No, yes, we all want to speak to you.' Susan indicated Alex, Ginny and Megan.

'Oh, I don't know if I like the sound of this.' Percy folded the newspaper and pushed it slightly across the table.

Ginny laughed. 'It's not anything bad. We just want to talk to you about something that's been on our minds for a while.'

'You don't like my beard?' Percy stroked his chin before picking up his mug. 'Or I've not been making my fair share of cuppas?'

'Ha ha, nothing like that.' Ginny looked around the room. 'We all like your beard and you make more than your fair share of drinks.'

'Let's just get on with it, shall we?' Alex crossed his arms. 'We think you should ask Flora out.'

Percy spluttered and lowered his mug before pulling a red handkerchief from his pocket and wiping his mouth. 'I'm sorry?'

'Just that. Just what Alex said. For as long as we've known you, you've held a torch for Flora and, well, now's the time to act on it.' Susan patted Percy's hand.

'I... No...'

'There's not any point in trying to deny it, Percy. We've all noticed it over the years.' Alex raised his eyebrows. 'And now you need to put your feelings into action and ask her out for dinner.'

Percy pinched the bridge of his nose. 'Is it that obvious how I feel?'

Megan looked around the table as everyone else nodded.

'Yes,' Alex said. 'It is.'

Frowning, Percy moved his chair a little. 'If it's that obvious, then does Flora know?'

Ginny frowned. 'I don't think so. Maybe.'

'No, no, I can't.' Percy held his hands up and shook his head firmly. 'I'm not jeopardising the friendship I have with her.'

'But if you never ask her out, if you never tell her how you feel, you won't ever get together.' Susan spoke softly, kindly.

'I know, I know all of that. But no, I can't. And that's final.' Percy pushed his chair away and stood up just as the kitchen door opened.

'What's final?' Flora paused in the doorway and looked around the room. 'Am I missing something?'

As he slowly sat back down, Percy's skin turned a deep shade of red.

'Ginny? Susan? Alex? Megan? Percy? What's going on?'

'Er, nothing. It's all good.' Alex grinned.

'Umm, there's clearly something I'm missing.' Flora crossed

her arms and lowered herself into her seat. 'Something you're trying to keep from me.'

'Right.' Susan stood up, resting her hand briefly on Percy's shoulder as she walked past him. 'I'm going to go and start cleaning out the kennels.'

'I'll help you.' Alex jumped up from his seat and followed her to the door.

'You've already done them today.' Flora frowned.

'I've got to go and check on Ralph,' Ginny added as she took her mug to the dishwasher.

Megan looked from Flora to Percy and pushed her chair back. 'Come on, Cindy, let's take you for a wander.'

As she walked out of the door, she could hear Flora quizzing Percy again. She closed the kitchen door quietly and clipped Cindy's lead to her collar.

She hoped Percy didn't think she had anything to do with the intervention. Yes, she'd mentioned their conversation to Ginny, but she had a feeling the intervention would have happened regardless of what she'd said.

'You look deep in thought.'

Megan turned around to find Jay and Sally walking across the courtyard towards her.

'Sorry. Yes. Hello, Rex.' Leaning down she fussed over the small Jack Russell while Cindy nudged her nose against Jay's leg and then Sally's.

'We've just been doing some agility training with this little one, haven't we?' Sally smiled as she pulled out a treat for Rex before giving Cindy one too.

'Aw, how is he getting on?'

'Great. He did really well.' Jay grinned as he knelt down and fussed over the dog.

'Maybe give Flora and Percy a few minutes in there.' Megan nodded towards the door.

'Oh really? What's going on?' Sally frowned and peered through the small window of the door.

'Ginny, Alex and Susan told Percy to ask Flora to dinner.'

'Oh, as in a date?' Sally raised her eyebrows.

'Yes. They told him he'd been taking too long and if he never asked her, then he'd never find out what she'd say.' Megan gave little Rex a final fuss before straightening her back. 'And just as they were speaking to him, Flora walked in, so she knows something is going on. Hopefully Percy will take this opportunity to talk to her.'

'That's exciting then.' Sally grinned.

'I'm not sure if he actually will or not. He looked a bit like a rabbit caught in the headlights.'

'Aw, bless him. I don't suppose he realised everyone knew how he felt?'

'No, I don't think so.' Megan made a face.

'It certainly shocked me to find out they weren't a couple.' Jay patted Cindy before standing up.

'Exactly. I almost think that if they do get together then not much, if anything, will change. They act like a couple already.' Sally smiled and looked from Jay to Megan and back again. 'Talking of which...'

Megan could feel her face warm as her lips curled into a smile. She looked across at Jay and took his hand. 'How did you know?'

'I may have mentioned our trip to the theme park.' Jay smiled.

'But I guessed the rest.' Sally grinned. 'I'm really happy for you both. You make a lovely couple.'

'Thank you.' Megan looked across at Jay.

'Well,' Sally said, passing Rex's lead to Jay, 'if the kitchen is out of bounds, I might just go and take a look at the agility see-saw. It was a bit wonky, wasn't it?'

'It was. Shall we take these two on a walk?' Jay nodded towards Rex.

'Good idea. Catch you both later.' Sally turned and held her hand up in a wave before heading back towards the paddocks.

'Shall we head down to the beach with them?' Megan indicated the two dogs.

'Maybe we could grab a drink from the chip van in the village first?' Jay said as they headed across the courtyard, the dogs following at their heels. 'You don't mind that Sally worked it out, do you? About us?'

'No, of course not.' She slipped her hand in his. 'Why would I mind?'

Jay shrugged. 'I just wasn't sure whether it would make things worse for you if Lyle found out. After the way he reacted before when he saw us together digging the foundations...'

Megan sighed. 'He can think what he likes. He will do anyway. I just want to get on with my life.'

'Good, good.' Jay swung the gate open, stepping aside to let Megan and Cindy through first before following.

* * *

'Now, this is the life.' Megan grinned as she sank to the sand. Cindy and Rex had played in the sea whilst she and Jay had paddled and now both the dogs were tired and in need of a rest. 'That's it, Cindy. Come and sit down and rest for a moment.'

Jay sat next to her and rolled his trouser legs down. 'You know, I'll miss this when I do get a job.'

'Me too. Although let's hope we'll still both have time to come and help out.' Megan stroked Cindy between the eyes as she flopped her long body against her.

'Most definitely.' Jay nodded and glanced over his shoulder. 'I wonder how Percy is getting on. Do you think he asked Flora?'

'I'm not sure. I hope so and I think it would have been tricky for him to get out of having *the* conversation... a conversation at least. Flora knew something was going on and if she'd overheard anything then I don't think he would have got away with not asking, but I'm not sure if she did.' Megan shrugged. 'Besides, if he really has been wanting to ask her out for decades then I'm not sure whether he suddenly will now.'

'If he doesn't, maybe we all need to get together and set them up. We could book a table at a nice restaurant and send each of them an invitation to an open night or something. I don't know.'

'Yes, that's a good idea.' Megan nodded. 'Maybe we should.'

'I think so. But, like you said, hopefully Percy will have asked her by now.' Jay shifted on the sand.

'Let's...' Megan frowned as the ringtone of her mobile filled the cove.

Please don't let it be Lyle. Please, not Lyle.

She pulled it from her back pocket and glanced at the screen. It was an unknown number. She closed her eyes, bracing herself just in case he'd now moved on to withholding his number.

'Hello?'

'Afternoon, is this Megan Trussel please?' It was a woman's voice. The tone cheery.

'Yes, I'm Megan.' Looking down, she drew a circle in the sand.

'I'm Primrose from the Ice Cream Parlour. We met the other day when you came in to put your card up on our noticeboard?'

'Hi, Primrose. Yes, that's right. Did you need me to take it down?' Megan used her fingernail to scrape off the top layer of sand from the circle.

'No, I was actually ringing to offer you a job.'

'A job?' Megan straightened her back. She could see Jay grinning beside her. 'Wow, that would be amazing.'

'Let me just tell you a little about the role before you accept or otherwise.' Primrose laughed.

'Yes, of course. Sorry.'

'Please don't be sorry. I need someone enthusiastic. The role would be behind the counter primarily and with perhaps a little help out the back with preparing the ice cream and things like that.'

'Okay, that sounds good.' But before she could let herself get carried away, Megan felt her heart sink. 'I've got to be honest with you. I don't have any retail experience. Not recently anyway. I mean, I worked at a newsagent for a couple of years when I was a teenager, but—'

'Don't worry. Our system is pretty straightforward. Nothing will take long to get your head around, I can promise you that. I just need someone reliable who can be flexible.'

'I can be flexible.' Megan looked across at Jay and crossed her fingers. He copied.

'Good, good. You see, my mum isn't too well and sometimes needs a little help, which is why I need someone who could, after training, be confident enough to run the parlour if I'm called away.'

'Oh, right. Yes, that would be fine.'

'Great. Could I ask you to pop in sometime and we can have a chat?'

'Yes, okay.' Megan glanced at Jay and waved her hand between him and Cindy before pointing up the beach to question if he was happy to head back.

Grinning, Jay nodded.

'I can pop in now if it's convenient? I'm just at the cove,

anyway.' Megan bit down on her lip. Did she sound too eager? Was there any such thing as being too eager when applying for jobs?

'Perfect. I'll see you in a little while then.'

And with that, Primrose ended the call.

'Eek.' Megan jiggled her legs up and down and laid the mobile on the sand. 'I've got a job! Hopefully, anyway.'

'That's amazing! Congratulations!' Leaning across the dogs lying between them, Jay cupped her cheeks with his hands and kissed her.

Megan reached behind the back of his neck and kissed him too. Yes, her new life was beginning to fall into place. Leaning back slightly, with her hand still resting on the nape of his neck, she grinned. 'If I *do* get this job, then it means I'll be able to save up, do an accountancy course and begin to build my own business.'

'It sounds as though you have the job already.' Jay tucked a loose strand of her hair behind her ear.

'Ah, I don't know. I still need to get through this interview-chat thing first.'

'You will. I'm sure she'll love you. And by the end of the day you'll have bagged yourself a job!'

'I really hope you're right. I literally thought it would take ages to find something.' Megan leaned towards him again, their lips touching.

27

After closing the gate from the lane behind her, Megan made her way across the courtyard towards Wagging Tails. She felt as though she could finally begin to move on. Primrose had offered her the job right then and there during their chat and had even given her a rota for when she'd be working, and although it was part-time, Primrose had promised her overtime on top of her usual hours. She'd have to take another look at the courses again tonight. She could even start thinking about names for her new business. Of course, she'd have to build her client base up, which made the job at the ice-cream parlour even more perfect. She could study and then eventually work on her new business around her hours at the parlour. And at Wagging Tails, of course. Sorting the books for Flora was still a priority, but she was sure she'd have enough time to fit everything in.

She looked to her right as she walked towards the reception area. The paddocks were empty, which was strange, as there was usually someone up in at least one of them with a dog or two. Perhaps Flora and Percy had finished their chat, and everyone was inside getting lunch.

Inching the door to the reception area open, she waited, trying to hear if the coast was clear or not, and on hearing chatter and laughter filling the building, seeping from the open kitchen door, she stepped inside.

'Hello, you,' she said, as Cindy came rushing out of the kitchen towards her, her tail wagging at full speed. Straightening her back, Megan folded the rota Primrose had given her and slipped it into the back pocket of her jeans.

'Hey, how did it go?' Jay walked into the reception area towards her.

'Great, thanks. I'm now an official employee of West Par Ice Cream Parlour and I'll be starting my first shift in a couple of days' time.'

Stepping forward, he pulled her into a hug. 'That's fantastic news.'

'Thanks. I literally can't stop smiling. It's only part-time, although she's pretty sure there'll be overtime, but I'll still have time to come here and also to begin my refresher course.'

'That's perfect then.'

'Megan, is that you?' Alex popped his head through the open door.

'It sure is.' She grinned at him.

'Come on in. We've got so much to tell you!'

'Ooh what?' Taking Jay's hand, she followed Alex through into the kitchen. Ginny, Sally and Susan were already sitting, mugs in front of them and a new packet of biscuits lying in the middle of the table.

'You look happy!' Ginny stood up and flicked the kettle on.

'I am. I've just got a job at the ice-cream parlour in the cove!' Megan grinned and sat down, Jay next to her.

'Congratulations! That's fantastic news!' Ginny hugged her around the shoulders.

'Thank you. I can't believe it. I thought it would take ages to find one. And Primrose, who owns it, seems really lovely too.' Megan looked down as Cindy placed her head on her lap.

'Oh, she is.' Alex smiled. 'And just think of all that ice cream!'

'Ha ha, yes! Plus, it's part-time so I'll be able to work on this...' She tapped on the laptop, which had been pushed to the middle of the table. 'And other stuff, too.'

'It sounds perfect. Congratulations.' Susan smiled.

'Thanks.' Megan took the mug of fresh coffee Ginny held out to her and looked around the table. 'So, what's this news you were talking about, Alex?'

'Well...' He paused.

Megan glanced around the room again. 'And where's Flora and Percy?'

'That's the news. They've gone out for lunch together!' Sally squealed.

'Together as in *together*?' Megan widened her eyes.

'Yes! Finally. It's only taken just over three decades.' Ginny laughed.

'Percy did ask her out, then?' Megan took a sip of her drink. 'I really didn't think he would.'

'Ah no, he didn't, but Alex here waded in with his size elevens to save the day,' Susan said.

'You did? How? What did you say?' Megan raised her eyebrows.

Alex took a deep breath and straightened his back. 'After a few minutes of us all leaving them to it, I popped in to grab a drink of water...'

'To get the gossip more like.'

'All right, Susan.' Alex shook his head and continued. 'Okay, to see if Percy had plucked up the courage to ask Flora out, which, obviously, he hadn't, so I did it for him.'

'What? How? What did you say?' Megan tilted her head. She couldn't imagine how he'd managed to get them together.

'I just said what we've all been saying all this time. I told Flora that Percy was in love with her and had been for umpteen years and that he wondered if she wanted to go out for lunch.' Alex shrugged nonchalantly.

'Just like that? And she said yes, I presume?'

'Yep. She looked as though she was about to cry, which I'm taking as she's felt the same way towards him for a long time too.'

Sally nodded. 'I told you she did, didn't I?'

'Yes, you did.' Alex laid his hands on the table. 'And that's that. Our lives here at Wagging Tails will never be the same again.'

Ginny laughed. 'Don't be so dramatic. I mean, you're right, they won't, but that's a good thing. I just can't wait until they get back to find out how their lunch date has gone.'

'What should we do, hang around and ask them or just get on with our jobs and pretend as though we don't know what's going on?' Sally asked.

Just then, the bell above the door from the courtyard tinkled. Everyone looked towards the kitchen door.

'I guess we might not have to wait to find out,' Alex stage whispered.

'To find out what?' Flora stepped into the kitchen.

Alex looked at her and then back to everyone else. 'Umm...'

'Who wants more coffee?' Standing up, Susan tried and failed to act normally. 'Flora, would you like a cup or have you had some on your lunch da—' stopping herself short of saying date, she grabbed Alex's mug and tried again '—day. Did you have coffee on your lunch today?'

Flora chuckled and sat down. 'Coffee would be lovely, please.'

Megan glanced quickly towards the door. Where was Percy?

As she caught Jay's eye, she was sure he was thinking the same thing.

Alex cleared his throat. 'So, where's Percy got to then?'

'Oh, I left him there.' Flora waved her hand dismissively.

'You left him there?' Ginny opened and closed her mouth.

'Oh no.' Susan clattered the teaspoon against the mug.

'What do you mean?' Alex leaned forward in his chair. 'You left him stranded on your date?'

Flora shrugged, a glint in her eye.

'You're pulling our legs, aren't you?' Ginny raised her eyebrows. 'I know you; you're joking with us.'

'Ha ha, yes, I am. The construction workers for the kennels have just arrived, so he's seeing to them.' Flora chuckled. 'Tell me I had you going though?'

'For a millisecond, maybe.' Alex held his thumb and forefinger slightly apart.

'I'll take that.' Flora grinned and took her mug from Susan. 'Thanks, lovely.'

'Oh, come on, you can't just keep us in suspense like this.' Alex tapped the top of the table.

'Okay, okay.' Placing her mug down in front of her, Flora held her hands up. 'I'm guessing you've gone and told everyone what happened, Alex?'

Alex shrugged.

'I thought as much.' She grinned. 'Yes, it went very well, thank you. And yes, we've decided to try to make a go of it.'

'You and Percy are an item?' Susan clapped her hands against her cheeks. 'I didn't think I'd ever see the day when you both admitted how you felt about each other.'

'Admittedly, it's taken a while.' Flora took a sip of her coffee. 'But that's only because we're such good friends and neither of us wanted to ruin the friendship.'

'I rest my case, I knew the feelings between them were mutual.' Sally grinned and looked around the table.

Flora smiled at Sally. 'But now that we've both admitted how we feel… mostly thanks to Alex here…' She held her mug up to him as he stood and took a bow. 'We've decided to take things slowly and if it doesn't end up working out, then we will remain friends.'

'Oh, I'm so pleased for you, Flora. For both you and Percy.' Susan rushed around the table and hugged Flora. 'It's been a long time coming, but now that it has, it's just wonderful.'

'Thank you,' Flora said, wiping her eyes with a tissue. 'See, look at me. If I'm this happy after one lunch date, what am I going to be like when we venture out again tonight?'

The room filled with laughter, and Megan looked around. This was perfect. It may have taken a broken marriage and a spell of living in her car, but now, she felt as though she was where she was supposed to be. She reached across and took Jay's hand.

28

Megan balanced the pizza box in one hand and closed the front door of the cottage with her foot. Flora was out at the cinema with Percy and Poppy had gone to dinner with Mack and some friends, so Jay had insisted on treating them both to a takeaway.

She paused just outside the living room door and took a deep breath, filling her lungs with the cheesy, tomatoey aroma of freshly cooked pizza. She could hear Jay switch the TV on, looking for something for them to watch. She pushed the living room door open and he immediately stood up to help her.

'If it tastes as good as it smells,' Megan said, 'then this might just be the best pizza I've ever had.'

'Yum, it does smell good.' Jay took the pizza box from her and laid it on Flora's coffee table, then wrapped his arms around her, drawing her closer.

She could feel his breath as he kissed the top of her head. 'Who'd have thought both us two and Flora and Percy would have got together?'

'I would. I knew from the moment I saw you at the induction day that we had a connection.'

'Really?'

Could she tell too? She'd been too nervous to even notice anyone other than Flora and the others in the Wagging Tails team, let alone anything else.

'Yes, really.' He hooked his forefinger beneath her chin and leaned down, their lips touching briefly.

'Aw, that's sweet.' She could feel a blush spreading towards her cheeks. 'I'll go and grab us both a drink.'

'Okay, thanks. I'll get the film on.'

In the kitchen, she took two glasses from the cupboard and poured them both a drink before taking her mobile from her back pocket. Her shoulders slumped as she saw Lyle had messaged again. Shaking her head, she navigated to it. She might as well see what he had to say. She wouldn't reply though. She wasn't going to let whatever he said ruin her and Jay's evening together.

The message opened as Cindy jumped up, resting her paws on the work surface.

'Get down, Cindy.'

When she looked back at her phone, she frowned. Huh. A photo of Lyle with one of their so-called friends, Hayley. His arm was wrapped around her shoulders, and it looked as though she was in the process of pecking him on the cheek. The words 'You're not the only one to have moved on' flashed beneath the photo.

Why had he sent her this? To make her feel jealous? Well, it hadn't worked. If anything, she just felt relieved – hopefully now he'd leave her be. Although she wouldn't hold her breath; knowing him, he wasn't going to let things lie.

He was with Hayley? That was the part that had her feeling strange. A tang of sadness crept over her. Out of everyone in their social circle, she'd felt the closest to Hayley. Or so she'd thought. Obviously it wasn't just her and Lyle's marriage which had fallen apart, Hayley's must have too. She took another look at the photo.

It had been taken in their house, her old home. Holding the screen closer, she squinted at something in the back of the photo behind them.

Was that what she thought it was? No, it couldn't be.

She gripped the edge of the work surface with her free hand. There was a photo frame on the mantelpiece, the same photo frame that had been there for years. The same photo frame that had housed her and Lyle's wedding picture. The only difference was now it wasn't the familiar image of her and Lyle staring back at her, her in her ivory wedding gown, him wearing a wedding suit. No, it was a photo of Lyle and Hayley.

She blinked and looked again. Not only that, but the photo had been taken in New York. At Christmas time. The Times Square Christmas tree towered above them. But that didn't add up... Lyle hadn't been in New York last Christmas. He'd been with her, Megan. It had been the Christmas before they'd visited New York. They'd visited with a group of friends. Including Hayley and her husband, Neil.

Lyle had been having an affair. Even back then. He'd been seeing Hayley behind her back, behind Neil's back.

Megan laid her phone on the work surface and closed her eyes. He'd been having an affair and yet he had the audacity to accuse her of doing the same thing with Jay, who she hadn't even known when she'd been with Lyle!

Opening her eyes, she reached out and turned her phone off, the screen fading to black as the power was halted. She shouldn't be surprised. She really shouldn't. Her and Lyle's relationship hadn't been right for years. This just offered an explanation. She should have seen it coming. She should have noticed. It was just one more example of Lyle being Lyle. Nothing should surprise her about that.

She placed her fingers against her temples and rubbed them. She could feel a headache coming on, but Jay was here, and she was determined to enjoy the evening, to celebrate her new-found job and his upcoming interview too. She could try to wrap her head around Lyle and Hayley later, but now she wanted to enjoy her evening.

After picking up the two glasses, she turned her back on the phone and headed towards the living room, stopping short outside the door. She could hear Jay's voice. He must be speaking on the phone.

'I know, I know... Yes, I understand... I'll come right away.' Jay spoke quietly, his voice edged with concern.

Megan stood, waiting for a few moments longer until she was sure the conversation was over before pushing the door open and carrying the glasses to the coffee table.

'I'm so sorry, Megan, but I'm going to have to run.' Jay stood up and ran his palm across his face.

'Is everything okay?' It hadn't sounded okay, not from what she'd heard.

'I'm not sure, to be honest. Leanne has broken up with Patrick.'

'Oh.' Megan frowned.

How did that affect him?

'Umm, and she and Mia haven't got anywhere to go. She's over at my house now, waiting in the car, so I'd better run.' Jay looked down at the unopened pizza box. 'I'm sorry, this was supposed to be your night, our celebration.'

Megan waved her hand dismissively. 'Don't worry about that.'

'Thank you for understanding.'

'Do you think they'll be staying at yours, then?' she asked as he made his way to the front door to slip his shoes on.

Glancing at her, Jay nodded. 'Yes, I've said they can move back in for the time being.' Trainer laces tied; he stood back up. 'I really am sorry. I was looking forward to this.'

'No, no, it's fine. You need to be there for Leanne and Mia.' She smiled and held the door open.

'Thanks.'

Megan watched as Jay rushed out, not even pausing to kiss her goodbye, and closed the front door behind her.

Sinking onto the bottom step of the staircase, she tucked her hair behind her ears and stared at the wooden door in front of her, trying to make sense of the evening.

She understood why Jay had rushed off. He doted on Mia and wanted to be there for her, to welcome her back into his home, to welcome Leanne back into her old home too. Their family would be together again. Mum, dad, daughter.

She let her head drop to her knees and closed her eyes. Why was she thinking like this? Jay wouldn't get back with his ex, not after the way she'd hurt him. She was certain of it. He one hundred per cent wouldn't. Although, he'd told her how painful it was living in the house without Mia, with all the family memories lurking in every corner. What if he did take her back?

Megan felt a wet nose nudging against her arm and opened her eyes.

'Hello, Cindy. Where's Dougal got to?'

Cindy walked into the living room wagging her tail, and paused to look back at Megan.

'Come on then, shall we let you both out into the garden for a while?' Pushing herself to standing, she followed Cindy back through the living room into the kitchen and to the back door. Sure enough, little Dougal was sitting on the doormat by the back door. 'You were right, Cindy. Do you need to go out, Dougal?'

After letting them out, Megan reached for her mobile again

and turned it back on, waiting until the screen had flickered to life before checking to see if she'd missed any messages. No, nothing. Nothing more from Lyle thankfully, but nothing from Jay either. She lowered her mobile back onto the work surface. What had she been expecting? Him to apologise again for running out of their celebration? Or for him to reassure her that he wasn't running straight into Leanne's arms? She shook her head. She was being daft. She knew she was. She knew it was only because of the photo Lyle had sent that she was even thinking that Jay would do anything like that.

She picked up her mobile and scrolled back through to Lyle's message, to that photo. Jay was nothing like Lyle. Nothing. Tapping the screen against her forehead, she pursed her lips. She knew what to do. She knew what she needed to do to put Lyle in his place and to hopefully stop him from contacting her again.

Leaning back, the edge of the work surface behind her digging into her back, she began typing:

> Thank you for the photo. I now have evidence that you and Hayley have been having an affair. Any future contact can now come through our solicitors. Megan

With her thumb hovering over the Send button, she reread the message. He wouldn't know what she meant by evidence, would he? Holding her finger against Delete, she watched the text disappear before trying again:

Thank you for the photo. I can clearly see from the picture in the background that you have been having an affair with Hayley behind my back (at least since our trip to New York). You'll be hearing from my solicitor. Do not contact me again. All future correspondence can be exchanged with our solicitors. Bye, Megan.

There. It was clear, to the point. Yes, she was doubtful this revelation would change anything, she'd still signed the prenup, but even if it didn't, hopefully he'd get the message and finally leave her alone. If she was lucky that would be the last she heard from him.

After letting Dougal and Cindy back in, she made her way to the living room and flopped onto the sofa. What did she do now? She had the whole evening. She glanced at her mobile again and shook her head. Jay wouldn't message her, not yet, not whilst he was settling his ex-wife and daughter into the home.

He would, though, eventually, wouldn't he? This wouldn't just be it for their fledging romance? She wouldn't blame him if he decided to try again with Leanne though. By his own admission, he'd been devastated when he'd discovered she'd been having an affair. His life had literally been pulled apart. But that didn't mean he'd forgive her and try again in their relationship.

No, it wouldn't.

Opening the pizza box, she picked up a slice. It was already cold.

How would she have felt if she'd found out Lyle was seeing Hayley before the whole drama with Wagging Tails? Before she'd seen his true character? Would she have been as devastated as Jay or would she have felt relief?

She took a bite and pulled the stringy cheese from the slice.

It wasn't the same, she decided. She knew that. It wouldn't

have been even if she'd been with Lyle. By that point, she hadn't been in love with him any more, so finding out about his and Hayley's affair wouldn't have been as life changing as it had for Jay.

No, that wasn't true. It would have been life changing in the way that she'd have still ended up homeless and penniless, but it wouldn't have been as emotionally traumatising as it would have been if she'd still been in love. As it must have been for Jay.

She threw the cold half-eaten slice of pizza back in the box and pulled a cushion onto her lap, hugging it to her. She'd watch something on TV, forget about Lyle and Hayley, and distract herself from worrying about Jay.

29

Megan pulled the laptop back towards her and began entering the details from the receipts. She looked at the pile of paperwork, invoices, and receipts she had left. She was over halfway through sorting the accounts although it would still take her a long time to finish, longer than it had to get to this point now she had her job at the ice-cream parlour to focus on too.

She glanced up when the kitchen door opened and in came Flora.

'Morning, lovely.' She grinned as she came in and flicked the kettle on. 'You were out of the cottage early today.'

'Yes, I just wanted to get cracking on this before I start my first shift at the ice-cream parlour.' Megan shook her head when Flora held up a mug, offering her a coffee.

'Of course, that's exciting.' Flora grinned.

Megan turned her mobile over, so the screen was flat against the tabletop. All she'd done since getting here was to check her mobile for messages from Jay. She knew he was busy, what with settling Mia and Leanne in the house as well as preparing for his job interview today. She wasn't expecting him to contact her. Not yet. Well, maybe he could have texted her last night after running out on their celebration meal, or this morning... No, he was busy. She understood that.

'How was your date with Percy last night?' she asked, trying to turn her thoughts to brighter things.

Sitting down, Flora ignored the click of the kettle behind her and smiled. 'It was everything I imagined it would be.'

'So you think you and Percy will go on another date?'

'Oh yes. Absolutely.' Flora nodded. 'Honestly? It felt right.'

'That's great then.' Megan smiled. She could see how happy Flora was.

'I sound like a teenager, don't I?' Flora chuckled. 'But really, it felt normal. It felt as though I've been with Percy for years. And I suppose we have been in a funny sort of way. Been together, I mean. We've been the closest of friends for years now, so I suppose this is just the icing on the cake, so to speak.'

'I'm really pleased for you. For you and Percy. You're perfect together.'

'Thanks, lovely.' Flora patted Megan's hand. 'How are things going between you and Jay?'

'Good. I think.' Megan nodded, unsure if she was trying to quell her own doubts rather than answering Flora's question. 'His ex-wife split from her partner last night, so she and their daughter have moved in with him until she gets back on her feet.'

'That's kind of him.'

'Yes, it is.' She nodded. It was. He was a kind man, a good man. Of course he'd let his ex-wife move back in. He wouldn't question it.

'Oh, shouldn't you be getting a wriggle on now? You're starting at ten, aren't you?' Flora pointed towards the clock on the wall.

Megan double-checked the time on her phone and stood up. 'Yes, I'd better.'

She began to tidy the paperwork.

'You get going, lovely. I'll do that for you. You don't want to be late on your first day.'

'Thank you.'

'No problem. Good luck with your first shift.'

'Thanks.'

As soon as Megan had moved and headed towards the door, Cindy had stood up from her spot under the table. Megan fussed over her before pulling open the reception door and stepping outside.

Percy and Susan were guiding the construction workers who were building the new kennels, and she could just about see Sally and Ginny in the bottom paddock. It felt strange walking away from this place during the working day. It would likely take her a while to get used to working somewhere else. She just hoped the ice-cream parlour would be as friendly and welcoming as Wagging Tails.

* * *

'Fantastic. You've got it.' Primrose smiled as Megan closed the till.

'Thanks. Sorry, I mixed up the order, though.' Megan watched as the young family made their way out of the door, ice creams in hand.

'Nonsense. Even I mess up orders and I've been here for years.' Primrose indicated towards the back room where the kitchen was. 'Do you think you'll manage if I go and start making some more ice cream?'

Megan glanced around the small parlour. A handful of tables and chairs were situated along the left-hand side whilst the right-hand side was left free for queueing customers. Huge menus covered the wall and were also hung behind the counter. A couple of teenagers were hanging about at a table by the window and an older couple were reading a newspaper on the table closest to the counter.

'Yes, I'll be fine.'

'Grand. I shan't be long and just shout if you're unsure about anything or need me, okay?'

'Yes, sure.'

Megan turned back to the door. She could see the cobbled walkway down to the beach from here. It wasn't busy, but the number of customers had been relatively consistent over the past couple of hours, with lunchtime proving to be the busiest time so far. She was surprised as the times she'd walked the dogs from Wagging Tails down to the cove, she hadn't seen many people, but she guessed some customers were local residents, some tourists who had happened upon the cove by chance and others dog walkers who might well be attracted to West Par for the cliff walks rather than the beach.

She smiled as a couple paused in front of the ice-cream parlour and watched as the woman passed two dog leads to the man before pushing open the door.

Megan stepped forward towards the counter. 'Afternoon. Welcome to West Par Ice Cream Parlour. What can I get you today?'

'Hi, could I have a chocolate brownie cone and a strawberries and cream in a tub, please?' The woman rummaged in her bag before drawing out her purse.

'Of course. Coming right up.' Turning, Megan began serving the ice cream. 'You've got two beautiful dogs there.'

'Thank you.' The woman grinned with pride. 'They're both rescues, and we feel very lucky to have them.'

The spaniel was sitting down, his tail wagging at a hundred miles per hour while a smaller dog was lying at the man's feet.

'Aw, that's lovely.' Megan passed the cone to the woman. 'They're not from Wagging Tails by any chance, are they?'

'Yes, that's right.' The woman nodded.

'I recently started volunteering there.' Megan grinned as she sat the tub on the counter.

'Really? It's such a lovely place, isn't it? And they do such a fab job. We adopted them both from there. I think they calm each other down.' Glancing over her shoulder out of the window, the woman laughed as the spaniel lunged on the lead, trying to chase a rogue beach ball that someone further up the walkway had let go. 'A little, perhaps.'

Megan laughed too. 'Oh, they're gorgeous.'

'Thank you.' After handing over the money, the woman picked up the tub and paused. 'And thank you for volunteering at Wagging Tails. We owe that place a lot.'

Megan smiled as the woman stepped outside and passed the man the cone before bending down and fussing over the two dogs. It was crazy to think how many lives Wagging Tails had impacted, humans as well as dogs. She hadn't really thought about that before. She'd always focused on what good they did for the dogs they rescued; she hadn't thought about how much they were helping people too by matching them with their perfect companion. They had such an effect on people's lives as well as that of the dogs.

'Could we get another couple of milkshakes, please?' One of the teenagers held their hands up, signalling Megan.

'Yes, of course. One strawberry and one banana, wasn't it?'

Megan waited until they'd given her the thumbs up before turning and beginning to make up the milkshakes. She hadn't used the machine on her own before. Primrose had guided her when she'd made the last lot. Frowning, she filled up the machine with frozen strawberries from the freezer beneath the counter before turning it on.

Glancing towards the window, she froze. Was that Jay? Yes, it was, and it looked as though he was heading this way. A small girl was pointing towards the ice-cream parlour and taking Jay's hand. Megan could see Jay glancing towards her and back at his daughter, presumably unsure whether the two of them should meet. He was a good dad; she could see that. He wouldn't want his daughter to meet Megan, a woman he had only just started seeing – not yet. He needn't worry though, it wasn't as if she was going to announce that they were dating or anything.

She turned her attention back to the milkshake, letting go of the lever just as the strawberry mix began running down the edge of the glass. One done, one to go. She was pleased she'd remembered how to work the machine. She wanted to prove to Primrose that she was a fast learner and that she could do this job. Primrose had taken a chance on her, giving her this job with next to no experience and after such a long gap in her employment, she wanted to repay her by doing well and, also, if she could show her she was competent then she'd give her that overtime she'd spoken about.

Just as she was finishing the banana milkshake, she heard the little chime ring from the entrance, announcing the arrival of a new customer. She picked up the glasses and turned. It was Jay and Mia.

She smiled and caught his eye. 'Hello, I'll be with you both in just a second.' She nodded towards the glasses.

'It's okay, I'll grab them.' One of the teenagers jumped up from his chair and took the milkshakes from the counter. 'Thanks.'

'You're welcome.'

Megan turned back to Jay and Mia.

'Mia,' Jay said, looking down at his daughter, 'I'd like you to meet my friend, Megan, who I've been working with at the dogs' home.' Turning back to Megan, he said, 'Megan, this is my daughter Mia.'

'Hello, Mia. Lovely to meet you. I like your headband. It's very sparkly.' She pointed to Mia's bright yellow sequinned headband.

'Thank you. My daddy got it for me for my birthday.' Mia took it off for a moment, looked at it and then slid it back onto her head.

'Your daddy has good taste then.' Megan smiled and indicated the menu. 'What can I get you both?'

Mia pulled her dad's arm, waiting until he'd bent down to whisper in his ear.

Straightening his back again, Jay grinned. 'Yes, you can have a milkshake and a cone. What flavour would you like?'

This time Mia reached up on her tiptoes to look above the counter. 'Can I have a chocolate milkshake, please?'

'Of course you can. That's a good choice.' Megan nodded. 'What ice cream would you like?'

'Umm, strawberry and chocolate.'

'Two scoops?' Megan turned to Jay. 'And how about for Daddy?'

'Ooh, there's so much choice.' Jay tapped his fingers against his chin.

Laughing, Mia tugged on his top. 'Choose, Daddy.'

'Okay, okay. I'll go for a mint choc chip cone, please.'

'Coming right up.' Megan turned and started the milkshake machine again just as the chime rang again. It was getting busy now.

'Mummy! Are you having an ice cream too?' Mia called.

With the milkshake machine whirring to action, Megan froze. She hadn't realised Leanne was here too. She'd assumed it was just Jay and Mia. Steadying her breath, she focused on pouring the milkshake. She just hoped Jay wouldn't make this awkward, them all being in the same room. She didn't want to get caught in the middle of anything. She turned slowly around, sure enough a woman, presumably Leanne, had joined Jay and Mia at the counter.

Megan swallowed before forcing a smile. 'Hi, what would you like?'

'Nothing for me, thank you.' Leanne stepped behind Mia and began undoing her braided hair. 'This is falling out. I'll plait it again, shall I?'

'Okay, Mummy.'

Megan lowered the milkshake and picked up a cone, catching Jay's eye in the process. She could tell by the pink tinge colouring the tips of his ears that he felt uncomfortable. She gave him a quick smile.

'Thank you,' he said as he picked up the milkshake.

'No worries.' Megan turned to Mia. 'Are we having sprinkles and chocolate shavings on your ice cream?'

'Yes, please.' Mia nodded just as her mum attempted to secure her plait again.

After adding the sprinkles and chocolate, Megan passed the cone to Jay.

Having finished tidying Mia's hair, Leanne placed her hands on her daughter's shoulders and smiled at her daughter. 'Guess what I brought for the beach?'

'My bucket and spade?' Mia turned around to look at her mum.

'No, but I did bring the beach ball! We'll need to blow it up first but then we can play.' Leanne patted the fabric bag slung over her shoulder.

'Yay!' Taking her cone from her dad, Mia said, 'Thank you, Daddy. Thank you, Megan.'

'You're very welcome.' Megan smiled and held out Jay's cone. 'And here's yours.'

'Thank you.' Tapping his card against the machine, Jay smiled at her, and then he turned towards the door.

Megan watched as the family left, Jay holding the door open for his daughter and ex-wife. She could hear Mia telling her mum about her, how she helped with the dogs with her daddy.

She could feel her stomach lurch as the three of them walked down towards the beach together. Forcing herself, she turned back to the milkshake machine and began cleaning it down, trying to keep her mind busy.

30

'So, what do you think?' Primrose dragged the mop across the floor.

'I've really enjoyed today,' Megan said as she scrubbed at a stubborn dribble of what looked to be mint ice cream on the counter and smiled. She *had* enjoyed it. With there always being either customers to serve or machines to clean or ice cream to restock, the hours had sped by and she could hardly believe that her first shift was over.

'That's good to hear. You'll be back tomorrow then?' Primrose paused and looked at her, the mop still in hand.

'I'd love to come back tomorrow.'

Did that mean she officially had the job then? Primrose hadn't said anything about today being a trial, but Megan had assumed it would be.

'If you'll have me, of course.'

Primrose chuckled. 'Oh, you've done a marvellous job and I hope you'll accept the job offer.'

'Yes, I will. Thank you.' Megan grinned.

'Good, good.' Primrose glanced outside. 'I'll just bring the chalkboard in, and I think we'll be ready to lock up.'

'I'll go and get it.'

Megan threw the paper towel she'd been using to clean the counter into the bin and rushed around the counter onto the shop floor.

Opening the door, Megan stepped outside and took a deep breath in, the warm salty air filling her lungs. It felt good to be back in a job, to be earning and to be working towards independence and her future.

She looked down at the A-frame chalkboard displaying a selection of the ice cream flavours written in Primrose's delicate cursive writing. It was the perfect advertisement to draw in passers-by on their way down to the beach. She carefully closed it and picked it up. It was heavier than she'd imagined it would be, but she guessed it needed to be to withstand the gusts from the sea on windier days. Turning, she headed towards the door, pausing as movement on the beach caught her eye.

It was Jay, Mia and Leanne. Jay and Leanne were standing opposite each other, throwing a brightly striped beach ball between them as Mia ran in and out of the waves that lulled up the beach.

Megan placed the A-frame back down and watched for a moment – as Mia circled around her mum, laughing as she then threw herself into Jay's arms, who picked her up and swung her around before passing her across to her mum.

They looked like the perfect family. To anyone passing by they did. All three of them were grinning from ear to ear and laughing. If she hadn't been told their history, then she would have thought so too.

Shaking her head, she picked up the A-frame again and carried it inside. Even when they'd been in the ice-cream parlour,

Jay and Leanne had been fine with each other, friendly. She couldn't imagine her and Lyle ever getting to that point, even being in the same room together and tolerating each other would be unlikely, but Jay and Leanne had seemed normal, had seemed happy in each other's company.

She stood the board against the wall by the door and glanced back out of the window. They did appear happy. It wasn't an act for Mia; she was certain it wasn't. If it had been she'd have been able to pick up on something, on some slight awkwardness or intolerance and the only time Jay had looked in the least bit uncomfortable was when he'd first come into the shop and introduced her to Mia.

'Perfect. Thank you.' Primrose appeared from the kitchen carrying her handbag. 'You can get off now, love. I'll see you at ten again tomorrow?'

'Definitely.' Megan took her bag from behind the counter and held her hand up in a wave before stepping back outside. She looked down towards the beach again. They were still there, Jay, Leanne and Mia. Still playing together. She turned and headed back up the lane towards the edge of the village and Wagging Tails.

* * *

'Is that you, Megan? We're in the kitchen,' Flora's voice called out.

Megan closed the front door of the cottage and slung her bag down by the shoe rack before heading towards the kitchen. Flora, Percy, Poppy and Mack were sitting around the table. 'Hi.'

'Hello, lovely. How was your first day?' Flora stood up. 'Do you want a cuppa?'

'No, I'm okay, thanks.' Megan shook her head. 'It was great, thanks. Primrose seems really lovely, and to be honest, the hours flew past.'

'Glad to hear you enjoyed it.'

'We're just deciding what film to see at the cinema this evening.' Poppy turned to her. 'Do you fancy joining us?'

'No, thanks for asking, but I think I'm going to head up and take a nap.' Megan smiled. Any other day she would have jumped at the chance and invited Jay along too but she just couldn't shift the feeling of unease about her and Jay's fledgling romance. Not after seeing him with Mia and Leanne this afternoon. She wouldn't be able to concentrate on a film and she'd be lousy company too. 'I'm shattered after today.'

'No worries.' Poppy smiled.

'Have a great night and I'll see you later,' Megan said, holding her hand up before leaving and heading upstairs. It was true, she was tired. She hadn't spent as long on her feet as she had today for a long time. Even when she and Jay had been digging the foundations, they'd taken numerous breaks, whereas the work at the ice-cream parlour had been constant.

She paused halfway up the stairs. She had forgotten to ask how the construction of the new dog kennels had gone. She turned to walk back down, but she could hear that conversation had already resumed, the four of them talking about the film choices for the evening. She'd ask when they got back. If the build hadn't been successful, they would have said.

Up in her room, she leaned against the closed door and rubbed her eyes. Despite images of Jay, Mia and Leanne on the beach replaying in her mind's eye, she might just have that nap now. She was tired enough.

Megan pushed herself away from the door and sank onto the bed, lying back against the pillows. The window was open, and a slight breeze was blowing, the floral curtains gently swaying.

Shifting position, she pulled her mobile from the back pocket of her jeans and checked for any messages. Nothing. Jay still hadn't texted her. Yes, she'd seen him at the ice-cream parlour, but he'd come in because Mia had wanted an ice cream, not to see her.

She reached her arms above her, gently laying her hands against her forehead. Now that Leanne had broken up with Patrick, should Megan even be dating him? This was his chance to get back with Leanne, to make his family whole again.

Yes, Leanne had cheated on him, had broken his heart, but that didn't mean he wouldn't forgive her, that didn't mean she didn't want to get back with him. Leanne had moved back into the marital home quite happily. Didn't that suggest something? Didn't that suggest that she hoped to get back with him?

Or was Megan just imagining things? Life wasn't that simple, was it? It wouldn't be easy for Jay to forgive Leanne for what she'd done to him, but equally, Megan didn't want to be the reason he didn't try. She and Jay had only been dating briefly whereas he and Leanne had years of history together, they had a daughter together. They had been married, been a family.

She couldn't compete with that. She didn't want to. Jay had been so happy on the beach. She'd seen that. He'd been relaxed and happy. In his element.

Pinching the bridge of her nose, she closed her eyes for a moment. She knew what she needed to do, and she knew she needed to do it now. Before she talked herself out of it, before he contacted her.

Sitting up, she leaned against the pine headboard and wrote a text.

> Thank you for a lovely time, but this isn't going to work – Megan

She pressed Send before she changed her mind and turned off her mobile.

Looking towards the window, she sighed. That was it then. She and Jay were over. She'd been daft to think she could just walk into a relationship with him, anyway. Things were never that simple. She should know that by now. Life with Lyle hadn't been simple. And before, when she thought it had, it turned out that he'd been having an affair with someone she thought was her friend.

Obviously, Jay would never have cheated on her, he was one of the good guys and now, with Leanne single again, he deserved the chance to get back with her, for Mia to have her family together again. Jay didn't need Megan standing in the way.

'Megan, we're off now, lovely.' Flora's voice wafted up the stairs. 'Have a good evening.'

Megan cleared her throat. 'Thanks. You too.'

She listened for the front door to click shut, and after it had, Cindy began to whine.

'Cindy, Dougal, I'm up here.' She stood up and opened her bedroom door for them.

Less than a minute later, Cindy had bounded up and onto her bed, quickly followed by Dougal. Megan smiled. She'd miss them when she moved out. Especially Cindy. She'd even missed her today at the ice-cream parlour. She was so used to her being there, right beside her at Wagging Tails, it had felt odd her not.

Sinking back onto the bed, she held open her arms as Cindy laid her head on her stomach. 'I've done the right thing, haven't I?'

Cindy looked at her for a moment, her deep brown eyes thoughtful, before she closed them.

It was done now. However much it hurt, it was for the best. She had to let him go, she had to.

31

Stirring, Megan strained her eyes in the dim evening light. She must have fallen asleep. She sniffed the air. There was a funny smell. What was that? She could feel Cindy moving beside her, pawing at her and nudging her arm with her nose.

'What's the matter, Cindy? Try to go back to sleep.'

Turning over, she closed her eyes again. She just wanted to sleep, to forget about Jay, about Lyle, about everything.

Cindy nudged her again, her nose wet against Megan's skin. Could she sense she was upset? She rolled back over and began fussing her behind the ears.

'I'll be okay, Cindy. Don't worry.'

A loud bark sounded from downstairs, penetrating the silence in the house. Maybe Flora and Poppy had just pulled up in the car. She closed her eyes again.

* * *

Megan stirred again, blinking the sleep from her eyes. The funny smell was there again. Stronger this time, and she could hear dogs barking. She pushed herself to sitting.

'Cindy? Dougal?'

Cindy jumped onto the bed and towered over her, her bark loud and constant.

'Okay, okay. I'm getting up.' Standing up, she paused. It wasn't just Cindy and Dougal's barking she could hear, there were others barking too. A little muffled, but there. It must be coming from Wagging Tails. Why would they be making all this noise at this time of the night? She hadn't heard it before, the barking, not from the cottage, not at this time. They usually only barked like this when they were being fed. Although this didn't sound like that, they didn't sound excited.

'Let's see what's going on, shall we, Cindy?'

Megan walked to the window and drew the curtains before opening and closing her mouth. An orange glow was flickering to the side of Wagging Tails, and it took her a moment to realise it was fire. Flames were licking up against the new kennels. That was what the smell was: smoke.

She grabbed her mobile and ran down the stairs, two at a time, before shutting Cindy and Dougal safely in the living room and flinging the front door open. As she ran across the driveway towards Wagging Tails she could see the fire was isolated to the new kennels. It hadn't leaped across to where the dogs were. Yet.

Pausing, she turned her mobile on, the screen taking an infinity to flicker to life. Once it had, she punched in 999 and waited.

She covered one ear with her phone, her other with her hand, trying to block out the noise from the dogs. She could hardly hear anything else.

'Fire, please. Wagging Tails Dogs' Home, West Par.'

After the call ended, she shoved her mobile back in her pocket and hoped they had all the information they needed.

Picking up the pace again, she neared the fire, holding her T-shirt over her mouth and nose. She stood and looked from the fire to the existing kennels and back again. The fire had completely engulfed the new kennel block. What was she supposed to do? Were the dogs safe where they were? Could the fire reach them?

Just then, an almighty crash filled the air, louder even than the barking from the dogs. She watched as one side of the new kennel block fell against the existing building, the flames licking against the roof.

Please don't take. Please don't take.

She kept her eyes fixed on the fiery debris that had landed on the roof, her heart skipping a beat as the fire slowly but surely took hold. She jumped from foot to foot. She was sure most roof tiles couldn't catch fire – they were made of clay, or whatever, they were flame retardant. There must be gaps in the tiles. That could be the only explanation. She hadn't learned much from Lyle's building trade, but some things she had.

She looked behind her, across the courtyard, towards the lane beyond. Where was that fire engine? It could have only been a couple of minutes since she'd made the call, though. They wouldn't arrive yet.

There was only one thing she could do, and that was to get the dogs out.

She ran the short distance towards the door and pulled on the handle, quickly remembering that Flora kept a key in a key safe on the wall to the side. After punching in the passcode, she took the key out and unlocked the door.

Inside the reception area, it took her a moment to catch her bearings. The room was dark, a dim light flickering through the small window in the door leading to the kennels, smoke filtering through from beneath the door. With adrenaline now pumping through her veins, she grabbed a handful of leads and pulled open the door to the kennels. The noise was deafening now she was inside, the terrified crying and barking of the dogs mixed with the noise of the flames from outside and above filling the space.

The smoke was thicker in here too and she turned the torch app on her phone on as the dim light continued to flicker on and off. She couldn't see any fire. It must still be contained on the roof or in the ceiling somewhere, but the windows opposite the kennels were open, great swathes of smoke pushing in from outside.

She hurried along the wall and pulled the windows shut before heading to the first kennel.

'It's okay. Let's get you outside, shall we?'

She quickly secured a lead to Rex's collar while deciding which dogs to approach next. She made her way down the row of kennels until she reached Splash – she knew they got along, and so did Ocean so she'd take them up to the top paddock before coming back to get the others.

Once she had the three of them out of their kennels and the leads in her hand, she glanced up at the ceiling again.

Please hold.

She rushed through the reception area, the three dogs following her quickly behind, and pulled open the door to the courtyard. A gush of smoke billowed in and, sticking her head down, she ran past the burning shell of the new kennels towards the top paddock, where she guided the dogs inside, dropping their leads before closing the gate again. She knew it wasn't a good idea for them to have their leads dragging behind them, but she needed to get the others out as quickly as she could.

As she was running back into the courtyard and past the fire, she stumbled on something and tripped. Throwing her hands out in front of her, she felt herself falling and her mobile skidding across the slabs of the courtyard. Megan had to grapple in the glow from the fire, but she managed to pick it up again. The torch was still on, thankfully. When she jumped back up, the smoke was even thicker than a few moments ago. She coughed as it filled her lungs.

* * *

Megan ran back towards the kennels. She could feel her heart pounding in her chest as she struggled to draw breaths in. She wheezed as she pulled the door open again, fighting to breathe as she hurried down the corridor towards Ralph's kennel. She knew he couldn't be kept with any other dogs, couldn't even be near them, which is why she'd left him until last. She'd take him over to the cottage. She'd put him in the garden while she ran inside to make sure Cindy and Dougal were still shut away.

As she pulled the door to the kennels open, the glimmer of blue penetrated the thick grey smoke. Help was here.

'Come on, Ralph. Your turn.'

Pulling his door open, she bent down, trying to clasp the lead to his collar. Her fingers were fumbling as she tried to listen to the sounds from outside. Would the firefighters realise she and Ralph were in here? Would they be able to put the fire out before any more damage was done to the kennels?

'That's it.' She couldn't hear her words above the noise of the fire, above the sirens. She wasn't even sure if any noise was coming out. She could hardly breathe, let alone talk.

That was it. She had Ralph on the lead now. She stumbled backwards, forcing herself to keep moving forward. She had to get him to safety. She had to get him out.

Just as she pushed the door into the reception area open, it gave way and she fell forward. She felt someone catch her, hold her up. She glanced in her saviour's direction.

'Jay?'

With her fingers gripping Ralph's lead, she let herself be guided outside and away from the fire, out of the smoke. The pulsing blue light of the fire engine blurred her vision, and she looked away from the firefighters as they began drenching the roof with water.

'Let's get you over here, away from the smoke.' Jay held her around the waist, gently cupping her elbows as he walked and she stumbled across the courtyard towards his car. He pulled the door open and lowered her into the passenger seat before kneeling on the floor in front of her.

She took deep breaths, filling her lungs with the fresh air and pushing out the smoke. Ralph put his front paws on her knees and nuzzled her chin.

'We need to get you to the hospital.' Jay took her hand in his. 'You need to be checked over.'

Megan shook her head. 'No. The dogs...'

'Where are they?'

'In the paddocks.' The words rasped from her throat. She couldn't leave them. They'd be scared and they'd need to be checked over. 'Is he okay?' She nodded towards Ralph. 'He was in there the longest.'

'He's fine, aren't you, boy?' Jay ruffled Ralph's ears. 'And Mack will check on him, on all of them, as soon as he's back. I've rang and Flora, Percy, Poppy and Mack are only a few minutes away. They'll be here in no time and be able to care for them.'

'But Ralph was in there for so long.' She began fussing him behind the ears before bending over and coughing.

'Ralph might have been in there the longest, but his kennel

was the furthest away from the fire in the roof whereas you were closer to the fire and inhaling the smoke.' He cupped her cheek. 'We really do need to get you checked over. Please.'

The last thing she wanted was to spend hours at the hospital. She just wanted to know if the dogs were okay. She needed to see them. She shook her head and stood up before sinking back into the chair. 'No, I need to check on the other dogs.'

'Megan! Megan!'

Looking up, Megan watched as Flora came running across the courtyard, Percy, Poppy and Mack close behind her.

'Oh, Megan, lovely. Are you okay?' Flora sank to her knees in front of her and looked her up and down.

'The dogs are in the paddocks. I had to tie Petal and Willow to the fence too.' Her voice came out as a hoarse whisper, her throat stinging as she spoke.

'Don't worry about the dogs, lovely. You rescued them.' Standing up, Flora cupped Megan's head with her hands and kissed her on top of her head before turning to Jay. 'I'll take Ralph. You get her to the hospital.'

Leaning her head back against the chair, Megan closed her eyes. She knew there wasn't any point in refusing.

32

'Almost there.' Jay grinned and looked across at Megan as he turned down the lane leading to Wagging Tails.

Megan nodded and pulled the sun visor down, the early morning's sun catching her eye. She'd feel better once she could see for herself the dogs were okay. Although she was dreading seeing how much damage the fire had caused. What would happen to the dogs if the kennels were ruined? Where would they all go? 'Good. I can't wait to check on the dogs. They really are all okay, aren't they?'

'Yes, they're fine. Mack has checked them all over and concluded that they're all in perfect health.'

Megan nodded. She still couldn't quite get her head around what had happened last night. Everything had been such a blur, from waking up to Cindy and Dougal barking to realising there was a fire, to getting the dogs to safety. She'd just been on autopilot. She hadn't been thinking, and now she was still trying to process everything. 'Thank you.'

'What for?' Jay glanced at her and frowned.

'For taking me to get checked over, for staying at the hospital with me.' He hadn't left her side all night, talking about silly little things, just trying to keep her mind off what had happened. She coughed. Although she'd now been discharged, the doctor had warned her to take it easy for a few days whilst her body recovered from the smoke inhalation. 'How did you know I was in there?'

'I came over to Flora's to talk to you about the text you sent. When I saw the fire and you weren't answering the door, I knew you'd be over there.'

He reached across and squeezed her hand before taking the steering wheel again and turning into Wagging Tails.

As the car pulled up, Megan looked out of the windscreen. The new kennel block lay in a heap, the wood crumbled and burnt, with no resemblance to the new building it had been before the fire. The original building, though, Wagging Tails, was still standing and Alex, Susan and Percy were balancing on ladders, pulling bright blue tarpaulin across the roof.

As Jay pulled the handbrake up, Megan watched as Flora rushed out of the door and across to them.

'Oh, lovely. It's such a relief to see you.' Flora hugged her tightly before holding her at arm's length. 'And you're definitely okay?'

'I am.' Megan grinned.

'She was given a clean bill of health? She didn't discharge herself?' Flora glanced across at Jay.

Chuckling, Jay closed his car door and walked around to them. 'The doctors have given her the all-clear. They advised her to take it easy for the next few days but apart from that she's fine.'

'Oh, thank goodness for that.' Flora drew her in for another hug before linking arms with her and leading her across the courtyard.

'Did the fire damage much?' Megan looked up at the roof. The ladders now stood empty, Percy, Alex and Susan having descended and disappeared.

'No, our luck must have been shining down on us yesterday. The roof needs replacing, but everything inside is okay.' Flora shook her head. 'Apparently, the roof should have been fine if it weren't for a couple of damaged tiles, which let the fire take hold. That'll teach me for putting off repairs.'

Megan nodded. 'That's a relief. And the dogs are definitely all okay? Even Ralph?'

'Yes, lovely, they're all fine. In fact, they've taken last night's drama in their stride, and you wouldn't even know anything had happened. They're all back to their normal selves. Thanks to you, that is.'

Megan shook her head. She had only done what anyone would have.

'I don't even want to imagine the outcome if you hadn't called the emergency services, or the dogs had been left in there any longer.' Flora looked down and pinched the bridge of her nose. 'Anyway, let's get you inside. I should think you need a good cuppa in a proper mug after the muck you get from the hospital.'

Megan smiled. The quality of the tea and coffee had been the last thing on her mind last night.

Jay held the door open for them both before stepping inside and closing it.

Megan glanced towards the door to the kennels. She could still smell the all too familiar whiff of smoke but with the windows open and a slight breeze blowing, she could imagine it wouldn't be long before it was cleared.

'In we go, lovely.' Flora pushed open the kitchen door and ushered Megan through first.

As soon as she stepped inside, a raucous cheer and a round of applause ensued as Percy, Ginny, Sally, Susan and Alex stood up and greeted her.

'You did a grand job, love.' Percy hugged her around the shoulders before going to stand with Flora.

'Thank you, Megan.' Ginny stepped forward and wrapped her arms around her.

'Thanks.' Megan glanced down at the floor and tucked her hair behind her ear. She could feel the hot flush of embarrassment rush across her face.

'Come and sit down. I'll pop the kettle on.' Susan pulled out a chair for her and tapped the back of it.

Sinking into the chair, Megan looked around her. All the people here seemed to care about her. They were more than acquaintances; they were friends, family. The atmosphere in this room was so completely different from the stuffy dinner parties she'd held or attended just a few months ago. She felt at home here. More at home than she ever had before.

Megan pushed her chair back and stood up. 'I'll be back in a moment. I just want to see the dogs.'

'Okay, lovely. We'll get you a drink and something to eat,' Flora said.

'Thank you.' Glancing behind her, Megan closed the kitchen door again before leaning against the counter and taking a deep breath. She rubbed at her eyes. Why was she crying? She was happy. She shouldn't be crying.

She heard the kitchen door open and close softly and wiped her eyes.

'Hey, are you okay?' Jay stood in front of her, cupping her elbows with his hands.

'Yes, I don't know. I just...' She shrugged. 'I think I'm just tired. I was just thinking how lovely everyone was, how at home I felt. I don't know why I'm crying.'

He stepped forward and wrapped his arms around her.

Sinking her head to his shoulder, she closed her eyes. Last night had been difficult too, for another reason, because Jay had been with her and all she'd wanted to do was reach out and take his hand, tell him that she wanted to be with him, but she hadn't been able to. She had to be strong; she had to stick by her decision. For his sake.

'I know this probably isn't the best time to talk about it, but can I ask why you don't want to keep seeing me?' Jay's voice was quiet, his tone uncertain. 'Why you sent that message?'

'Because it's the right thing to do.' She spoke into his shoulder, her voice muffled against the fabric of his T-shirt.

'Okay. I understand.' She felt him nod. 'But just so you know, it wouldn't have been my decision.'

What did he mean?

Leaning back, she looked up at him. 'I did it for you.'

Frowning, he let his arms fall to his sides. 'In what way?'

'So, you could get back with Leanne or at least have the choice of getting back with her. So you can be a family again. For Mia.'

Looking away, he shook his head before meeting her gaze again. 'I'm not getting back with Leanne. That's never been an option.'

'But you looked so happy on the beach. The perfect family.' She swallowed as the image of the three of them came to mind again.

'I was happy, yes. But I'm not getting back with Leanne. We broke up because she was having an affair. There's just no chance of us trying again. Besides, she'll sort it out with Patrick before long. This happens at least every six months or so.' He ran his fingers through his hair. 'It's you I feel a connection with. It's you who I want to be with.'

'Really?'

'Yes, really.' He nodded.

'Oh.' She looked at the floor. Had she really completely misunderstood the situation? Had she jeopardised what she and Jay had for nothing?

'And I'd like to give us another go. If you want to, of course.'

She looked out of the window, the fire-wrecked pile of wood from the new kennels staring back at her.

'I don't know. What if things have changed and you and Leanne do want to try again? I don't want to be the one standing in the way of Mia's parents being together.'

He took her hands in his. 'I understand and I'm really touched that you'd do that for me, for Mia, but the truth is Leanne will be getting back with Patrick...' he glanced at his watch '...probably in just less than forty-eight hours' time. The relationship I have with her is just friendship. I wouldn't want anything else now. The best thing for Mia is for her parents to be amicable, to get on. That's the best gift we can give her.'

'You're sure?' Megan looked into his eyes. She knew he was telling the truth. She could see in his eyes that he and Leanne wouldn't be getting back together.

'I'm positive. That scenario is so far off the cards that you'd need a telescope to have any chance of spotting it.' He chuckled.

Megan nodded.

'So, what do you say? Would you like to give our relationship another chance? See what the future holds for us?'

'Yes, yes, I would.' Megan smiled. 'I'd also like a shower. I stink like a chimney.'

'Yes, you do.' Jay looked at her, his lips twitching as he tried to keep a straight face. 'But that won't stop me from doing this...'

As he tucked his forefinger beneath her chin and tilted her

head gently towards him, Megan leaned forward, her lips touching his. Yes, she was excited to see what the future had in store for them.

EPILOGUE

Megan pulled open the gate to Wagging Tails and held it open for Jay.

'It feels strange us both popping in after a full day's work and not volunteering here full time, doesn't it?'

'It sure does.' Taking the gate, Jay closed it before falling in step with her and taking her hand. 'Do you fancy grabbing lunch tomorrow after your exam? We can go somewhere nice.'

Megan groaned. She'd almost forgotten. Not that she had any excuse to forget, she'd been studying the accountancy refresher course at Trestow College for the past few months and the number of hours she'd been poring over books and revision guides over the past few weeks had all but put a hold on her and Jay's social life. Instead, Jay had been joining her at Flora's kitchen table and spending the time researching species and habitats for his job at the local nature reserve between quizzing her and helping her with her revision.

'Hey, you'll smash it. I know you will.' He squeezed her hand.

'Fingers crossed.' Holding her free hand up, she crossed her fingers.

'And then you can start setting up your own accountancy business.'

'Yes.' She nodded. 'I forgot to tell you, Primrose asked if she could be my first client today!'

'She did? That's amazing! Congratulations.' Pausing in the middle of the courtyard, Jay wrapped his arms around her and began kissing her.

Wrapping her arms around his waist, she kissed him back. Their relationship had gone from strength to strength since the fire and she was still getting used to the fluttering in her stomach every time she saw him. These moments though, when he kissed her, held her hand, hugged her, all of these little actions which showed how he felt about her, she wasn't used to them. Lyle had never been affectionate, not when out and about and not even around the home. Looking across at Jay, she smiled. This, the relationship she had with Jay, was so entirely different to what she was used to. And she liked it. More than liked it. Leaning back in his embrace, she grinned at him.

'Thanks. I just need to think of a name now. Megan's Accounting is a bit dull.'

'Ha ha, now that will be the fun part, thinking of a name.' He pointed towards the edge of the courtyard by the Wagging Tails building as they began walking again. 'Oh, look, the new kennels are up.'

'The new kennels take two.' Megan watched as Flora and Percy carried bedding into the new kennel block. 'Let's just hope they stay up for a little longer than the last one.'

Jay chuckled. 'Oh, I'm sure they will. And I'm sure Susan and Percy have been breathing down the electrician's neck this time.'

'I bet. No more fires then.'

'No, let's hope not.' Jay grimaced before pausing again. 'Actually, before we go over and take a look, I've got something I've been meaning to tell you, and this seems as good a time as any other.'

'Ah, now that sounds serious.' Megan frowned and turned to him.

'It is.' Looking down at the floor, Jay ran his fingers through his hair.

'You're worrying me now. Just tell me! Please!'

'Okay, okay.' Looking up at her, he met her eyes before taking her hands in his. 'I've been meaning to tell you this for a few weeks now, but I've fallen in love with you, Megan.'

Shaking her head, Megan laughed before cupping her hands around his cheeks. 'You had me worried.'

Letting a deep breath out, Jay relaxed his shoulders before intertwining his fingers with hers and drawing her closer. Taking his hand away, he reached up and gently brushed a loose strand of hair from Megan's eyes before cupping her cheek.

As their lips met, Megan felt the familiar rush of warmth running through her body. He loved her! Leaning slightly back, her lips millimetres from his, she whispered, 'I love you too, Jay.'

Pulling away, he grinned, his eyes glistening with happiness. 'Well, that's a relief.'

Megan linked arms with him and they began walking again. 'Did you actually think I was going to tell you that I didn't?'

'No, but...' He shrugged. 'It's nice to hear the words.'

She grinned. Everything was perfect. She couldn't be happier with her life now. It was miles, quite literally and figuratively, away from her old life with Lyle and she'd forever be grateful for Wagging Tails for changing her course.

'Ah, there you two are!' Letting the door to the new kennel block close behind her, Flora came rushing across to them, hugging them both in turn. 'Come on, come in and take a look at the new kennels!'

'They look great, even from the outside.' Jay grinned and held the door open for them.

'They really do.' Megan stepped inside and looked around. A small corridor down one side of the building led to four kennels of a similar size to the ones in the main kennel block. Each kennel had an opening at the end leading to an outside area. Although relatively small, the area would allow the dogs to lie or play in the sun. 'Ooh, it looks really nice in here.'

'It sure does, doesn't it, love?' Percy stood up from where he'd been setting the dog bed, before leaning back down and pulling the bed an inch to the right.

Flora checked her watch. 'Right, we've got about half an hour before Sylvia drops off four new dogs from the pound. Shall we go and get a cuppa?'

'You've filled the new kennel block already?' Megan asked as she followed Flora outside.

'Oh, yes. Did you really think she'd leave them standing empty for even a day or two?' Percy closed the door behind them before wrapping his arm around Flora's waist.

Megan laughed and shook her head. 'No, I don't suppose I did.'

Flora glanced back at the new kennel block. 'It just feels so wonderful to be able to rescue four more dogs than we could before. This is really going to make a difference.'

'You bet it will.' Jay pointed ahead and nudged Megan's arm. 'It looks as though someone's eager to see you.'

Looking towards the window of Wagging Tails, Megan grinned. Cindy was jumping up and down at the window. 'Aw, I miss her when I'm at work.'

'I know you do, lovely. She misses you too.' Flora touched her on the forearm. 'She waits at that door, usually lying across the doormat, waiting for you.'

'She's such a gorgeous soul.' Megan smiled. 'And I can't believe what a difference Sally's training is making to her separation anxiety. You wouldn't have been able to leave her alone in the reception area like this a few months ago.'

'No, you wouldn't.' Flora nodded. 'She'll be ready to be rehomed in no time.'

Megan nodded and swallowed, a lump forming in her throat. That's all she'd ever wanted for Cindy, a loving home, but she sure would miss her. When she was volunteering here or whenever she was over at the cottage, Cindy was glued to her side. It would feel strange her not being there.

Jay glanced from Megan to Cindy at the window and back again. 'Flora, we'll catch you up in just a moment, if that's okay?'

'Of course it is, lovely.'

'We will?' Megan paused and waited until Flora and Percy had walked a few metres ahead before turning to him. 'Is everything all right?'

'Yes, it is.' Jay looked at the ground and rubbed the back of his neck. 'I was going to wait until tomorrow at dinner, after your exam, to talk to you about this, but this feels like the right time.'

'Oh.' She frowned. What was it he wanted to talk about now? Him telling her he loved her had been surprise enough, what else did he want to say? She took his hands in hers. 'I'm listening.'

'Now I know this probably sounds rash, but I've been thinking about it for a while now and I've been waiting for the right time to talk to you about it.'

'Go on...' Megan ran the pad of her thumb across the back of his hand.

'Okay, I will.' He glanced away from her before catching her eye again. 'I'm just going to come out with it and if you think it's a crazy idea, then that's fine. I won't be offended.'

'Jay, what is it?'

He took a deep breath in, his gaze unwavering. 'Will you move in with me?'

Opening and closing her mouth, Megan felt her stomach flip. 'Move in with you?'

'Yes, we've been seeing each other a while now, and although I know it's not been that long in the great scheme of things, I think we know each other by now, really know each other.' He shrugged. 'I think it would be great.'

She grinned. She didn't even need a moment to think about it, moving in with Jay felt like the most natural step to take in the world. 'I'd love to.'

'Great, great. Which leads me to the next suggestion I'd like to make.' He looked across at Wagging Tails as Flora and Percy reached the door. 'Why don't we adopt Cindy? She loves you so much, and as you said, her separation anxiety is improving all the time.'

'Really?' Dropping his hands, she reached around his neck.

'Yes, really. You'll be working from home soon enough and we can get a dog walker until then, so she's not at home alone for any length of time.' He shrugged. 'I think it could work.'

Megan shook her head. 'I don't know what to say. You've thought of everything. That would be perfect.'

Jay smiled and tucked her hair behind her ears. 'You moving in will be perfect, adopting Cindy will be the icing on the cake, so to speak.'

'I love you.' Cupping his cheeks in her hands, she leaned forward and kissed him.

As he kissed her back, he began to chuckle and moved away slightly. 'I think she likes the idea.'

Following Jay's gaze, Megan watched as Cindy came charging out of the door and sped across the courtyard towards them.

'Did you hear that, Cindy? You're going to have a new family.'

* * *

As Megan and Jay took their seats around the table, Cindy squeezed between them both and laid her head on her paws between their chairs. Megan looked around the kitchen. Everyone was there, sitting, laughing and chatting. Flora passed around mugs of coffee and Percy shook biscuits from a packet to a plate before passing it to Alex who slid it towards the centre of the table.

Pushing her chair back, Susan stood up and made her way across to a cupboard before pulling out a large cake and setting it at the head of the table.

'Now we have everyone together, I thought we should celebrate the new kennel block having finally been replaced.'

'Ooh, that's beautiful, Susan.' Ginny looked at the cake. 'You're such an amazing baker.'

'Yum, that does look good.' Standing up, Alex leaned over and scraped a little icing off the bottom of the cake before sticking his finger in his mouth. 'It tastes good too.'

'Oi!' Swatting Alex's hand away, Susan chuckled. 'Who wants a slice then?'

As a chorus of 'me please's and 'absolutely's rang through the room, Megan looked down at Cindy, who opened her eyes slightly and cocked her head to one side before sinking back into a deep slumber. Catching Jay's eye, she nodded towards the large dog between them.

'I think the news of her having a new home has worn her out.'

Chuckling, Jay reached across and squeezed her hand. 'Maybe we could go shopping for some things for her this evening? Even if we just start window shopping before everything is finalised.'

Megan nodded. 'Yes, we'll have a ton of stuff to get before she moves in.'

'What's this then?' Percy glanced at Megan and Jay.

Placing her hands on the table in front of her, Megan looked at Jay before turning to Percy and Flora. 'Jay asked me to move in with him and we were wondering, well, hoping, that we might be able to adopt Cindy. Please?'

Grinning, Flora clasped her hands together. 'That would be wonderful. Cindy dotes on you and I think she's found her perfect match.'

Jay blinked and raised his eyebrows, his lips twitching at the corners. 'And what about me?'

'Ha ha, you know what I mean, lovely. We all know you and Megan are perfect for each other and now Cindy will have her happy-ever-after too. With both of you.'

'Yes, that's wonderful news. Moving in with each other and adopting Cindy. Congratulations.' Reaching across the table, Percy patted Jay's forearm.

'Thanks. So we stand a chance of being able to adopt this one here then?' Jay glanced down at Cindy who was still sleeping peacefully at their feet.

'Stand a chance? I've already mentally signed the adoption papers!' Flora chuckled.

'Now we have two things to celebrate. Well, three, the newly rebuilt kennels, Cindy's adoption and Megan and Jay moving in with each other.' Alex took a slice of cake from Susan and held it up. 'Cheers. Here's to Wagging Tails and a long future of helping more dogs, and humans. Happy days ahead of us all.'

'Thanks.' After taking a plate from Susan, Megan waited until everyone else had a slice in their hand before raising it in the air. 'Cheers to happy days.'

'Happy days.' The chorus filtered around the table as Flora, Percy, Ginny, Susan, Sally and Jay joined in with Alex's toast.

WELLINGBOROUGH DOG WELFARE (WELLIDOGS)

I'd like to take this opportunity to give a huge shout-out to Wellidogs, a no-kill shelter based in Grendon, Northamptonshire. The dedicated team rescue dogs from the pound and those abandoned or handed in to them. They work tirelessly to provide the gorgeous dogs in their care a safe home, full bellies and, above all, love and kindness.

At Wellidogs, dogs are given a second chance. They are shown patience, training and affection. The wonderful dogs are assessed, trained and given the opportunity to find their forever home, the home they deserve.

As with Ralph at Wagging Tails, they have resident dogs who, for various reasons, have made their home at Wellidogs. These beautiful dogs will spend the rest of their days secure in the knowledge they will forever be loved and cared for at Wellidogs.

Please, if you are considering rehoming a dog, then check out the deserving dogs at Wellidogs, waiting hopefully to be welcomed into a home just like yours. https://wellidog.org/

As a local charity they rely on the generosity of their supporters and the general public to continue rescuing and rehoming the dogs so if you can support them by liking their Facebook page, joining their group, or liking and sharing their posts, or donating, I know they'd be ever so grateful.

Facebook page: https://www.facebook.com/wellidogs

Facebook group: https://www.facebook.com/groups/welling boroughdogwelfare

I'd like to give a little mention to two absolutely gorgeous greyhounds who, like Petal and Willow, were surrendered to Wellidogs by a local racecourse. As with Wagging Tails, Wellidogs are routinely asked to take on a large number of retiring greyhounds and do their utmost to accommodate those that they can. The two greyhounds I met and walked at Wellidogs, Gill and Jack, were the most gentle little (or relatively tall!) dogs who had shared a kennel their entire racing life and I'm happy to report that, thanks to the wonderful team at Wellidogs, they were rehomed together – there really can be happy endings!

ACKNOWLEDGEMENTS

Thank you, readers, so much for reading *Happy Days Ahead in the Cornish Village.* I hope you've enjoyed returning to West Par and the Wagging Tails family as well as following Megan on the next stage of her journey and seeing her find happiness with Jay. I know I have enjoyed writing about the wonderful dogs at Wagging Tails as well revisiting Flora, Percy and the rest of the team.

A huge thank you to my wonderful children, Ciara and Leon, who motivate me to keep writing and working towards 'changing our stars' each and every day. Also thank you to my lovely family for always being there, through the good times and the trickier ones.

I'd like to thank Vicki and Lynn at Wellidogs (Wellingborough Dog Welfare – www.wellidog.org) for welcoming me into the home to meet the wonderful dogs they have at Wellidogs and for letting me volunteer. Thank you to Jasmine, Aidan, Amy and Ash for giving me more of an insight to volunteering at a dogs' home.

I'd also like to take this opportunity to say a huge thank you to each and every person who works or volunteers at a dogs' home or rescue centre. Thank you for caring for the dogs in your care, and for relentlessly fighting for their future and happiness. You are wonderful beyond words.

And a massive thank you to my wonderful editor, Emily Yau, who reached out and believed in me – thank you. Thank you also to Sandra Ferguson for copyediting *Happy Days Ahead in the Cornish Village*, and Shirley Khan for proofreading. And, of course, Clare Stacey for creating the beautiful cover. Thank you to all at Team Boldwood!

ABOUT THE AUTHOR

Sarah Hope is the author of many successful romance novels, including the bestselling Cornish Bakery series. Sarah lives in Central England with her two children and an array of pets and enjoys escaping to the seaside at any opportunity.

Sign up to Sarah Hope's mailing list for news, competitions and updates on future books.

Follow Sarah on social media here:

[f] facebook.com/HappinessHopeDreams

[X] x.com/sarahhope35

[O] instagram.com/sarah_hope_writes

[BB] bookbub.com/authors/sarah-hope

ALSO BY SARAH HOPE

The Cornish Village Series

Wagging Tails in the Cornish Village

Chasing Dreams in the Cornish Village

A Fresh Start in the Cornish Village

Happy Days Ahead in the Cornish Village

Escape to... Series

The Seaside Ice-Cream Parlour

The Little Beach Café

Christmas at Corner Cottage

LOVE NOTES

LOVE IN EVERY CHAPTER

WHERE ALL YOUR ROMANCE
DREAMS COME TRUE!

THE HOME OF BESTSELLING
ROMANCE AND WOMEN'S
FICTION

 WARNING:
MAY CONTAIN SPICE

SIGN UP TO OUR
NEWSLETTER

https://bit.ly/Lovenotesnews

Boldwood

Boldwood Books is an award-winning fiction publishing company seeking out the best stories from around the world.

Find out more at www.boldwoodbooks.com

Join our reader community for brilliant books, competitions and offers!

Follow us
@BoldwoodBooks
@TheBoldBookClub

Sign up to our weekly deals newsletter

https://bit.ly/BoldwoodBNewsletter